THE
THREE
WISHES
OF JAMIE McRUIN

THE THREE WISHES OF JAMIE McRUIN
by Charles O'Neal was awarded a five-thousand-
dollar prize by The Christophers. In sponsoring a
book contest, The Christophers offered awards for
books of high literary merit reflecting Christian
values. The judges for the contest were Myles
Connolly, Father John S. Kennedy, Clare Boothe
Luce, Fulton Oursler, and Mary O'Hara.

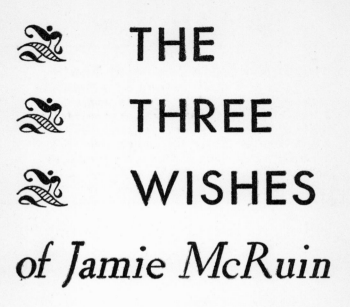

THE

THREE

WISHES

of Jamie McRuin

BY CHARLES O'NEAL

Julian Messner, Inc. New York

49-10831

PUBLISHED BY JULIAN MESSNER, INC.
8 WEST 40TH STREET, NEW YORK 18

PRINTED IN THE UNITED STATES OF AMERICA

To Patricia

Wife and queen of my heart,
whose inspiration lingers along
these pages like sunlight over
the ground—

THE
THREE
WISHES
OF JAMIE McRUIN

PART ONE

*Once upon a time when cows were kine and eagles
of the air built their nests in the beards of giants,
a little green-coated boy, with a stick in his hand
and a bundle of bannocks over his shoulder, went
out on the rocky roads of the world to push his
fortune. . . .*

I

HIGH up on a hillside overlooking the sea, and where the grass curled green and a breeze from the west stirred the branches of the yew trees to gentle gossip, Jamie McRuin lay pleasantly dreaming. Jamie was fond of dreaming. Where else but in a wishing world could be found the life of unfettered freedom for which he hungered. He had taken to dreaming as other Irishmen took to drink, and at times grew almost as drunk upon dreams as they upon poteen.

Twenty-four years of life beside the bare Connacht rocks and the spitting mouth of the ocean had given Jamie the face and eyes of a bard. His features were bold and regular, and his skin of surprising whiteness for one who spent most of his hours out of doors. Under the worn edges of his cap, his hair curled thick and black. His eyes were closed now, but their lids twitched pleasantly and his lips formed faint, intangible outlines of the wonderful words he was speaking somewhere in the dark woodland of his dreams.

Far below, and nestling at the foot of a row of toothy hills known in the west of Ireland as the Twelve Pins, stood the small stone and sod cottage where Jamie lived with his father, Old Dan, his younger brother, Dennis, and his older sister, Kate. Their handful of acres was set apart by hedges and a ragged stone fence, but was alike in appearance with a dozen others surrounding it; alike in size and alike in poverty. The year was 1895. Even the years were alike in Connacht.

The narrow path winding up the mountain was no wider than a sheep's width. Kate McRuin paused on it in her slow climb and squinted across toward Dunriggan Gap—a devil's cauldron, said to be without bottom and through which the waters from the upper lakes plunged headlong to the sea.

"Jamie . . . Jamie McRuin . . . !" Her voice rose like a tattered kite and hung for an uneasy instant on the buoyant air, then dropped away to be swallowed by the muffled booming of the snarling, white-lipped ocean.

"Och, he's gone again," she muttered wearily, "and out of this world, where only them that rides the moonbeams— the flahooly ones—can find him." Drawing her shawl tighter about her, she continued the climb.

It was a grand dream that Jamie was dreaming when Kate intruded upon it. He had dreamt it twice before . . . and well known it is throughout the depth and breadth of Ireland that a dream dreamt three times is bound to come true!

Standing beside the sleeping boy, Kate felt a tug of jealousy. Whatever of beauty there had been in the family, it had passed her by and settled upon Jamie. The endless work and worry of an Irish peasant household made Kate appear older than her thirty years. Care of her father and her two younger brothers had fallen upon her when the mother died. Kate was sixteen then; and from girlhood into womanhood, she had cooked, cleaned, scrubbed, mended,

and helped in the fields, until her hands and feet had tough-
ened into leather, and her face and voice grown thin and
harsh together. Now her voice was sharp and edged with
bitterness as she roused him.

"Would you mind waking now, Jamie McRuin! Come
back to the roof of the world where the potatoes still grow
in the ground and not on fairy bushes. There's company
waiting for you at the cottage."

Jamie stirred and opened his eyes reluctantly. They were
of the deep blueness of a rain cloud trapped by the sun,
their color warming or deepening according to his mood.

"Hello, Sister Kate!"—there was a lilt of music in his teasing voice. "Sure you looked like the Fairy Queen standing
there with the sun making a halo behind your head. I've
been having tea with her."

"Tea with the Fairy Queen is it?" Kate snapped. "And
did she tell you that high dreaming and low living are sisters in Ireland? That you and your dreams have let the
farm go to thistles and that it's ruined we shall all be if you
don't turn your hand and marry and settle down, as every
decent man should?"

"We spoke of marriage," Jamie conceded loftily. "I'm to
have the girl of my choice."

Kate's exasperation found expression in a snort of deri-
sion. "And never a word of a crock of gold or silver the
depth and breadth of your face?"

"Kate darling, would you have me strive and sweat until
my back is knobbed and bent as a blackthorn stick, to have
what I can get just by closing my eyes on a grassy hillside?"

"Aye, and what's to become of the rest of us while you
live on in your silk and satin dreaming?"

The hurt in Kate's voice sobered Jamie. "Who's at the
cottage?" he asked, changing the subject.

"Cousin Tavish," Kate replied. "All the way from Kilkahoon since morning he's come—and to see you!"

Jamie whistled apprehensively. Owen Roe Tavish was the community matchmaker, or Speaker, and a distant relative. His presence at the home of an eligible young man was the harbinger of matrimony.

"Sure now it sounds as if Old Dan has made up his mind."

"Someone had to, since you seemed incapable of making up your own," Kate sniffed.

"Has Cousin Tavish found a likely girl then?" Jamie queried.

"Yer-a-noe," Kate retorted evasively. "You're to have a look."

She led the way down the mountainside, and, tease as he might, Jamie could draw no further information from her.

The question of Jamie's marrying had been a familiar and pressing topic in family meetings. The fortune his bride was to bring would restock the farm and provide Dennis' passage money to America; and maybe enough left over for Kate to find a husband and a home of her own.

Jamie had argued that Dennis should keep the farm while he went adventuring to America, but Old Dan would not hear of such a thing. "America, is it?" he would bellow! "Sure and I'll not be giving up my eldest to that benighted country. America has bled Ireland white enough already— skimming the cream of our young manhood year after year till there's nothing but skim milk left. They'll not be getting my Jamie."

There the matter had rested, and escape for Jamie seemed farther away than ever. What it was he wished to escape, Jamie himself was not sure. He only knew that he hungered in his heart for some wonderful experience not to be found beside the bared teeth of Connacht rocks and the spitting mouth of the ocean.

Owen Roe Tavish and Old Dan McRuin were waiting in the yard of the cottage as Kate and Jamie came down the mountain. Jamie's father was a typical west country Irishman. He dressed in sturdy homespun and wore a crumpling, high-crowned hat that seldom left his head, and carried a heavy blackthorn stick that seldom left his grasp. His hair was thick and black, though the frost of years had begun to make inroads, and his eyes were slate-blue like Jamie's.

It was a warm March day and the two men had been enjoying a glass. Tavish's small, fiercely bright blue eyes sparkled with the satisfaction of a job well done. The marriage broker was a solid, compact little man, with great, aggressive eyebrows that rose and fell according to his mood. He had an authority of manner which made him seem inches taller than he was, and his superior education gave him a power of words and speaking unmatched in the entire countryside.

Marriages in rural Ireland were not easily arrived at. They had to be coddled and nursed, and finally arranged with a shrewd eye for the prospects of the boy on one hand and the dowry, or "fortune," of the girl on the other. The "arranging" was Tavish's job, and he took his work with the utmost seriousness.

"Sure now," he would say, "the business of helping young lovers find each other is better put in the hands of a grown man with experience than left to chance, or a cupid with wings, buzzing around like an insect, and shooting arrows into respectable, God-fearing people."

Without his practiced hand and tactful soothing of ruffled dignities, marriages would have been seldom in that part of Ireland. Poverty and pride, which shared most Irish firesides in common, were the twin rocks between which Tavish was forced to pilot his frail, romantic skiffs; and for every voyage that ended safely at the altar, he took justifiable satisfaction

—plus a reasonable commission based upon the size of the bride's dowry.

As his call upon the McRuins was a professional one, the Speaker was attired for the occasion. He wore his best vest, a rich double-breasted affair of green-and-gold brocade, while the remainder of his apparel consisted of a tight-fitting pair of homespun trousers; a short, buff-colored cutaway coat; and a tall green hat that had long since lost its resiliency of texture and color.

"God and Mary salute you now, Cousin Tavish," Jamie called out when he and Kate were near the cottage, forcing a cheerfulness he did not feel. "Sure had I known that a visit from you was Kate's reason for bellering, I'd have leapt on my white steed and been here quick as lightning through a gooseberry bush."

Tavish's great eyebrows lifted with pleasure and his sharp little eyes twinkled. "Would you now?" he said, and turned to Old Dan. "Didn't I tell you, Dan—the boy's a darling. The catch of the county! And I'm not saying it because we're kin!"

Old Dan McRuin grunted his agreement. Jamie was his favorite of the children. "He's the flahooly one," he would proclaim proudly. "Sure he puts a thread of poetry around every word he utters."

"Lucky's the lass as will get him," he agreed now.

"I'm doubting if any of the county girls are good enough for our Jamie," said Kate spitefully. "He's been hobnobbing with the High Queen of the fairies and she has promised him the girl of his choice."

"Has she, now?" said Tavish impressed. Old Dan, too, was interested.

"Indeed she has!" Jamie assured them. "Not only am I to have the woman of my choice," he continued mysteriously, "but two other wonderful wishes besides."

"You don't say," said Tavish, observing Jamie shrewdly.

"Be that God's truth, lad?" demanded Old Dan. "Three wishes!"

"Aye, Father, three wonderful wishes!" said Jamie, and waited tantalizingly.

It was the sort of bait few Irishmen could resist. "Well . . . out with it, lad! How did it come about? And mind you . . . give us the truth of it!" Old Dan was childishly eager.

Taking his time, Jamie related the story of his dream. He had rescued three bags of fairy gold from three old crones who had stolen it, and he had returned it to the Fairy Queen's grotto. In gratitude, the Fairy Queen had granted him three wishes. "And don't be forgetting 'twas the third time I had dreamt it," he reminded his listeners. "Sure there be more to it than an empty snooze on a grassy hillside. Three times I saw Queen Una . . . and three times she spoke to me!"

"Three times you saw the Fairy Queen . . . and three times she promised you three wishes?" queried Old Dan in awed tones.

Jamie was beginning to enjoy the role of storyteller. "First off, she offered me her hand in marriage," he said with mock modesty. "It seems the men among the fairy folk are not such-a-much. The ladies like to bring in a little new blood occasionally."

"And what did you say to that? Was she very beautiful, lad?" Old Dan exclaimed eagerly, caught up in the wonder of the tale.

"Aye, Father," Jamie assured him, "with the sort of glowing, golden beauty that went out of Ireland when the foreigners came in."

"And what did you say to the proffer of marriage?" Tavish asked. "You turned her down?"

"That I did. I said I had responsibilities in the land of the living . . . but thanking her kindly at the same time."

Kate snorted derisively. " 'Tis nice that he admits it, if only in his dreams."

"Silence, girl," Old Dan snapped at her. "What happened then?"

" 'Twas than she granted me the three wishes," said Jamie with calculated indifference.

Even Owen Roe Tavish was impressed. "You don't be saying!" he exclaimed.

There was a moment of uneasy silence. "Well . . . well . . . say it out! What did you ask her?" Old Dan demanded.

Jamie kept them waiting. "First," he said at last, "I asked for travel: Enough to make a man homesick . . . for every man should know and experience the wonder of movement. . . ."

"Aye . . . aye!" Tavish and Old Dan agreed together. " 'Tis a good wish!"

"Next, I spoke for the woman of my choice . . . to be as beautiful as the Fairy Queen herself, and who would love me always," Jamie continued.

"Sure every man wishes for that," Tavish observed piously, while Old Dan nodded agreement. "And for the third wish . . .?"

"For the third wish . . ." Jamie paused dramatically, "I asked for a wonderful son! One who would have the gift of poetry and speak in the ancient tongue!"

There was a moment of stunned silence, broken by a low moan from Kate. "No money . . . no money!" she repeated. "He didn't ask for riches! Poor as we are, he didn't ask for so much as a shilling!"

Her wailing released a flood of argument and protest from Tavish. Even Old Dan, who thought everything Jamie did was perfect, was disappointed. "Wonderful sons are not necessarily got by wishing, Jamie lad," he said reproachfully. "Couldn't you have asked for something a little more practical?"

"Like riches?" said Jamie. "Sure the riches I'll earn myself, Father! When I get to America, checks that long I'll be sending home . . . and that's what I told the Fairy Queen."

Mention of America snapped the spell of the tale that Jamie had been weaving. Another wail came from Kate. "You see, Father! He's not given it up! He still wants to go to America! He's going to desert us all."

"I've said it before and I say it again," roared Old Dan, "he'll not go! America'll not get my Jamie! And that's my final word!"

Jamie pleaded. "Father . . . my heart is set upon going! Think of the promise made me by the Fairy Queen! The first wish was for travel . . . and you yourself said it was a good wish! And Cousin Tavish, too!"

"Aye, that I did," agreed the speaker with a sly wink at Old Dan, "and travel you shall have!" He clapped Jamie affectionately on the shoulder. "Arm and arm we'll go tomorrow to the fair at Kilkahoon . . . and that's travel enough for any man, eh, Dan McRuin?"

Jamie's father grunted a sour assent. "But what of my other wishes?" Jamie protested. "And a trip to Kilkahoon by shanks' mare is not calculated to make a man homesick."

"Sure the woman of your choice you'll be having, too, Jamie lad," Tavish assured him blandly. "Leave that to me. And who is better qualified to choose for you the girl of your choice than your own cousin, Tavish, who has made it his life's work? Guided by those magic words of the Fairy Queen, and with the wonderful powers of persuasion gifted me from my grandfather, Dermott Tavish, who once split a rock with the sound of his voice calling his brother,

Sheamus, who had run afoul of the drink and thought he had lent his shadow to the Devil and was out on the hills trying to get it back . . . we'll to the fair to choose the fair, and once chosen—I promise she'll be yours, and there's my hand on it. Pour us a drink, Kate, and we'll toast the lucky girl!"

Kate moved to obey, but Jamie shook his head despondently. "You've a power of building a nest in a body's ear, Cousin Tavish," he said, "but when you've done there'll be nought to my wonderful wishes but the common furniture of life."

Tavish brushed aside Jamie's despairing protest. With a drink in his hand, he proposed a toast. "And for your third wish—the wonderful son—sure you'll be having that—in God's good time, for you're a lad to flash his antlers in the air, Jamie. Up romance!"

With another wink at Old Dan, Tavish downed his drink. The facts of life, he thought to himself, must be faced in this world; our dreams we keep for the next.

By suppertime Tavish was mellow with whisky and love of his work. He spoke glowingly of the girl he intended to find for Jamie; her beauty and wit and the number of pigs, cows, and sheep she would bring with her. "She'll be as lovely as the girl he courts in his mind," he promised.

Meanwhile Dennis, a sour, dark-tempered, perverse lad, who resented his older brother's favored position, had come home. He had been helping a neighbor mark some pigs and now he noisily washed the blood from his hands at the washbasin just outside the door. When he finished, he dashed the water carelessly into the yard, calling spitefully to Kate: "Och, I forgot to say, 'Take care of the water.' Sure now bad luck will have the lot of us before the week is out."

He took pleasure in violating Kate's many superstitions—

one of which was to call a warning to the Little People when water was thrown out. Otherwise they might be lurking about underfoot and get wet and put a curse on the house.

Spindly and bucktoothed, Dennis was given to wrapping himself in moody silences from which he emerged vindictive and quarrelsome. "Be on your guard," he warned Jamie maliciously, having listened to Tavish. "Take no girl like a pig in a sack. Make her walk and trot as you would a horse. Remember what happened to Napper McBroom."

"What happened to the Napper?" Jamie inquired.

"Sure they showed him the girl sitting in a chair all wrapped in shawls and blushing pretty as a pomegranate," declared Dennis, "and after he said he'd have her, who should come hobbling to meet him at the altar but the same girl. She'd only cne leg."

"Dennis," said Tavish, giving him a look that throttled, "if they knew in America the kind of plague about to be visited upon them, sure they'd hold public prayers that your voyage would be long and your ship a leaky one. Now hold your lip."

Old Dan was disturbed. "Cousin Tavish would never let a thing like that happen," he said reprovingly.

"I only warned Jamie to be careful," Dennis retorted sulkily. "Anyway, the system of marrying for money and not for love in Ireland is out of date."

Tavish's great arching eyebrows rose upward in shocked surprise. "And where now have you been hearing such radical and unpatriotic talk?" he demanded.

"I didn't hear it . . . I read it in a book," said Dennis smugly.

"Dennis . . ." the Speaker waggled his finger sententiously, "books are the invention of sinful men. They should be kept from the hands of simpletons like yourself. Now be silent or you'll be getting the full weight of my tongue."

Dennis subsided, but Tavish refused to be mollified. His professional pride was hurt. "And who knows the pedigree of every girl from Bantry Bay to Derry Quay better than I do?" he demanded. "Just let anyone try to put something across on Owen Roe Tavish! Sure I'll raise such a wind as will blow the tails off the horses."

Kate had been busy at the hearth inside the cottage. Now she called them to the evening meal. "The praties are ready now . . . come along to the supper."

Seated about the bare, rectangular wooden table with a great bowl of steaming potatoes in the center, Tavish's good humor returned. As guest of honor, he received a boiled duck egg, and he praised Kate's cooking until her plain red face grew redder with embarrassment and pleasure.

"Would you look at that mountain of laughing potatoes," he crowed. "Sure now, you have to be born in the west of Ireland to know how to boil potatoes like that. See how the skin is cracked just a smile or a wink to whet your appetite for what's inside."

He reached for the strip of salt bacon that was hanging suspended from the beam above the table. Rubbing the greasy meat against his peeled potatoes to flavor them, Tavish passed it along to the others.

When the meal was finished, Tavish declared it sumptuous and said he would stay the night. He chattered on while Kate cleared away the dishes. Old Dan fell asleep, with ashes from his pipe spilling down his vest and threatening to set him on fire. Dennis joked awhile with the Speaker, yawned, and climbed the ladder to the small loft where he and his older brother slept.

"God keep you," he mumbled.

Jamie had sat silent through the meal, his mood wavering between elation and despair. He was excited at the thought of going to the fair at Kilkahoon; of strutting among the colleens and perhaps saying to Tavish: "I'll take that one. Speak to her father." But a feeling of depression outweighed his other emotion. Common sense warned him that there was more to marrying in Ireland than the choosing of a girl. The pretty ones were usually spoken for or had no fortune . . . and a girl with no fortune was worse than no girl at all.

"You'll have no luck with me tomorrow, Cousin Tavish," he warned. "I've a bad name in Kilkahoon. Every time I've gone to the fair, there's been fighting and skull cracking—and I've been in the thick of it."

"Sure fighting and a little fun is nothing to hold against a young man with muscles," Tavish reassured him. " 'Tis all one at fair time."

"But how do I know the girl of my choice will have me?" Jamie persisted.

"Sure now wouldn't she be daft to say 'no'? You're a darling . . . that's what you are . . . a darling, and lucky's the word for any girl that catches your eye, Jamie. Now go to bed. . . . Tomorrow we must look our best."

Kate put Tavish in the west room to sleep with Old Dan. The two old men went arm in arm to bed, more to prop each other up than from any excess of affection. Tavish, who was quite full of liquor by this time, hummed a little song.

"Good night to you, Katie McRuin," he said kindly to the hard-working girl. "Pray for us all."

"Soft sleep to you, Cousin Tavish," she answered simply.

There had been little in the thin living provided by the farm for Kate McRuin except work and prayer. She was an exceedingly devout girl, with blessings for every household task. As she made the bed in the west room for her father and Tavish her lips whispered: "I make this bed in the name of the Father, the Son, and the Holy Spirit; in the name of the night we were conceived; in the name of the day we were baptized; in the name of each night and each day, each angel that is in Heaven."

So, too, whenever she milked the cow she prayed in rhythm to the hissing streams of milk:

> The blessing of Mary and the blessing of God
> The blessing of the sun and the moon on her road
> Of the man in the east and the man in the west
> And my blessing with thee, and be thou blest.

At the finish of the milking she never forgot to send a small squirt over her left shoulder for the Gentle People, who were always there to demand a share of every milking.

When the men were asleep she tidied the main room, put away the dishes, and polished the pots. Then she greased Jamie and Tavish's boots and rubbed them until they shone. Finally she banked the peat fire with the prayer: "I save the seed of the fire tonight, even so may Christ save me. On the top of the house let Mary, in the middle, let Brigid be. Let eight of the mightiest angels round the throne of the Trinity, protect this house and its people till the dawn of the day shall be."

Her last act was to throw out the dishwater, with her warning admonition to the Gentle People to: "Mind the water." Then she retired to her small bedroom; said a prayer for herself and for Jamie's mission on the morrow, and went to sleep.

Next morning early Jamie and Owen Roe Tavish set out for the fair at Kilkahoon. Tavish stood outside the gate with his arm across Jamie's shoulders and recited: "Once upon a time when cows were kine and pigs were swine and the eagles of the air built their nests in the beards of giants, a broth of a boy called Jamie McRuin, with his good friend

Tavish to guide him and speak for him, set out on the rocky road for Kilkahoon to push his fortune."

They passed out of sight of the cottage, with Kate whispering prayers and crossing herself, as if Kilkahoon was a thousand miles away and the journey fraught with peril.

Dennis sneered: "There goes our Jamie being led to the altar like a lamb to the butcher."

"For shame," cried Kate. "'Tis for you and the passage money to America that he's doing it."

Old Dan clutched his blackthorn stick and measured a swing at his son's head. Dennis promptly ducked out of range.

"Would you be listening to Kate, now. 'Tis for me, she says! But divil a word of her making sheep's eyes at Waddie O'Dowd every market day, and passing notes at chapel!"

"Dennis!" Kate's pink face flamed a deep scarlet.

"Waddie O'Dowd!" exclaimed Old Dan, momentarily distracted. "Passing notes . . . and in the chapel?"

"Like homing doves . . . back and forth between the pews," said Dennis.

Old Dan scratched his head, puzzled. "Sure I didn't know Waddie O'Dowd could read?"

"That what's written between the lines he reads well enough," said Dennis derisively.

"Kate . . . daughter . . . explain yourself," the old man roared, transferring his displeasure from Dennis to his daughter.

But Kate had fled weeping inside the cottage, her sobs swallowed up by the deeper sobbing of the ocean.

II

ON the road Jamie and Tavish mingled with groups and families thronging on foot or in carts to the fair at Kilkahoon. There were well-to-do farmers who rode horseback, and caravans of tinkers, with their shabby wagons and strings of colts, dogs, and children. The tinkers were the pariahs of the countryside, cursed by Saint Patrick; for when the good saint had found the lump of gold with which he eventually purchased his freedom from slavery, he had taken it first to a tinker. The tinker had called it worthless, saying: "Give it me. It is solder and without value." Since that day the tinkers had lived homeless, roaming the lanes like gypsies, without roofs or walls they could call their own. They lived by trading horses, poaching, and occasionally mending a pot or pan.

Roughs along the road shouted vulgar insults at them as they passed, and received equally profane replies. There was a special curse for outsiders that the tinkers taught their children. "You build houses . . . aye, like the crows, you put stick and stick together. May we see a scatter of the sticks

and the kites achase through the woods. You live man and
wife, you say—like goats—two and two together . . . for
fear ye should reach to the hedgetops and the wild taste get
in your blood."

When a stretch of the lane grew rocky, Tavish and Jamie
removed their shoes and strung them about their necks to
prevent scuffing against the stones. "We must look our
best," Tavish declared, "and a man's best begins with his
feet."

Farther along Jamie stubbed his toe painfully on a sharp
rock, but Tavish reminded him philosophically that a dam-
aged toe would mend. "Had you been wearing your brogues,
lad, sure now they would have been ruined indeed."

The streets of Kilkahoon were a tumult of gaiety and
business activity. There were English horses and Irish hob-
bies displayed in the streets alongside great Belgian and
French draft animals. Booths for linens and fine Irish
woolens and lace were hung with their wares close beside
pens of fat, black Angus cattle, bleating goats, and prize,
uncomplaining sheep. Jugglers and ballad singers performed
in the streets and three-card men pretended to be drunk,
to trap the unwary.

"Stay close at my side, Jamie lad," Tavish warned; "and
keep your two fists in your trouser pockets so the roughs
will know we're not looking for trouble. There'll be no time
for bloody noses and broken heads this day. We've more
important things to do."

The fair presented a wonderful, laughing, lively scene and
Jamie's eyes drank it in. Bonnie girls singly and in groups
darted laughing through the crowd, their skirts and shawls
swishing.

"Look at them . . . just look at them," Tavish purred.
"Ah . . . that I were two and twenty this day."

He guided Jamie along the crowded street, calling attention to various girls whose charms were outstanding. When Jamie displayed more than a casual interest, however, Tavish quickly found some fault to discredit the candidate who had caught the young man's eye.

Jamie thought Standish Moynihan's daughter an exceedingly pretty girl. He pointed her out to Tavish as she stood tapping her foot in time to the bagpiper's tune.

"There's the glimmering of a fading beauty there," the Speaker conceded, "but you must look deeper than the surface in choosing a wife, lad. Moyna Moynihan has that fearsome a reputation. Why man, she stood with a club over her father and three brothers until they signed the liquor pledge. And since that day not one drop of liquor has been allowed in the house. And do you know where her aging father, with scarce the strength to get out of his chair, has to go to smoke his pipe? Out to the shed, no less, in the foulest kind of weather. That's the acid test of a wife, my boy: how she treats her father."

With various and comparable calumnies that came easily to his tongue, Tavish led Jamie past the tempting girls that caught his eye. He brought him at last to the combination livery stable, feed and harness shop of the Tinker Shanahans. The Shanahans had formerly been tinkers, but had given up the road and had grown rich in the feed and harness business. Their chief interest remained in horse trading, however, an occupation at which they had few peers.

The family was large, consisting of Old Timothy, who lived in semiretirement and on friendly terms with no one or thing, except his pipe and ever-present bottle. There were eleven sons who conducted the business, and one daughter, Tirsa, the youngest. The brothers were divided roughly into three categories by public opinion. Jimmie Pat Jackie, Hees, Patch, Tydd and Tone, were the five dark, dour, grim-faced brothers who were never known to smile. They were known perversely as the "laughing" Shanahans. Five other brothers —Fash, Lafe, Ryall, Dan, and Synne—were equally dark in coloring, but for business purposes put on a great show of joviality while they took a customer's teeth in a horse trade. Of these two groups the second, or the "black" Shanahans were the more distrusted. The most feared of all, however, was Randal, the youngest, who was known with supreme euphemism as "softhearted." It was said of him that Randal had a human heart served for breakfast, like a kipper, when business was good and he could afford it.

Jamie had known of the Tinker Shanahans for years, as who hadn't, but never experienced any dealings with them. The family was famous and fearful but it was whispered that the most frightening of the lot was Tirsa, the daughter. There was a local joke which warned anyone trading horses with the Shanahans to be on guard lest Tirsa be substituted for one of the animals.

"Why have we come down here, Cousin Tavish?" Jamie asked.

"Sociability . . . nothing more," Tavish assured him.

The Speaker buzzed among the brothers and their customers, laughing, joking, occasionally whispering to Randal, the "softhearted," who kept regarding Jamie much in the manner he would study a horse being offered for sale.

Jamie thought it odd, the unusual interest that the brothers were taking in him. Far back in his mind a suspicion was born and began to grow. Old Timothy limped out, with an ash stick in one hand and a bottle in the other, to beckon them into the house. Jamie followed at a respectful distance, while Timothy, Tavish, Randal, and Fash, one of the "black Shanahans," led the way.

The Tinker Shanahans, married and not, lived with their families in one large, two-story tatterdemalion house at the rear of the shop. In the dim, gloom-filled parlor, where the smell of the near-by livery stable penetrated challengingly, the men sat down. The bottle was passed from hand to hand without benefit of glasses and Jamie found himself more and more the subject of conversation.

"Och, he's a sober lad, industrious, but with spirit, and a good hand with a horse," said Tavish. "I wish my poor tongue could describe to you the charm of the small estate which will be his when he decides to take a wife. The acreage is small but the soil is that fertile, you've but to drop the seed potato into the ground and step back to avoid being bowled over by the maturing plant."

The Shanahans were more interested in the livestock on Jamie's farm. They wanted to know the number of pigs and chickens; the number and breed of horses; and how much milk the cow gave.

Tavish answered these probing questions with a jovial expansiveness that made Jamie think the Speaker was describing some other farm than that of the McRuins'. Finally the Shanahans appeared satisfied. They rose and retired to the rear of the house. When they were gone Tavish clapped Jamie on the shoulder.

"Fortune has indeed smiled upon us this day, Jamie, my boy," he gloated. "The pulchritudinous cream of Connacht girls has consented to be courted by you."

The suspicion that had been growing inside Jamie now became a certainty. "You're not by chance referring to Tirsa, daughter of the Tinker Shanahans?"

"Chance?" crowed the Speaker. "I couldn't have thought of a better word myself—for 'twas chance alone that brought us to the House of Shanahan this day."

Jamie had his doubts about the latter part of Tavish's statement. They had come straight to the Shanahans with directness of homing pigeons. His mind grasped at the small fragments of descriptive gossip he had heard about Tirsa, seeking to form a mental picture of the girl. A moment later the daughter of the house entered, demurely clinging to her father and Randal.

It would have been more fitting if the two men had been clinging to her, Jamie thought, and some of the furtive rumors about Tirsa's appearance came back to him. It had been said that her mother was frightened by the Irish giant when she was carrying the child. At any rate, she appeared taller than any of her brothers, and they were all men of considerable stature.

There had been other whispers, too—no Irishman in his right mind would speak out against a girl with eleven fierce brothers—about her terrible temper and tremendous strength. But now she exuded coy femininity like a lady Goliath.

After flashing one avid look at Jamie she dropped her eyes and steadfastly refused to raise them again, despite the hail of flattery poured over her by Owen Roe Tavish, who seemed determined to outdo himself as a king of compliments.

"I have acted as Speaker for many a lad in love, but this is the first time such unmatched beauty has left me speechless," he declared. "Speak up, Jamie boy, isn't that the truth of it?"

Jamie opened his mouth to say something but could only gulp in air. From Tirsa came a sharp, explosive laugh, more related to the whinny of a horse than any human sound. Without a word of leave-taking, Jamie rose and hurried from the house.

" 'Tis shyness," Tavish explained, "the shyness of young love. Ah . . . 'tis a beautiful thing is nature, the way one heart speaks to another when a boy and girl meet and are at once in love."

With that observation which came easily to a man in his

profession, the Speaker shook hands all around. Arrangements were made for another meeting at the McRuin farm
to seal the bargain—in this way the Tinker Shanahans would
have an opportunity to check on Jamie's inheritance. Then
Tavish took his leave.

Jamie was waiting disconsolately outside. "Cousin Tavish,"
the boy said soberly, "I've been taught to respect my elders
like I've been taught my catechism. I would no more think
of defying my father than I would of defying the priest. But
Tavish, that girl is bewitched."

"That's it . . . that's it," exclaimed Tavish enthusiastically. "What a gift for words you have, Jamie. Bewitching
. . . that's the word for her. I couldn't have said it better
myself."

"I didn't say 'bewitching,' I said 'bewitched,'" Jamie protested. "She's monstrous."

"Shush, lad. That's no way to speak of a girl with a family
all brothers." Tavish put his arm about Jamie's shoulders
and led him away from where the remainder of the Shanahans had never paused in their haggling over horses. "Come
now, with our business attended to, we'll do the fair."

But the light had gone from Jamie's eyes and the lightness
from his feet. When he had come to the Kilkahoon fair, the
entire countryside had worn a smiling face. The dancers
seemed scarcely to touch the ground, and the birds overhead
added their voices to the music of the pipers. Now the music
had lost its lilt and the smiles were gone from the faces of
the people. Moyna Moynihan and the girls who had looked
so pretty before, now looked drab and old before their time.

Tavish tried to raise the boy's spirits. "What a fortune the
girl will bring. The Shanahans will pay plenty to be rid of
her. This is one deal they'll not get the better of. There'll be
lashans of money, enough for Kate to marry her Waddie
O'Dowd—sure now he'd leap at the chance if he thought

she'd bring so much as a red-eared cow—and to send Dennis to America, besides."

Jamie gave no answer. He left Tavish at the fair and strode homeward, scuffing his boots against the rocks of the road, not feeling or caring. His high hopes were shattered and the dream of three wishes had turned to gray dust. In his heart Jamie knew there was no escape. Family obligations and loyalties shaped a pattern and the pattern shaped his destiny. It had been so in the past . . . so would it be in the future. He would marry the Shanahan girl who whinnied like a horse; Dennis would go to America; and Kate and Waddie O'Dowd would have a home of their own.

With a pain inside him like an unhealed wound, he clenched his fists and walked the road, dragging his coat in open invitation to battle, hoping to meet some face he could smash or a head he could break his knuckles against.

III

EXACTLY one week later was the time the Tinker Shanahans had agreed to visit the McRuin cottage and seal the
terms of the marriage contract with a handshake and a glass
of whiskey. The day was a busy one for everyone in the
household, including Owen Roe Tavish. Kate had the red-
ding up of the place to do, plus the baking of cakes for the
guests. Jamie and Dennis raked and tidied the yard and
patched and repaired the fences. To the Speaker fell the
task of supplying two horses, six pigs, and an extra cow,
which he had assured the Shanahans were a part of Jamie's
inheritance. Separating an Irish farmer from his livestock,
even for a few hours, was no easy task. It required all the
charm that the silver-tongued Tavish could muster, with a
leavening of threats added for the reluctant ones.

" 'Tis something I've never done before," he would say,
fixing a farmer with a hypnotic eye, "asking a man for the
loan of his cow and pig. But 'tis for love! Now if you're
against love—if you're not wanting me to have the lend of
your animals, say so at once, and we'll part as good friends
as ever. I've never misused any man's cow in my lifetime—

nor any man's pig or horse—you know that as well as I do—
and your father knew it before you."

By a mixture of promises and threats, and by assuring the
reluctant owners that their animals would be back in their
pens by feeding and milking time, Tavish succeeded in filling
the McRuin yard with livestock.

"There now," he said, well pleased with his contemplated
fraud, "to match that the Shanahans will have to give a
share in the business."

"Isn't it a bit cheating and dangerous besides to be telling
the Shanahans that all those animals are ours?" Old Dan
inquired dubiously.

Tavish shrugged. "Aye, 'tis low, knavish trickery, Dan;
sure, I'd never stoop to such flagrant dishonesty if it were
not for my own kin."

"But won't the Shanahans be suspicious?" Old Dan persisted.

"Aye, they will that . . . being the crooks that they are,"
retorted Tavish, with bland inconsistency. "Sure the Shanahans wouldn't trust their own mother. The point about
cheating in matrimonial matters is to cheat so extravagantly
that when the Shanahans disbelieve half, which they will,
we're still fifty per cent to the good."

As the sun passed the meridian the cottage was spick and
span with readiness. The borrowed horses, pigs, and cow,
respectively, stomped, grunted, and chewed lazily on her
cud. Old Dan McRuin fumbled in his near-empty tobacco
pouch for a fresh pipeful. Kate scolded him peevishly, saying there would be no tobacco for the guests. The shadows
of the trees outside began to lengthen and a midafternoon
stillness stole across the hills. Dennis shuffled his feet nervously and Kate sat primly, clasping and unclasping her
hands.

"Maybe they're not coming," Jamie said, making no effort to conceal the hope in his voice.

"Not at all," replied Tavish. " 'Tis a trick of the trade. They don't want to seem anxious, and if we look frightened they'll drive a hard bargain. So rest easy. Before the night falls the contract will be made. Jamie will have the girl of his choice, Kate will have her fortune so she can marry, and Dennis will hoist his sails for America and quicker than a cat's wink will be sending home letters fattened with American dollars."

Tavish was right about one thing. The Tinker Shanahans did arrive, all thirteen of them, with Tirsa, at midafternoon. The eleven brothers swarmed over the place, sounding the animals, testing the soil, and engaging in whispered conferences with each other. Tirsa and her father remained in the house with Owen Roe Tavish and the McRuins. The atmosphere was friendly but tense. Kate passed her cakes and accepted praise of them with a scoffing "tsch, they didn't turn out well at all." The whiskey jug went around and Timothy Shanahan insisted that his daughter have a swig. " 'Twould not be good manners to refuse, girl," he said.

Tirsa took a ladylike swallow, leering at Jamie the while. Old Dan offered Timothy a pipeful of tobacco, and the two old men fell into a long harangue about tobacco and the smoking of it, with Tirsa and Kate interposing an occasional comment.

"I'll tell you something about myself," said Dan. "The weed is my great vice. I've been known to burn three ounces of it at one sitting."

"Och, 'tis much too much," agreed Timothy Shanahan.

"I tell him he does wrong," said Kate. "But does he listen—" she shrugged.

"Sure, it must be bad for the lungs," Tirsa said, then giggled.

"No constitution can stand it," admitted Old Dan. "Sure, I be killing myself with every puff."

The drink had loosened Tirsa's tongue. "I don't mind the smoking at all," she chattered, "that is, if the tobacco is good. Father smokes like a chimney, as do my brothers, although their wives complain something fierce. I don't mind at all, I say. I'd even smoke myself if it were considered ladylike! Fancy me with a seegar, now—" she exploded into her high, whinnying laugh.

Jamie sat glumly through the hail of words. The brothers, led by Randal, drifted into the cottage. The liquor jug was refilled again and again and passed from hand to hand as the talk grew louder and the atmosphere thicker. The Shanahans had scant praise for the McRuin livestock. However, they assured Jamie they would show him how to sweeten his animals so they would bring profitable exchanges at the market. This would be done for him as a member of the family, and for a small commission, of course.

"And now," said Tavish, above the clash of conversation, "we come to the subject of this meeting: On the one hand, a girl with a beauty the like of which ties men's tongues to the roofs of their mouths, and on the other, this boyo here, who has wandered for days under an enchantment. Will the boy and girl leave the house while the more delicate details come up for discussion?"

Obediently Tirsa and Jamie rose and left the cottage. They wandered along the quicks that separated Jamie's land from the neighboring farms. Tirsa, who had chattered like a magpie inside the cottage, now was silent. Jamie's attempts to draw her into conversation yielded nothing but another series of her amazing giggles. He spoke of his terrible temper and hinted at other habits too frightful for delicate ears to hear. But Tirsa remained unimpressed.

"Don't forget I grew up with eleven brothers," she reminded him. "I know what boys are like."

In desperation, Jamie sought a new tack. "We'll be very poor," he warned. "All of your fortune will go to getting a husband for Kate and sending Dennis to America. There'll be nothing left to fix up the farm with. I couldn't afflict such poverty on a nice girl like you, and that's the truth of it."

"Then Father will take you into the horse trading," said Tirsa with assurance. "There's enough in it for all."

"Sure my health would never stand that," Jamie protested quickly, " 'tis my lungs!" He coughed feebly in verification.

Tirsa was instantly all sympathy. "Och, wirra! My brother, Fash, was bothered with the lung trouble. I rubbed his chest with horse liniment and fed him on crushed eggshells, and he was well in no time at all," she assured him.

Jamie winced. " 'Twould never do for such a frail one as myself," he said, coughing again. "Sure I'm not long for this world, they do be telling me . . . and that's a fact."

Tirsa was not to be dissuaded. "I've other remedies—taught me by my mother—secret ones! You'll be yourself again before the year is out," she promised.

Jamie made one final despairing effort. " 'Tis unfair for a sweet girl the likes of yourself to be burdened with a rough-neck such as I. At fair time, when I'm with the drink taken, sure I'm that crazed I might raise my hand to you."

Tirsa's giggles changed to a derisive snort. "Och . . ." she hooted, "I could bend you with one hand . . . drunk or sober."

The sun was gilding the hilltops when Tavish called the young couple back to the cottage. " 'Tis set . . . 'tis all arranged," he exclaimed with jubilation. "The Shanahan and the McRuin have shaken hands on the match. Come in . . . come in, and share a loving cup with your be-trothed, Jamie, my boy."

Like a young whale that is caught in the shallows, Jamie

continued to struggle. "Go inside," he said to Tirsa, "I've a word to speak with Owen Roe Tavish."

Tirsa obeyed. "Don't be long," she called coquettishly.

"I'll not," said Jamie grimly. "Now, Cousin Tavish," he said, turning to the Speaker, "the wind of a word with you."

"I've no time now, lad," said Tavish nervously, "later . . . later. . . ."

" 'Twill be now or never," Jamie warned. "Cousin Tavish . . . I can't go through with this terrible thing. . . ."

" 'Tis too late . . . 'tis over and done! The papers are all signed! Reconcile yourself, Jamie lad. 'Tis no worse than a cold plunge, is marriage! Once in, the water is said to be reasonably comfortable . . . besides, no man should live without the jewels of love!" Tavish concluded piously.

"I'll not let you do this to me," Jamie cried, seizing Tavish's arm. " 'Tis wicked! I could never love the girl. There's someone whose portrait I've worn in my heart as long as I can remember. We've never met, but she's mine—promised me by vows made beyond the rim of the world. To marry another . . . 'twould be a double crime: One against the Shanahan girl . . . and one against the girl who's waiting for me somewhere . . . and who someday I'll meet. . . ."

The boy's passionate protest shook Tavish's smug assurance. "Every man courts someone in his heart, Jamie," he said seriously, "but how many meet or marry her? One in ten thousand thousand. Only someone God loves very much. . . ."

Kate came from the cottage. "Is anything wrong?" she asked, her eyes moving from Tavish's face to Jamie's.

"Jamie here will none of the Shanahan girl," Tavish answered with a shrug of weariness.

"Go back to the guests, Cousin Tavish," Kate said quietly.

"Don't be too hard on the lad, Kate. 'Tis a hard thing to

be young, and have three wishes . . . and to give them
up . . . all in the same day." He patted Jamie's shoulder
affectionately, then moved slowly away toward the cottage.

When he was gone, Kate turned to face Jamie. "Now
then," she demanded sharply, "what is this? Dan McRuin
himself, and the Shanahan have signed their names and
given their hands. 'Tis settled!"

Jamie's face was a picture of anguish. "Kate . . . if you
love me . . . spare me! Get me out of this," he pleaded.

Pity, like a clutching fist, tightened about Kate's heart.
She strengthened her resolve with a show of harshness.
"Have you thoughts only for yourself? And what's to become
of the rest of us if you don't marry with the girl?" she
demanded.

Jamie raised his arms in a gesture that was without hope.
"Kate . . . darling sister . . . believe me! I am that ready
to give up my three wishes! To trade my dreams for the
common furniture of life . . . but not with. . . ." He
waved despairingly toward the cottage. "That laugh . . .
sure it would drive the river from its bed . . . make soft
the hard, and grind the great sea stones to pebbles! What
would it do to me, and through all the years that are to
come."

Kate drew the boy about to face her. "You've always had
great love for the mysteries of life, Jamie brother, but little
liking for the facts. Will you look at these hands and tell me
what you read there?" She extended her hands but Jamie
turned his face away.

"I've not the power to read what's written in the hands,"
he protested.

"Sure then you're blinder than I thought," Kate said
sharply. "There are facts written in the palms of these hands,
Jamie. They are as hard and calloused as your boots. If you
looked closely enough, you'd see there all the years of toil

and drudgery I've put in since Mother died. Sixteen I was then. For fourteen years I've cooked and washed and mended—even worked in the fields! And believe it or not, my brother, I've also dreamed a few dreams. . . ."

Jamie looked at his sister and seemed to see her for the first time. "Och, Kate, forgive me! I'm that blind I didn't know!" he said humbly.

His sudden softness brought Kate to the verge of tears. "I didn't dream of three wishes," she continued, "only one: to have a home and husband of my own. Are you going to deny me that?"

Jamie wrapped her gently in his powerful arms. "Och, my darling . . . my sister and mother in one . . . sure, you'll have your wish, and Waddie O'Dowd, too, though what a lovely girl like yourself, and with a fine fortune that is to be, wants with that great lump of nothing, I'll never know. . . ."

He kissed her soundly on both checks and brushed away her tears with his two thumbs. Then, arm in arm, like friends who had lost each other and found themselves again, they went back into the cottage.

The interior of the cottage was hot and the Shanahans had been drinking steadily. It was plain that Owen Roe Tavish had driven a hard bargain for there was no gaiety in their faces. Only the elder Shanahan seemed quite content. Old Timothy was a small man compared to his towering children. With his pipe cold and his eyes blurry with liquor, he talked on and on, while Dan McRuin listened sleepily, contributing an occasional, "Yer-a-noe" or "May the saints preserve us," to the one-sided conversation.

"Eleven sons and one daughter . . . and all of them like their mother," Old Tim was saying dreamily. "She was a moveless kind of a woman, Dan . . . rocklike, when the kindness went out of her. It was because of her I gave up my tent and the roads of Ireland. She had a hankering for the town and a piece of land and the respectability that went with it. Aye, she was hard as the back of her hand with the children. When I was angry I let them feel the rough side of my tongue, but once a year in the spring she lined them up and gave them a hiding whether they deserved it or not— like you would give a dose of spring tonic. . . ."

Owen Roe Tavish strutted before the Shanahan brothers with pardonable pride. It was not every day that anyone bested the Shanahans in a business transaction. So he gloated in mellow happiness while the brothers glowered.

Outside the cottage a sudden flurry of noisy activity was creating considerable confusion around the barnyard. Chickens squawked and cackled. The pigs grunted and squealed. The borrowed cow bellowed, and the horses whinnied excitedly. The mounting disturbance caught Jamie's ear. He glanced toward Dennis, but his brother was conversing animatedly with Tirsa. Tavish was within reach so Jamie tugged at his arm.

"Something's gone wrong out in back," he whispered. Beckoning the Speaker to follow, he went outside.

Something had gone wrong, indeed. Tavish had exuberantly forgotten his promise to return the borrowed livestock by feeding and milking time. Between the Shanahans' late arrival and the celebration of the marriage contract, the time for feeding and milking was long overdue and half a dozen irate neighbors had descended upon the McRuin farm to reclaim their animals. The resulting confusion soon spread to the cottage and the Shanahans streamed out to see what was creating the disturbance. One look was enough to tell them they had been hoodwinked. Their bitterness knew no bounds.

Tavish and Jamie had gone to the byre, trying to dissuade

the angry neighbors from reclaiming their animals. "The black curse of a thousand Cromwells on the lot of you!" the Speaker had roared when his pleas were rejected, "and a special one on the man who invented neighbors."

With the Shanahans boiling from the cottage lusting for blood, he hastily drew Jamie behind a shed.

"Wisdom is the better part of valor, lad," he whispered. "We must give time for hot heads to cool."

They hid behind the hedge of a neighbor's field and darkness lent them a cloak. Jamie wanted to return to the cottage and have it out, but Tavish was firm against it. " 'Tis not your blood they're after as much as mine," he said. "It's the being took they can't abide . . . and I'm the one that took them. Timothy has given Old Dan his hand and they can't go back on that. They'll cool off . . . just give them time."

But the Shanahans showed no sign of cooling off. Despite the pleas of Tirsa, who would have been satisfied with Jamie if he hadn't a farthing, and Old Timothy's inclination to laugh at the manner in which his sons had been outsmarted, only blood and broken bones would satisfy them. Dividing into three groups, the brothers systematically ranged the countryside. News of what had happened spread before them like fire in a thatched roof, and the entire district turned out gleefully to watch the hunt. It was bright moonlight and Jamie and Tavish found themselves harried like rabbits, first this way and that. Finally they were driven toward the gap of Dunriggan, the deep ravine, impassable except for a narrow, swinging footbridge.

The bridge was a flimsy affair constructed of thin boards interwoven with hemp, and dangerous even in daylight. There were no guardrails, and the narrow, suspended platform swung wildly to and fro, with merely a single line passing shoulder high from one side of the gap to the other, to steady the wary passenger. Only the practiced and the intrepid could maneuver such a bridge in safety.

Jamie had crossed the bridge many times, but for Owen Roe Tavish the adventure was fraught with peril. A small, droll sign affixed beside the bridge caught his eye. "Those falling from the bridge," he read the dubious assurance aloud, "have small risk of drowning, as they are usually killed outright by the fall."

"Sure that does it," he announced. "What man dares, I dare, but yon contraption was made for angels or monkeys, and since I'm neither, I'll stay here and take my medicine. I'll lay about me with the weight of my tongue, backed up with a stout ash stick, and before I'm done in, sure I'll raise knobs on Shanahan heads that will outlast the memory of this day."

Tavish's talk was brave but when the Shanahans drew near, giving voice to threats and imprecations like hounds baying on a scent, his resolve melted. Making the sign of the cross and closing his eyes, he permitted Jamie to lead him over. Safe on the opposite bank, his courage returned. He answered the Shanahans ranged along the opposite side of the gap, threat for threat, and challenged them to cross.

"Are you that anxious to give us the wake, Randal Shanahan, that you'll risk your precious tinker's neck on this side of the bridge?" he taunted. "Come along then . . . the lot of you . . . one at a time. Me and Horatius, here, will keep the bridge; and a shirtful of sore bones the first Shanahan across will get that he'll keep till his dying day."

The Shanahans went into a council of war and determined to rush the bridge. They collected as many stout sticks as could be found; then armed with these weapons, they bunched close behind Randal and started across.

Tavish's flow of stout words stopped. "Jamie lad, they do be coming across. What are we to do?"

"Let them come," said Jamie. "Sure you've been inviting them."

"The invitation was rhetorical, Jamie lad," Tavish pleaded. "Do something. They be coming across fast as the Devil can drive them."

Jamie waited until the brothers were well into the center of the bridge, then whipped out his knife and laid its sharp edge on the single-strand guide rope.

The Shanahans paused transfixed. With no hand rope to cling to they would all be toppled into the swift-flowing stream below. "Make another move to cross," Jamie warned, "and I cut the rope. And don't be trying to back up either. Sure I like you the way you are: midway between Hell and Heaven."

The brothers remained frozen in terror. Above their heads hung the empty, spangled sky. Below them the river roared and gnashed at the perpendicular rocks lining the shore. Beneath their feet the frail hanging bridge danced and quivered. Eleven pairs of hands clung to the slender lifeline, while eleven pairs of eyes were fixed in desperation upon the shining blade of Jamie's knife poised above the guide rope.

On the shore, Tavish danced with glee. "Go to it, Jamie," he crowed, "give it a whack. Good riddance to the bad lot of them."

Randal sought to reason with Jamie. "Couldn't just one of us come across and talk it over?" he asked. "All we want is fair treatment. Sure there has been great misrepresentation in the marriage contract."

Tavish stepped forward authoritatively. "If there's to be further negotiations, lad, I'll handle them."

The now thoroughly cowed Shanahans quickly declared their willingness to abide by the original marriage contract. They even agreed to add an extra pig as compensation for all the trouble they had caused. This settled, the brothers began a hurried but careful retreat from the bridge. When they were back on the other side, Jamie put his knife away.

"Now stand in the shape of the Irish cross," he called, "and swear by St. Kevin that you'll do us no harm when we reach the other side of the gap."

The brothers obeyed. They stood each in the shape of an Irish cross, with feet close together and arms outstretched, and swore as Jamie directed. But Fash Shanahan had not formed the sign of the cross. He hid behind Synne, one of the "black" brothers. Neither Jamie nor Tavish noticed that his arms were not outstretched and that he did not make the oath.

They were in the center of the bridge, moving carefully because Tavish was still frightened, when Fash stealthily drew his knife. He struck the thin guide rope a mighty blow, severing it with the one stroke. Jamie and the Speaker teetered helplessly on the bridge for a long moment, then plunged together into the dark and swirling waters of the gap. Neither of them uttered a sound.

The Shanahans stood in stunned wonderment as the two men were swept swiftly down toward the sea. Only a few of them had seen Fash strike the guilty blow. "Brother Fash acted with spirit and foresight," said Randal promptly. "Had he waited until they reached this side of the gap . . . one of us might have broken his oath."

But the five "laughing" Shanahans disapproved. They thought it was a dirty Irish trick and said so. Hot words were exchanged between the groups of brothers, and the words soon gave way to blows. While Jamie and Tavish floundered perilously in the deep, swift-flowing stream below, the brothers battled over the ethics of the situation above. When the issue had been fought to no decision, and that which passed for harmony among the Shanahans restored, Jamie and Tavish had disappeared. Overhead the stars remained. The deep rush of the river shook the earth and filled the night with tumultuous sound. But of Jamie and the silver-tongued Tavish there was not a trace.

Sobered and to a degree saddened by the double tragedy, the brothers started toward the McRuin cottage. On the way Randal recounted sadly to the neighbors thronging the hills how the guide rope on the bridge had snapped, spilling Jamie and Tavish into the dark waters and darker death. The tale was told and retold until the brothers came to believe it themselves, arriving finally at the cottage in a state of reasonably good conscience.

Death is a constant caller to the Irish. Old Dan and Kate and Dennis took the news better than Timothy Shanahan and Tirsa. Tirsa flew at her brothers, screaming that they had done her out of a husband. Old Timothy raised his heavy ashwood stick, threatening to open the skulls of each and any of his eleven sons who had laid violent hands upon Owen Roe Tavish or Jamie.

The Shanahan boys towered above their father, but the force of his anger made them humble. Meekly they swore by all the saints that the two men had fallen to their deaths from the bridge. "Not one of us laid so much as a little finger on them," Randal said truthfully.

"That we'll take oath on," said Fash.

"Be you certain they're dead? Why did you not wait and seek out the bodies?" demanded Old Timothy.

"The people of the district are searching the gap with torches, all the way to the cove," Randal explained. "Having seen the accident, we hurried back with the news."

"Aye, he's gone," said Old Dan. "He's dreamed his last dream. 'Tis said Queen Una dwells beneath the water; maybe he'll meet her there."

The old man's simple grief touched everyone in the room.

Kate sobbed quietly, wiping her eyes with the heel of her hand. Dennis sat clenching and unclenching his fists, his dark brow furrowed. Tirsa had stopped crying and sat glowering at her brothers, her eyes filled with hate. Timothy Shanahan placed his hand upon Old Dan's shoulder.

"I have lost one of my own sons," he said solemnly, "and that portion Jamie would have had under the terms of the contract will still be his, just as if he had lived to marry Tirsa." Kate, her grief in a measure assuaged, dried her eyes and began to lay out Jamie's things in preparation for the wake.

IV

JAMIE pulled the battered and half-drowned Tavish from the waters of the gap just before they both were swept out to sea. In his limbs was the weariness of death, and blood flowed down his face from a long cut over his eye. The two men rested awhile upon the rocks at the mouth of the gap, then, leaning upon each other for support, made their way slowly up the cliffs and toward the cottage. There was no bitterness in their hearts against the Shanahans. Gratitude for being alive had driven all other emotions out. Tavish moaned and mumbled as Jamie helped him along the rough and stony paths. The moon had gone down and inky blackness was settled over the hills. Occasionally in the distance a torch flashed, and voices hailed each other across the glens, but Jamie and the Speaker avoided any contact with the searchers. For all they knew, the Shanahans might still be on the prowl.

"Sure this is one night the witches brewed," Tavish said between his groans. "Oh . . . them Shanahans. The ancients had a way to deal with the likes of them. A forest of trees

41

. . . and the Shanahans chained and spread-eagled among them, a Shanahan to every two trees. Then the trees were cut to fall away from each other—and at the same time. Och—the result would be beautiful to contemplate."

"Save your breath," said Jamie wearily, " 'twill make you easier to carry up the cliff."

At the cottage Kate had made extensive preparations for the wake. With Timothy Shanahan paying the bills she could afford to spend more or less lavishly. Two borrowed coffins were set up on saw horses before the fireplace, grim proxies of the bodies which had not yet been recovered. Jamie's personal belongings were placed neatly atop the pine box designed for his remains. On top of Owen Roe Tavish's coffin was the Speaker's tall hat, the only part of his apparel available for the occasion.

The news of the wake and its promised munificence had spread swiftly over the district. In a poor community such as this, a good wake was a welcome diversion. The thought that there would be plenty to eat and drink was enough to draw mourners who ordinarily would have given the two departed souls no more than a casual "God rest them."

By the time Jamie and Tavish had limped into view of the farm, the cottage was crowded with people, with more and more arriving and pushing their way inside to be near the whiskey. The sound of voices raised in lament reached the two men as they crossed the pasture.

"Is it the water sloshing around inside my head, or do I hear the sound of keening?" Tavish mumbled weakly.

" 'Tis likely we are both drowned and this is but a bad after-dreaming," Jamie grunted.

"Och, no, lad. No dead man ever ached in the places I do," Tavish replied.

The two men crossed behind the barn and crept up to the

low, rear window. One glance into the murky interior revealed the situation. Mourners were packed about the empty coffins like herring. Tirsa was seated at the head of Jamie's coffin, assuming the position of chief mourner, and Dennis sat beside her comfortingly. The women keened softly, and occasionally a man's voice rose above the subdued murmur.

"Aye, he was a boy to warm the inner cockles of the heart," said one.

"My arms are around you, Dan McRuin; aye, and around every member of his family this night," said another.

"He goes uneaten by the tooth of time, in all the pink of his young manhood," declared a third old man, who had walked miles in darkness to join the wake.

Outside, Owen Roe Tavish listened resentfully. "There's no mention of me," he whispered.

"They'll get to you when the whiskey starts working," Jamie assured him.

"That should be soon," Tavish muttered, watching the fresh bottles supplied by the Shanahans pass from hand to hand. He licked his lips thirstily. "Maybe we should make our resurrection known."

"Not yet," said Jamie.

He was afraid to give words to a wonderful thought rising within him. Inside the house, Randal Shanahan sounded the praises of Owen Roe Tavish.

"He was a man of extrahuman powers," Randal was saying. "Shifts and dodges were unknown to him. The country will not soon look upon his like again."

Tavish purred agreement as more and more men, their hearts warmed by a mixture of liquor and sorrow, gave voice to extravagant praise. They recounted occasions when the magic of his tongue had drawn recalcitrant parents together when all seemed lost because the property settlement stood in the way of true love.

"Sure Cupid has lost a string to his bow," a poetical little woman added to the chorus.

"He was one to stand against the sort of marriage too common in Ireland, where property and not true love is the consideration," said another.

"Sure, now that should be me epitaph," Tavish agreed modestly.

"Do you know," said Jamie slyly, "a terrible thing has just been made known to me."

"Shh, Jamie," Tavish hushed him, "I can't hear all the wonderful things they're saying."

"Come with me behind the byre; we've got to talk this thing over," Jamie whispered.

Reluctantly the Speaker followed him. "I never dreamed Standish O'Gorman held me in such high repute," he mused. "When I spoke for his daughter's hand for Fergus McFey, he threatened to use his stick on me. Well, I suppose a man has to die to know rightfully how his neighbors value him."

Behind the byre Jamie drew the Speaker to a spot where the sea-wind no longer licked at them with a tongue of ice. The old man's clothes were sodden wet and his teeth chattered like dice in a box. "I'm ready to go in now," he sighed. "The immortal part of me has had all the praise that is good for one man. The mortal part hankers for a steep drink of whiskey to take the chill out of me bones."

Jamie shook his head. "Tavish," he said, "We can't go back. It's too late."

"What do you mean by that, Jamie McRuin?" Tavish bristled.

"Don't you see, man, we could never live up to those wonderful things they've said about us in there? We're immortal. If we come walking in now, every man and maid in that house will turn against us. My own father is reconciled to my death. Tirsa is ready at a minute's notice to hold hands with my brother, Dennis, and he to take my place. The Shanahans all have guilty consciences, for which they have paid handsomely. If we appear now, everything turns to dust and ashes. My father would say, 'Look at the great bowsie, for all his dreams, he hasn't the wit to stay dead when it is best for all concerned.' Every man in the place would be kicking himself for any compliments he might have paid us. The Shanahans will reach for their sticks. Sure 'twould be one fearful muddle and we would never live down the disgrace of it." Jamie paused to observe the effect of his words.

Tavish checked his chattering teeth long enough to say, "Very well, Jamie, you stay dead. 'Tis more becoming the young to die heroically, anyway. I shall tell them all how you saved this miserable carcass at the expense of your sweet, young life. Such an epitaph you'll have as will be sung from one end of Christian Ireland to the other. 'Twill be my masterwork. Words I have been saving up for my own funeral will go into it."

"Very well," said Jamie, "go on back in there. Feel the weight of their anger. You'll soon see what it means to be a dead hero come to life. For every one of the good things they've said about you, ten bad ones will spring to their lips. How do you suppose Standish O'Gorman will feel about forgiving you when he sees you alive? Do you think he will forget that not a month ago you tricked him into doubling his daughter's fortune by telling him Fergus McFey was getting money from America? And don't forget the sticks of the Shanahans are aimed more at you than at me."

Owen Roe Tavish was momentarily sobered. "A man must give serious thought on his immortality," he admitted.

He limped slowly toward the cottage, with Jamie following close at his heels. "Are there any cases sadder in all the

history of the red world," the boy persisted, "than where
the men were given up for lost, only to return and find
they'd done better to stay dead?"

To prove his point, Jamie mentioned the case of Enoch
Arden, and conjured up names of ancient Irish kings who
had left their lands, and, after being reported dead, had returned home to misery and unhappiness. Where fact and
legend failed, he was not above inventing cases in which the
resurrection of such men had proved grimly anticlimactic.

Inside the cottage, Old Dan, warmed and consoled by
the plenty of good whiskey, and touched by the solicitude
of friends and neighbors, had risen to make a speech.

"Two mounds of gentle earth are waiting for my son and
cousin—Jamie and Owen Roe Tavish," he cried, gesturing
toward the empty coffins. "God be on the road with them
this night, I say. You—my friends and neighbors—are here
to bid them farewell, and with the tears washing down your
faces. . . ."

There were cries of agreement and approbation from the
mourners. Encouraged by the show of interest, Old Dan
continued. "Och, Owen Tavish," he apostrophized, "yours
was a mouth that never uttered an injustice. There be those
of us who feared your sharp tongue and superior learning,
got when you were studying for the priesthood when you
were but a lad. . . ."

A surprised murmur rose from the crowd inside the
cottage. " 'Tis God's own truth," continued Old Dan, "my
cousin, Tavish, was a spoiled priest!"

His words were greeted with a shocked silence. Outside
the window, Tavish clasped his hands to his head and
moaned. "Och . . . the idiot . . . the omadhaun! Hold
your tongue, Dan! I'm here . . . alive . . . !"

"Hush, man," cried Jamie, clapping his hand over the
Speaker's mouth, " 'tis too late! The words have fled . . .

from mouth to ear! By tomorrow your secret will belong to every man and woman in the county."

"I'm the ruined man this night—that I am," the Speaker groaned. "Who now will trust their matchmaking to a spoiled priest?"

Inside the cottage, Old Dan droned on with confessional zeal. "My lips have been sealed all these many years with the dark secret of why you left the Jesuit school. Fell in love with Ireland's pagan past, did my cousin; with Conchobor and Cuchulainn; with Balor of the evil eye, and Deirdre and the sons of Usnech; with great Queen Maeve and Finn of the Fenians, and Niall of the Nine Hostages . . . until the shadow of the whitethorn fell across the path to the cross . . . and he was lost for a while. . . ."

Jamie put his arm about the shoulders of the broken Speaker and led him back to the byre. His thoughts were a surging mixture of exultation and sadness. An avenue of escape had suddenly burst wide open for him, but at such a bruising cost to the old man beside him.

"There is a time for everything, Owen Roe Tavish," he said gently, "and the time has come for us to disappear."

"But Jamie, where is an old man like me to go? We have no relations outside Ireland . . . only our cousin, Power O'Malley, in far-off Georgia."

"Then to far-off Georgia and Cousin Power O'Malley we'll go," said Jamie. " 'Tis where Dennis was going. We'll take his place."

"Are you daft, man? And where's the money to come from?"

"How much will it cost?" Jamie demanded.

"Pounds and pounds, boy; lashans, more than dead men can lay their hands on."

"I wonder," said Jamie with meaning. "Come on."

The exhilaration that had swept through Jamie drove the

weariness and the aches and the chill from his body. He led the way back to the window. Inside at the wake, offering time had come. Though it was hardly a proper wake without bodies or proof of death, and no priest present, the conscience-stricken Shanahans insisted upon coming forward and placing generous contributions upon the empty coffins.

"Give deeply, man," Old Timothy Shanahan said to Randal. "The size of the offering shows your regard for the departed."

There was sly irony in the old man's words. Timothy knew that Randal and his brothers might give freely with words but would bitterly resist parting with money. He took his stand beside the coffins to shame them into generosity. Such an example set by the closefisted Shanahans spurred the others, now mellowed by an excess of whiskey. They trooped to the coffins and emptied the contents of their pockets upon the lids, voicing their bereavement at the untimely passing of the deceased.

Outside the window Jamie and the Speaker watched the tangible tribute to their virtues mounting sizably upon the lids of their separate coffins. Tavish, who loved the sight of money, even upon a coffin, clucked appreciatively. "You're right, Jamie, we could never go back now. To see all that lovely offering go back to the Shanahans would break my heart."

"Do you think there's enough for the passage to Georgia?" Jamie whispered.

Tavish was horrified. "You mean pilfer the burial offering from our own coffins? 'Tis a ghoulish thought. Besides, Father Finley wouldn't like it at all, at all."

Jamie explained that they would only be borrowing the money. "We will repay Father Finley . . . and with interest that will make his poor box jingle."

The Speaker continued emphatic in his disapproval, but a

gleam of acquisitiveness had come into his eyes. "I wouldn't consider doing such a low, knavish trick. Besides, how would we get the money off the coffins without being seen?"

"Leave that to me. We will bide our time and the whiskey will do the rest," said Jamie.

An hour went by, during which more and more of the watchers departed, or dropped off into fitful slumber. The Speaker's teeth were hammering so that Jamie feared the noise would attract someone's attention.

"Your teeth are clicking like bones in a box, man," he said. "Are your clothes that damp?"

"Me clothes are dry but their wetness has settled in my bones, Jamie," Tavish answered miserably. "I need the fire of liquor to drive it out."

The sky had a cold grayness before Jamie dared to venture inside the cottage. Most of the neighboring women had slipped away home and Tirsa and Kate had gone into the bedroom to sleep. The men were sprawled on the floor or on chairs, drugged by a mixture of weariness and alcohol. They muttered occasionally or stirred in their sleep, but Jamie could not wait any longer. He took off his shoes and crept through the open door of the cottage, stepping across the bodies of sleeping men. From the rear window Tavish watched, prayerfully. Swiftly Jamie gathered the offering from the coffins. The paper notes rustled softly and the silver coins clinked. The noise seemed shattering in the still room. The money gathered, Jamie turned to go, when Tavish "whished" to him from the window. The Speaker was making violent motions toward a partly filled bottle of whiskey left on the table. Jamie tiptoed to the bottle, gathered it in his hand, and started again for the door. Suddenly he found himself directly before his father's chair.

The old man was slumped down, his head tilted back, and mouth slightly ajar. Abruptly his bright blue eyes opened and stared straight into Jamie's. No other part of him moved. Even his mouth remained partly open.

Jamie froze in his tracks, scarcely daring to breathe. "Is that the ghost of my son, Jamie?" the old man asked simply.

"Aye, Father," Jamie answered softly, trying to sound as he thought a ghost should.

"Dear Jamie," his father continued, "drowned and battered by the stones . . . his clothes torn and wet. How's your mother, son?"

"I haven't seen her yet," Jamie whispered. He tried to think of some way to escape from Old Dan, who seemed set to carry on a long ghost-talk with his missing son. "I've got to go now, Father, Tavish is waiting."

"Where?" asked Old Dan, with childish curiosity.

"With three angels, just beyond the Knockmealldown Mountains," Jamie said urgently. "Their names are Generosity, Gratitude, and Promptness, and Promptness doesn't like to be kept waiting."

"God rest your soul, Jamie, and the blessings of Brigid be upon it. Kiss the little hands of Mary for me. Tell your mother I'll be with her soon."

Jamie's eyes flooded with tears. His father's words had been spoken like a prayer, which indeed they were. The old man's eyes closed and a half-smile tipped the corners of his lips. A ray of light from the promised sunrise transfixed his face for an instant. . . . Impulsively Jamie stooped and kissed the old man's forehead.

Telling about his dream afterward, Dan McRuin proudly said that even the kiss of a dead McRuin was warmer than that of most living

PART TWO

A damsel fair with curling hair and such beauty as went out of Ireland when the foreigners came in. . . .

V

THE road that wound southward through the greening
Georgia hills was the dull red color of a robin's breast. Surface dust rose in a soft, pink cloud about the feet of two
foot travelers and remained hanging in the warm spring air
minutes after the men had passed. They trudged steadily
ahead, their eyes upon the uneven surface of the road and
their feet scuffing out a kind of grating rhythm. The afternoon sun beat down and the weight of their heavy homespun garments brought a steady trickle of perspiration on
the faces of the younger man and his older companion.

Jamie spoke without slowing his stride. "There's a bridge
ahead, Owen Roe Tavish. Maybe now there'll be a river."

"Sure the sound of running water will be the sweetest
music heard this side of Heaven," the old man grunted,
"though after swallowing half of Dunriggan Gap, I never
thought to say it."

With Jamie leading, the two men left the road before
it reached the bridge and descended to the bank of a wide,
shallow stream. They followed it a hundred yards or more to

where a thicket of willows and alders shielded them from the road; there they drank thirstily and removed their dusty shoes and drew the legs of their trousers above their knees. While Jamie washed his face and arms, Tavish thrust his feet into the stream, letting the water purl about his ankles.

"Don't stand too close, Jamie lad," he said. "The cold water striking my hot feet may bring a rush of steam that will scald you. Like the great Cuchulainn of olden times, who would come from a battle in such a heat of rage that the servants had to dip him in three vats of cold water before his temperature returned to normal . . . there was always danger of someone being scalded to death."

"I could boil water for tea just by dipping in my big toe," said Jamie. He thrust his feet knee-deep into the stream and lay back on the gravel with a sigh of comfort.

"How far would you say we'd come, Cousin Tavish?" he asked.

"As a man who calls anything over and above ten miles 'a long way' and lets it go at that . . . I'd say we'd come a long way."

"And how much farther do we have to go?"

"As a man who believes that only one journey ever really ends—and that one to the graveyard—I'd say a long, long way."

"How do you feel?"

"I can speak only for my feet. They're in Heaven."

"Now why is it that an Irishman can never give a straight answer to straight question?" Jamie mused.

The Speaker was indignant. He raised himself upon an elbow to state that Irishmen, being of poetical natures, naturally preferred saying things in an obscure manner.

"It makes their meaning so much clearer than if they had put it in plain language in the first place," he concluded.

"Then tell me how many days since we sailed from Galway?" Jamie persisted.

"Days? 'tis years you mean," Tavish retorted. "That trip
. . . och, that trip . . . with the ocean maneuvering to
drown us each day, and me too sick to make a fight of it."

"I never thought you'd live through," Jamie agreed.

"I didn't. I died and rose up again."

Jamie laughed. The weeks of hand-to-mouth travel spent
with the spirited old man had bred a new respect and affection for Tavish. "Right now there be a kind of sweet weariness in my bones . . . but a kind of excitement, too," he
said. "The days we've been on the road seem like hours spent
under an enchantment. Each morning as we started out the
wind would whisper: 'Step livelier, Jamie McRuin, you're
walking to meet the Spring. Around some bend in the road
ahead she's waiting . . . with the odor of early violets on
her breath.' "

"Och," Tavish sighed, "the stories I'll be telling at home
of the wonders of the Western world. Sure I'll walk the lanes
with an eight-foot stick, and my pockets clinking with gold
and silver."

"Shall we put on our shoes—point their toes Atlantaward
—and follow where they lead, Cousin Tavish?" Jamie
invited.

"Leave me close my eyes another minute," Tavish
pleaded. "It reminds me of a weir at home where I fished
as a boy." The old man was silent a moment, then he said
seriously, "You must promise me something, Jamie!"

"Anything, Cousin Tavish."

"No, I'm that serious. If I should die . . . I wouldn't
want to lie buried in any but Irish soil. Promise me you'll
take me home when that time comes?"

"I will, Cousin Tavish," Jamie said softly. "I swear by the
gods my people swear by! Owen Roe Tavish shall lie in sweet
Irish earth when his time comes."

The promise soothed the old man. He lay back and closed
his eyes again. "Just two minutes more, Jamie. I'll fall asleep

to the music of the water . . . then I'll wake and be ready
to go," he said.

Jamie stretched himself upon the bank and gently
scratched his back against the gravel beneath him. The days
since leaving Ireland had piled one upon the other until
they had lost their separate identity. A sense of wonder and
excitement had fused time and space and the elements into
a sort of magic backdrop before which he and Tavish
marched, yet remained apart from. Their money had run
out in Virginia and they had traveled shanks' mare the rest
of the way, except for an occasional short lift. But to Jamie,
in retrospect, the miles had not seemed to weary him, nor
the rain to wet him. Cold had not chilled, nor hunger weakened him. Sure, the Fairy Queen has woven a spell around
me, he mused. I'm insensible to the wear and tear of every-
day life . . . a kind of superbeing. 'Tis a very satisfying
thought.

He turned his attention downstream to where a great
splashing was taking place in the brook. A hundred yards
below a man was watering a string of twenty or thirty mules.
The animals were tethered into groups of five or six to
simplify handling, and as fast as one bunch was watered
another was herded into the stream. The man in charge was
a skilled hand with animals. He prodded the stubborn mules
into the water, let them drink their fill, then urged them
scrambling up the bank with sharp cries and the stinging
slap of a rope.

As Jamie watched admiringly, a young girl approached
the watering place carrying two heavy wooden buckets. The
man tending the mules motioned her to go farther upstream.
"The mules have riled the water," Jamie heard him call out.

The girl turned and came toward Jamie and Tavish's
resting place, making her way slowly through the tangle of
shrubs and willows. She disappeared momentarily and Jamie

watched for her reappearance with a mild glow of interest. He was hungry for the sight of a pretty girl. She was bare-headed and occasionally her yellow hair glinted in the sun as she moved gracefully through the green willows. Her figure was slim and straight and poised as a young colt's, while the heavy bucket in each hand balanced her movements.

Jamie appraised the topography of the ground opposite and decided there was only one place the girl could get down to the stream. That was where he and Tavish were cooling their feet. He began to follow her progress with mounting expectancy, watching for the red-and-white checked dress as it bobbed in and out among the willows like a red-and-white float in a smooth green sea.

"How would you like to see a bonnie girl, with hair the color of gold and beauty of the sort that went out of Ireland when the foreigners came in?" he whispered to Tavish.

The Speaker's eyes snapped open and he sat eagerly up-right. "Where?"

The girl's bright gingham dress was obscured momen-tarily, and Tavish peered about vainly. " 'Tis not like you to be teasing an old man," he reproached Jamie.

He lay back and closed his eyes again. "There be few things that the sight of a pretty girsha wouldn't cure," he sighed.

The corners of Jamie's mouth twitched and he kept his eyes on an opening in the willows opposite. A few seconds later the girl appeared. She set one bucket down and was preparing to fill the other when she saw the two men. There was no fear in her start of surprise, but immediately she turned to go.

Jamie stood up. "Please stay," he called.

Tavish sat up, blinking at the apparition on the other side of the stream. "Is she real . . . or are we under a spell?" he muttered in Irish.

The girl on the opposite bank stopped and faced the two men. Jamie saw that she had large, hazel eyes that tipped upward at the outer corners. Her features were small and regular, from the perfect forehead down to a tiny, determined chin.

Jamie didn't want to speak again for fear any words he might say would drive the girl away. He waited for Tavish to say something, but the old man was still entangled in his dreams and half believed himself under an enchantment.

"Don't be afraid," Jamie said to the girl.

Her lips curled upward into a smile and she tossed her corn-yellow hair. "Afraid . . . of two Irishmen having a foot bath?"

Tavish hastily withdrew his feet from the stream and covered them with his hat, tittering foolishly.

"Do you live hereabout?" said Jamie, emboldened.

"We are horse traders and our camp is just below in the piney woods," the girl answered.

Tavish regained his tongue. "Irish horse traders," he exclaimed. "Sure now, my cousin, Power O'Malley, him that we're on our way to visit in Atlanta, wrote us about you in the old country. What is your father's name, lass?"

"Shiel Harrigan."

"I knew some Harrigans in Kerry."

"My father's family came from Cork."

"You haven't told us your name," said Jamie.

"Hold your questioning tongue," Tavish scolded. " 'Tis not right and proper to ask a young girl's name alone in the willows."

The girl turned her wide, wise hazel eyes full on Jamie. "My name is Maeve," she said.

Jamie had never heard silver bells but the voice of the girl on the opposite bank taught him how they should sound. "I must go back to the camp," she said, "they're waiting for the water."

Tavish and Jamie splashed quickly across and dipped the two buckets into the stream. "I'll be carrying these for you, Maeve," Jamie said boldly.

The girl hesitated. "Our people don't welcome strangers. One of you may come," she conceded.

She looked from Jamie to Owen Roe Tavish. "The old one."

Tavish purred a sound of satisfaction as Jamie dejectedly set the buckets down. "I'll be ambassador for the both of us, Jamie; never fear, lad."

He hefted the buckets preparatorily, spat on his hands, then seized them and set off after Maeve. She led the way through the willows but flashed a warming smile at the disgruntled Jamie. A moment later Tavish was back.

"I forgot my boots," he explained.

When they were gone out of sight, Jamie laid his head disconsolately on the sand. As a person who lived by and for his emotions, he had never sought to analyze them. There was never time. Feelings light and dark, gay and sad, stormed through him in such a violent flood there was little time for analysis until the flood had subsided. Then it was too late. Now he lay on the sand with such an aching love for a girl, whom he had first seen but a few brief minutes before, that his muscles twitched spasmodically and tears smarted in his eyes. He knew with the certainty of youth and first love that the girl with the golden hair and the eyes that were merry and wise at the same time was the one the Fairy Queen had promised him. Her portrait fitted the empty frame that had hung on the wall of his secret heart.

In the hour that Tavish was gone, Jamie felt nothing but the soft, poignant ache of ecstasy. His stomach was empty but there was no sensation of hunger. He did not hear the brook babbling over the stones, nor the doves in the wood, nor the crows complaining in the green, young corn. In that one hour he courted and won Maeve in a waking dream, bore her to the priest in a carriage spilling with flowers, and heard her bound to him by spoken vows unsaid since the time of the Druids: "By the sun and the moon and the whole earth, is Maeve wed to Jamie. May the air bless them, and the water and the wind; the sea, and all the hours of the sun and moon. And fruitful their union be!"

Jamie came awake when Tavish called from the opposite bank. He sat up groggily and put on his shoes. "We're invited to stay the night and ride into Atlanta in style," Tavish crowed. "Come along with you. Whisha, man, you've waded across with your boots on. You act like you've been drinking."

"If I could bottle the stuff on which I'm drunk," said Jamie, "I'd be the richest man in the world. Better . . . nor I nor the world would know the need of money."

"What sort of blather-am-skate is that?" said Tavish. "Come along."

With Jamie following at his heels, the Speaker recounted what he had learned at the horse trader's camp. "They have small liking for strangers," he said. "The dogs would have torn me to pieces had it not been for Maeve. There's a colleen for you; a princess right out of a fairy story. There be five or six families with such a plather of children and dogs that they only sort them at nightfall."

Jamie made no comment and Tavish continued. "Would you believe it, lad, offshoots of the tinkers, they are! Living in tents like they do at home—but rich! Not a family of them has touched solder to pot in two generations. Horses and mules and Irish lace, with an occasional piece of tweed, is what they trade in now."

The six or seven tents of the horse traders were ranged in a semicircle about large community stoves and tables. The pine trees gave additional shelter and the ground was smoothly carpeted with pine needles. Chairs and benches were spread about under the trees. Some were rugged, home-made affairs, but here and there velvet-upholstered and over-sized leather Morris chairs sat incongruously under the sky.

The tent houses were large, rectangular canvas affairs, all dark green in color, with a heavy center pole and four shorter poles to uphold each corner. It was a warm spring day and the sides of the tents were rolled up, leaving the interiors open and revealed. On the high center pole of each tent was hung a crucifix. At one end, and dominating the interior of every tent, was a giant double bed, neatly made and covered with a rich spread of Irish lace. The beds varied between mahogany, brass, and fumed oak, but in size and grandeur they could have been the pride of any Victorian bedroom. Each tent was further equipped with large com-modes or chiffoniers and mirrors, while cots and smaller beds for the children were pushed out of sight beneath the master bed.

In a poverty-ridden community, there was no sign of poor-ness here. The children were loved and well fed. It showed in their racy wildness and lively tongues. They spoke a jab-berwocky of English and Gaelic, and filled the camp and woods surrounding it with quick, ringing laughter.

The uniqueness of the scene was lost on Jamie. Tavish introduced him to the men of the camp and he acknowl-edged their friendly greetings in a semidaze. There was Shiel Harrigan, who was the leader of the camp and Maeve's father; Tade Hennessy, Brave Dan Devlin, Jaunting Jim Donner, Me-Dennis O'Ryan, and Foxy Fergus O'Flaherty. In the brief hour that Tavish had been loose in the camp, he had learned every man's nickname and history. His gay spirits and countless stories captured the affections of the men and the woods echoed with their laugher.

Jamie had spun himself into a cocoon of dreams. He was present but took no part in the common activity of the camp. His eyes were on the women who stayed modestly separate from the men. It was nearing the supper hour and they were busy about the stoves and tables preparing the evening meal. Jamie could see Maeve moving among them. He heard his voice joking and making casual conversation with the men, but his attention never strayed from the girl with hair like sunshine. Not a movement or gesture of hers escaped him. The smallest act became endowed with a peculiar grace of its own and found a sort of musical accompaniment in his heart.

"How can I go on, loving her more and more, when even now the length and breadth of me is one great ache?" he asked himself.

One thought troubled him. What if Maeve did not take his love seriously. What if she laughed and said no man could care for a girl in a few short hours. How would he convince her?

Someone touched his shoulder. It was Shiel Harrigan, Maeve's father. "The supper is on," he said. "You'll sit at my table. We eat ahead of the women here."

Jamie followed him to a plain, rough table near the stoves. Harrigan was a broad, well-built man of medium height. In his weather-beaten face were only occasional traces of the beauty his daughter had inherited, but their eyes were alike; tilting upward at the corners, and appearing young and old, wise and gay at the same time.

Tavish sat on Harrigan's right, Jamie on his left. An older woman, whom Jamie took to be an aunt or cousin, set a jug and three glasses on the table. Harrigan poured three drinks and proposed a toast to the visitors.

> Here's health and long life to you;
> The woman of your choice to you;
> Land without rent to you;
> And death in Erin.

To Jamie, in whose state liquor could have only a sobering effect, the words seemed deeply prophetic.

He sat silent throughout the meal, aware only of Maeve's form flitting between the stove, the tent, and the table. He hungered to look at her but dared not, for fear his secret would spill from his eyes. She must know, or at least suspect his feelings, he thought. There seemed to be no other young man of marriageable age in the camp—a fact for which Jamie felt extreme relief. For a few tortured minutes when Tavish was introducing him to the men, he was afraid Maeve might have been bespoken by one of them.

Tavish regaled the company with news and gossip of the old country. Though few of the horse traders had been born in Ireland, they listened avidly to Tavish's stories as if every character and hill and stone was known to them intimately.

Dan Devlin brought out a set of Irish pipes and played the old familiar songs: "Eilleen Aroon" and "Like Hares on the Mountain." Maeve stood where the warm glow from the fire touched her face and sang in a high, sweet voice:

Were I and my darling, O heart-bitter wound,
On board of a ship for America bound.

Jamie was grateful for the dark. It cloaked the depth of emotion that suffused his being and left him weak. One by one the children fell asleep and were gathered up by their mothers and tucked into bed. The women soon followed. The sides of the tents came down with sharp, rustling sounds and the lamps within cast dim silhouettes upon the canvas walls.

Maeve and her aunt, whom she called Bid, were the last to go. The girl flashed Tavish and Jamie a smile. "God be between you and harm," she called, and disappeared into the shadows.

"If I live twice two hundred years, I'll never forget the wonder of this night," Jamie promised himself.

The men sat awhile smoking and conversing in low tones. One by one they knocked out their pipes, muttered a quiet "God bless . . ." and slipped away.

Harrigan led Jamie and Tavish to an open wagon some distance from the tents, near the rope corral in which the horses and mules were tethered. There was a thick layer of straw in the bed of the wagon and the chief of the horse traders furnished an armful of quilts.

"You'll be comfortable the night," he said. "God keep you."

"Sure, I could sleep on two flat rocks in the middle of a stream with never a drop of wet, I'm that worn out," said Tavish. "Put your hand in God's, Shiel Harrigan. It was a day of days when we set eyes on your lovely daughter."

When Harrigan was gone the two men removed their shoes and wrapped themselves in the quilts. Jamie had no desire to go to sleep. The hunger in his heart made him wakeful. He lay staring upward at the spangled sky and finding in every pattern of stars the outline of Maeve's face. The fine, lace-edges of the pine boughs above seemed wisps of hair that caressed her cheeks, and the wind in the upper branches became her human sigh.

The aching knot in Jamie's breast became intolerable and he sat up with a strangled cry. "Tavish," he said, "are you awake?"

The older man stirred and mumbled a grudging "No."

"Listen carefully," Jamie continued, "in the morning you shall speak to Shiel Harrigan . . . first thing."

"Oh, I will . . . I will," grumbled Tavish sarcastically. " 'The top o' the morning to you, Shiel Harrigan,' I'll say. 'And how's your morning's morning this morning? Did you rest well, God grant?' Oh, I'll speak to him . . . never fear. Now go to sleep."

"I mean speak to him for Maeve . . . for me."

"Oh, to be sure . . . to be sure," Tavish scoffed. Then he sat upright. "Jamie . . . do you know what you're saying? Sure, now, you're dreaming. 'Tis a nightmare you're having, and small wonder . . . sleeping so close to the horses."

"It's no dream. My heart is worn to a silk thread for the love of her."

"If you ben't dreaming, then I pray God 'tis me. Marry with Maeve, is it? Sure, you've spilled your wits somewhere back along the road, my fine buachail."

Jamie seized the old man and shook him savagely. "Are you forgetting I've been promised the woman of my choice? Sure then, I choose Maeve. Think you I've traveled half the world around to find her and then not say out what's in my heart?"

"All right, Jamie, all right; compose yourself, lad. Sure, I'll speak for you," Tavish soothed him. "God's darling, you are, but don't forget we're little better than ghosts now, with nought but the clothes on our backs and given the length and breadth of us for a place to sleep down with the horses out of cold charity. 'Tis all well and good to speak of fairy promises and dreams and wishes. But when the talk is of marriage, you'll find the old ones standing out for money and hens and feather beds. With a stem of sense, you'll know what I'm saying is true, lad."

"I can read it in her eyes. She'll have me, in spite of her father's money and his hens and his feather beds," Jamie said.

A buoyant assurance swelled inside him. He believed his own words. The force of his love would sweep everything before it. Una's promise would be kept. Hadn't his first wish —for travel—been granted? Hadn't he been led straight to Maeve? Now the rest was up to him. The path of destiny lay sharp and clear and strewn with rose petals.

"When she knows what's in my heart, she'll have me," he proclaimed confidently.

Tavish had been thinking. "The situation is delicate and calls for care," he said. "These are a people who do not take favorably to outsiders. If the wind of a word of this gets out, sure the two of us will be turned loose to find our way to Atlanta as best we can. So . . . we'll not speak until we're but a day's ride away. That will give us time to impress Shiel Harrigan and the others with what a lovely boy you are. With luck, and in the small while we have, and if the Devil hasn't baked Harrigan with too hard a crust, we might . . . remember, I only said 'might,' win from the man a charitable listening to our suit."

"Hear the words of a man who has looked into tomorrow and has the gift of prophecy," Jamie assured him. "Maeve's father will open his arms to me, as to a son."

Tavish settled himself once more to sleep. "Who can reason with a young man," he sighed, "when the lightning of love has struck?"

Jamie lay staring into the wide and starry sky, relishing his wakefulness. The seconds were so rich in exquisite happiness he didn't wish to lose one to oblivion. Contentment, like a warm, enveloping blanket, settled over him and the soft thumping of hoofs in the corral near by lulled him finally to sleep.

Tavish was snoring gently when Jamie awakened at dawn. The smell of wood smoke stung his nostrils pleasantly. The women of the camp were stirring already. The thought of Maeve sent Jamie leaping from his bed. Without waiting to put on his shoes, he opened the ropes and began to herd the mules and horses into the stream, using the same technique he had observed the day before.

As he was finishing, Maeve's soft, silvery laugh sounded behind him. "Sure now, you're waking the creatures out of a sound sleep to water them," she teased.

It was easy to laugh with her, Jamie found. He took the buckets she had brought. "The stream is murky here. Come, I'll take you to a magic spring, where the water is of such marvelous sweetness, 'tis said that whoever drinks it falls in love with the first person they see."

Maeve wrinkled her nose playfully. "Oh, the blather. I know the name of every spring from here to Atlanta and I never heard the tell of such a place! What would be the name of this wonderful spot?"

"The Spring of the Seven Sisters! There's a legend about the place that's God's own truth. A prince of the underworld who lived hereabouts, fell in love with the youngest of seven sisters. When he invited her to come and share his underground palace, she laughed in his face, because he had long green hair like the moss that grows at the bottom of the stream, and pink eyes like a rabbit, and a red nose like a bog-Irishman who has lived all his life on praties and poteen. . . ." Jamie stole a look over his shoulder at Maeve, following at his heels.

"Oh, the blather-am-skate," she hooted, "there's not an ounce of truth in the whole of it." But the tale had caught her fancy and her eyes sparkled with interest.

" 'Tis true as truth," Jamie protested. "It was written in a book."

Maeve was impressed. "What happened when the youngest sister refused to marry with the wicked prince?" she asked.

"He determined to capture her against her will and placed a spell upon the water, so that when the youngest sister drank at the spring, she would fall in love with the first man she saw. . . ."

"Which would be the prince with green hair," prompted Maeve.

"Sure that was the way he planned it, but plans often go awry. The youngest sister was very beautiful but she had six older sisters who were plain enough to frighten kites from a cornfield. When the seven of them came to the enchanted spring, they drank in the order of their ages: the oldest first, and so on. Well, the wicked prince was hiding beneath the water, and when he heard the oldest sister drinking, he sprang to the surface, thinking to show himself to the youngest. Instead he was seen by the ugly oldest who promptly fell madly in love with him. Six times the underworld prince appeared and six times he was seen by one of the ugly sisters, until they were all six in love with him. Only the youngest, the one he wanted in the first place, was left."

"What happened?" demanded Maeve, enchanted as a child by the story.

"They were all drowned," said Jamie placidly. "The six ugly sisters were so mad for the love of the wicked prince, they flung themselves into the water trying to reach him. And the youngest was drowned trying to rescue her sisters."

" 'Tis terrible," Maeve protested. "Why did the youngest have to die?"

" 'Twas the fault of the book. Sure books do terrible things to people," Jamie teased.

"But the youngest was beautiful. She oughtn't to have died."

"Aye . . . she was the beauty of the world. With hair as blond as sunshine . . . like your own," Jamie said softly.

Maeve's cheeks flushed a bright pink. They had reached the point of their meeting the day before. "I must go back now," she said. "They'll be wondering why I'm so long in bringing the water."

"Don't you want to drink at the magic spring?" Jamie asked.

Maeve shook her head. Her manner had become cool and

distant. "I have no time for magic springs . . . or stories of underground princes and the like." She turned and walked swiftly toward the camp.

Jamie filled the buckets and followed slowly, hurt and humbled. A sharp word from Maeve had turned the surging happiness within him into a weight of misery. His bantering lip-liveliness was gone and the buckets which had danced in his grasp before, now dragged at his arms like leaden weights.

The camp was in the midst of breakfast when they returned. Maeve took her place among the women, while Jamie sat again beside Shiel Harrigan. No comment was made about his carrying water for the chief's daughter, but out of the corner of his eye Jamie saw the woman Maeve called Aunt Bid speak sharply to the girl.

The aunt was a tall, dominating spinster, whose eyes saw and registered everything with an old maid's acumen. She had taken over the rearing of Maeve ten years before when the girl's mother died, and had guarded her dead sister's child with a zealousness that scarcely could have been equaled had Maeve been her own.

The horse traders broke camp after breakfast and were on the road in an hour. They moved southward toward Atlanta, traveling steadily but easily, so as not to weary the animals. Their camp sites along the way were already laid out, having been used many times before, and the problem of making and breaking camp had been reduced to a minimum by the speed and precision gained from years of practice.

Tavish rode in the lead wagon, with Shiel Harrigan, Maeve, and Aunt Bid. Jamie had to content himself with the second wagon, driven by Jaunting Jim Donner. He caught glimpses of those ahead from time to time, and heard Maeve's silver laughter at Tavish's endless sallies, but he was as removed from her as if they dwelt in different planets.

In the evenings after camp was made, a festive air infected the horse traders. It increased as they drew nearer and nearer to Atlanta. Jaunting Jim explained to Jamie how other camps of horse traders were making their way toward the Georgia capital from all over the South. There they met during the last week in April to bury those who had died on the road during the year and whose bodies had been sent ahead for burial. There would be one great mass funeral. Marriages would be performed, betrothals announced, and babies christened, in one all-embracing festival. The young people would meet, mingle, and court one another.

" 'Tis a fair and funeral all rolled into one," Jaunting Jim said. "None of our people would miss it, unless they were laid out in a box—and then they'd be there in spirit."

At night, when the supper things were cleared away, there was music and dancing. The children were taught the ancient group dances and songs, so they would be prepared to take a part in the celebrations. Those who had yet to be confirmed studied their catechisms.

Tavish had endeared himself to everyone. The children called him the shanachie, or storyteller, and begged him not to leave them when they reached Atlanta. Jamie had exchanged no word with Maeve since that morning by the stream. He flung himself into the work of the camp, more to keep occupied than to impress Shiel Harrigan with his potentialities as a son-in-law. Tavish nodded his approval as Jamie sweated at loading and unloading the wagons; fed, watered, brushed, and curried the animals until their coats shone.

On their last night out from Atlanta, Tavish took Jamie aside. "Tonight I will speak for you," he said solemnly.

Jamie shook his head in acute misery. " 'Twill be of no use, Owen Roe Tavish. She'll have none of me."

"Whisha . . . where's all your proud confidence now, lad? Are you giving up without a fight?" the old man scolded. "No man that Owen Roe Tavish speaks for is beaten until the last word has been spoken."

"It's in my bones," Jamie said. "She'll have none of me."

The boy's despondency was so real that Tavish set himself to cheer the lad up. "And why not?" he demanded. "She may be the likeliest girl that ever shook a foot on short grass, but does that mean you're not her match? You that was the darling among the colleens at home. Sure many a red cheek grew redder when you walked into the chapel of a Sunday morning. Not have you? Why, she's that lucky we'll consider the match—and I'll tell Shiel Harrigan as much."

The Speaker's exuberance won a wan smile from Jamie. "Bless you, Owen Tavish, for what you're trying to do. Sure you're a man who can lie finer than the truth."

"Watch for a signal when I've spoken to her father. You have my hand on it, the girl will be promised you before the fire is banked for the night." With that the old man stalked away, muttering with determination.

In spite of his doubts, Jamie's hopes rose. Maeve promised to him? And why not? Hadn't he Queen Una's word for it? He set about his evening chores with a lighter heart than he had had for days, grateful that powers more than human were helping to shape his destiny.

He watched Tavish and Harrigan stroll away from the camp after supper and fear and hope tied at "tug-o'-war" inside him. The two men were gone a long while. The women and children had retired when Harrigan returned—alone. He went directly to his tent without speaking to anyone.

Minutes passed and Tavish did not appear. Finally Jamie went to look for him. He found the old man at the horse corral stroking the velvet nose of a colt. Standing beside him, Jamie towered almost a head taller than the little Speaker. Tavish seemed shrunken, and the spirit had gone out of him. Even before he spoke, Jamie knew what the answer was going to be.

"I've gone and lost her for you, Jamie," the old man said.

James heard the words as if from far off, and his own voice answering: "I dreamed too high, Cousin Tavish."

"I won't have you be thinking that," the old man protested. "Harrigan had nought to say of you but good. 'Tis only—well, the girl is promised to another. They're to be wed in Atlanta."

The words came with the finality of final judgment. Why hadn't Tavish added: "And may the just God have mercy on your soul"? Jamie thought. They were supposed to say something like that when a sentence of doom was pronounced on a man. Far back in his brain he heard a small, clear voice: "From this moment you are a dead man, Jamie McRuin," it said. "Others you may fool but not yourself. Sure you'll walk and talk and breathe the air—and take to the drink, maybe. You'll smash your great fists into men's faces and feel their blood on your knuckles, but you'll be dead for all that. You've been killed inside, Jamie, and from now on you're a walking corpse."

It was true. Maeve was lost to him. The sweetness locked inside him which had needed the chemistry of her touch to draw it forth, now turned bitter as gall. A terrible rage seized Jamie. He wanted to hurt someone . . . something; but mostly himself. An outward pain might ease his inner suffering.

Tavish's hand was on his shoulder but Jamie shook it off. "I've no need for your pity, Cousin Tavish," he said. "Save it for the man she's going to marry . . . when he meets up with these." Jamie shook his fists level with the Speaker's eyes. "The beating I'll give him will serve as a wedding present." He turned and staggered into the woods like a drunken man. Tavish watched him go until the darkness swallowed him.

"Jamie . . . Jamie . . . don't you know that beating with your fists will never mend the ache of love?" the old man said softly.

It was hours later when Jamie walked slowly into the clearing where the tents were pitched. His clothes were torn and stained with blood from his cut and battered hands. He looked as if he had been in a terrible fight. Silently but without stealth, he moved toward Maeve's tent. The sharp-eared dogs started up, then growled sleepily and lay back down.

Before Harrigan's tent Jamie hesitated, but only for a moment. Some instinct seemed to guide him to where Maeve lay sleeping. At the spot he sank to his knees and pressed his face against the tent wall, as if in silent prayer. There he remained like a suppliant at the altar, giving no thought to his personal danger, or of the recklessness of his act. Had Maeve's father or any man in the camp discovered him, they would have felt justified in shooting him.

"Maeve," he whispered the name no louder than breath. "It is I, Jamie . . . come to beg your forgiveness and say good-by. I wouldn't cause you a minute's unhappiness, even by loving you, could I but help myself. O my darling—my treasure—my hands are that broken and bleeding from bashing the trees in the wood. Every tree seemed to wear the face of the man you're going to marry. . . ."

Inside the tent there was a slight rustle. The flap of the tent swished back softly and Maeve appeared in her nightgown. Without speaking she came to Jamie's side and took his arm, drawing him gently to his feet.

"Come away," she said kindly. "Is it in your mind to destroy us all?"

She led him to a bench near the stoves and sat him down.

A soft glow from the banked fire fell upon his wracked and tortured face.

Maeve said nothing, but took a cloth and wet it in one of the wooden pails. Gently she bathed his torn hands and face as a mother would a child.

"I should have spoken that day by the stream and told you I was to marry with Travis Bunn in Atlanta. It was cruel of me to keep silent." Her voice was tender and wise and seemed filled with ineffable music.

"Was it so plain then, that everyone could see my feelings for you?"

"Women have an instinct about such things. I knew and yet I pretended not to know. Aunt Bid warned me . . . she even spoke to Father. I laughed at them . . . said it was foolishness. Now I'm sorry for you've hurt yourself."

"The scratches will mend."

"They're on the outside. Things inside take longer."

"Maeve . . . if it were otherwise . . . if you were not promised to Travis Bunn . . . ?" Jamie was not allowed to finish the question. Aunt Bid had slipped from the tent and now bore down upon them swiftly and silently, her stern face dark with anger in the dim light.

"Would you shame your father in his own camp?" she hissed at Maeve. Keeping her voice low so as not to arouse the camp, she turned on Jamie, lashing him with her tongue.

"Are you crazed, man? Destroy yourself if you've a mind, but don't drag an innocent young girl down with you."

For some reason which he could not fathom, Jamie felt comforted. He gazed at Aunt Bid in her long, flowing flannel nightgown, her feet bare and her sparse gray locks twisted into curlers, and felt a perverse impulse to laugh. Instead he rose and bowed politely.

"May God preserve you, ma'am," he said. "Sure and you're looking well."

Maeve choked back a laugh and Bid turned on her fiercely. "It would serve you both right if I let your father find you here . . . and you in your nightgown."

"And isn't that what you're wearing?" Maeve said, with demure slyness.

Aunt Bid was torn between righteous rage at such effrontery and confusion at finding herself in the presence of a man while clothed only in her nightgown.

"There's been nothing said or done here this night for which anyone has call to feel ashamed," Jamie said loftily. "I did but beg Maeve's forgiveness for loving her, and her promised to another. Can there be harm in that?"

He raised his voice as he spoke, and in fright Aunt Bid gathered Maeve to her and began a hasty retreat.

"The man is drunk or mad or both," she exclaimed.

Jamie followed them. "I said I loved her, but 'twas no secret. You knew it . . . her father knew it . . . and she knew it. Now let the world know it: I love Maeve. There . . . it's been said, and the words are still warm with the breath of me. When I'm walking the streets of the world sad and tormented, she will know that I am rich inside for having loved her."

Jamie's voice had risen to a small shout as Maeve and her aunt vanished into the tent. He stood for a moment, arrogant as a conquering rooster. A flood of exhilaration swept over him. There was no explanation for the sudden change; it came like a summer storm, with thunder and swift lightning, to cleanse him of the vapors of despondency.

Tavish hurried from the corral to his side. "Have you been drinking, man? Sure I heard you proclaiming great words in my sleep. Come to bed before you wake the camp."

Jamie clapped his arm affectionately about the old man. "Cousin Tavish," he announced, "you're embracing a happy man."

"Sure now I know you're drunk . . . or crazed. Come to bed."

"Aye . . . drunk I am," said Jamie, "but not on whiskey. I'm drunk on the wonder of the world."

The horse traders made their Atlanta camp just off the Chattanooga Turnpike in a pleasant stand of longleaf pine. The location had served them many times before, and the tents, stoves, and elaborate camping paraphernalia carried in the wagons were soon in place. When the work was done, a welter of bathing, shaving, hair cutting, and shining of boots followed. The girls gathered at one end of the camp after their baths, where mothers combed, brushed, and braided hair until the children winced and cried out in pain.

The boys were herded together at the other end by Brave Dan Devlin, who was handy with a set of mail-order clippers. Brave Dan wasted no time on this ritual of the annual or semiannual haircut. He clapped a saucepan on the head of each squirming child, using its metal edges as a general outline to follow, and clipped off all exposed hair as if he were shearing sheep. The results were mildly spectacular, since the same saucepan served, without regard to the size of head being shorn.

Jamie took over Maeve's task of fetching water for bathing and shaving. It kept him busy the entire morning. "I hauled enough water this day to wash a regiment of Hottentots," he told Tavish. "There's scarce enough left in the stream to bathe a canary."

In midafternoon Father Kerrigan, the parish priest, drove into the camp. He was a small, round-faced clergyman with shrewd, merry eyes. At his appearance the brattle of camp activity died down. The children crowded eagerly but respectfully around him and the older men and women pushed forward to shake his hand.

The priest's memory for names and faces was remarkable. He remembered the names of men, women, and children, as if these nomadic members of his flock were regular attendants at chapel, instead of merely annual visitors.

The children squealed with delight when he produced small presents of candy and licorice. When the greetings were over, Shiel Harrigan and the men of the camp took him aside to discuss details of the week's activities. Jamie and Tavish were not included in these plans and stayed politely apart.

Maeve had not been among the group that greeted the priest. She and Aunt Bid had been busy putting the finishing touches on her wedding dress. Bid, with her mouth crammed full of pins, pulled and pleated and tucked, all the while keeping up a steady chatter of reproof for Maeve's conduct of the night before.

"An upstart . . . a nobody, not fit to latch your shoes, and there you were ready to lick his boots," she mumbled.

Maeve surveyed herself unconcernedly in the bureau mirror. "He had hurt himself in the woods. All I did was wash his hands and face. 'Twas the least I could do after letting him think I had not been spoken for."

"All you did was risk your happiness in this world and your immortal soul in the next," the old lady snorted. "What was it to you that the omadhaun had gone about smashing trees with his fists."

"Did any man ever love you so much that the pain of it drove him to beat his poor knuckles to the bone?" Maeve asked.

"A regiment," lied Bid, "but I was too smart to be fooled by their sleuthering. Mark what I say. Lovers' oaths are writ in running water. Besides, in two days' time you are marrying with Travis Bunn, a good man and steady. It's not proper that a young girl on the eve of her wedding let her mind go wandering off in a long, sweet spring."

Maeve was moved to contrition. She turned and put her cheek against the older woman's. "Forgive me, Auntie Bid. It was thoughtless of me to be so willful. My father has given his word, and I will marry with Travis Bunn on the day set. Now then get on with the fitting."

Shiel Harrigan entered the tent and stood watching. "Father Kerrigan is here," he said. "He wants to see you."

"Should I go like this?" Maeve asked.

"And why not? He'll see you like that on the last day of the rituals," said Harrigan. "Run along now, and don't keep the priest waiting."

He watched her go fondly. "I wish her mother could have seen her in that dress."

"I for one will be glad to see her out of it," said Bid. "That wanderer from the old country has quite turned her head."

"Jamie McRuin?" Harrigan shrugged. "Blather . . . Maeve has always been a deep one. Water under the ground . . . with more wisdom in that little head than in yours and mine put together."

Bid grunted. "Nonetheless I'll be glad when Travis Bunn has taken the responsibility for her off our hands," she said.

Maeve made her way through the crowd about the priest and knelt for his blessing. Father Kerrigan made the sign of the cross and then extended his hand. "You'll be a married woman in two more days, Maeve Harrigan. At high noon the day after next. Is that agreeable with you?"

"Yes, Father."

"Travis Bunn is a good man . . . and you're a fine girl, Maeve. But remember one thing: An Irishman is only as good as the wife he gets."

Maeve flushed but said nothing. From the corner of her eye she saw Jamie standing at the edge of the trees. Even at a distance the dark scratches on his hands and face were visible. The memory of his absurd solemnity, bowing to Aunt Bid and saying, "God preserve you, ma'am . . . you're looking well," came back to her and she smothered an impulse to laugh again.

Father Kerrigan caught the flicker of her smile and misunderstand it. "Mind you, there's to be none of this 'Jumping the Budget,' or any of your pagan fandangoes before the wedding," he said smiling. "What happens afterward . . . well, if St. Patrick could put up with your pantheistic didos, I guess I can stand it."

While one of the men was watering his horse and turning the buggy around, the priest went swiftly from tent to tent and blessed each one. Shiel Harrigan was also busy. He circulated among the men and when he shook Father Kerrigan's hand, a sizable wad of bills was pressed into the priest's. " 'Tis small, Father, but there'll be more when the others come."

"You've never been backward about sharing your profits with the Church," the priest replied. "And speaking as an individual and not a priest, keep an eye out for a younger horse for me. Old Brian Boru, here, is almost as old as his namesake. He'll be departing for 'horse Heaven' any day now."

Shiel Harrigan promised to shop around and, with a farewell wave of his hand, Father Kerrigan drove away. On the main road to Atlanta, he gently clucked the old horse into a trot and held him to the pace with persistent urging. He had another stop to make and no desire for night to overtake him on the road.

VI

THE Proddy farm, which was Father Kerrigan's next stop, could hardly be called a farm. It was forty acres of gullied red clay hills, stumps, and Jimson weed, but Jesse Proddy clung to it with the tenacity of a boll weevil clinging to cotton. The land had been stripped bare and now was worn by wind and rain. Jesse Proddy, with only one mule and a deep aversion to staying at any one job longer than twenty minutes, seldom had more than a few acres under cultivation. How he and his family managed to survive was a riddle to the countryside.

The Proddy house, or shack, was a three-room affair perched precariously upon wooden stilts that gave early indications of succumbing any day and pitching house and inhabitants down the hill toward the Chattanooga Turnpike. The farm buildings consisted of a barn, a tool shed, and chicken house, the boards of which, along with the house, had weathered to a uniform, field mouse gray. The shallow well had been dug conveniently near the barn and pigpen, so that seepage from those pools of filth could make its typhoid-bearing way directly into the farm's water supply.

The Proddys were Father Kerrigan's principal problem. The joke of it, if such things could be considered as jokes, was that the Proddys were not Catholic. In fact, whenever Jesse Proddy spotted the priest's black buggy coming up the hill, he quickly herded as many of his six children as could be found away from the house and into a patch of jack pines that marked the lower edge of his property.

"That fiend o' Rome in his black suit is jest so much black smallpox to me," he would say to anyone who would listen.

Father Kerrigan had first heard about the Proddys a year before. One afternoon a young woman had called at the priest's house and asked him to deliver five dollars to Hester Proddy, Jesse's wife. Upon questioning the girl, the priest learned she was the Proddys' oldest daughter, Bernice. The girl had left home three years before when she was fifteen and had been supporting herself one way and another ever since.

"I know we ain't Catholic," Bernice said. "We ain't anything. But I don't know any other way to get this money to Ma. If I sent it by letter Pa would get it and have it drunk up before the postman had reached the next mailbox."

Father Kerrigan promised to deliver the five dollars the following day. Hester Proddy was alone in the house when he drove up. She was a frail little woman who couldn't have weighed more than a hundred pounds and was fast becoming an invalid from overwork. She seemed confused at having a visitor whose hands and face were clean. When the priest told her who he was and explained the nature of his visit, she kept referring to him as "Preacher" Kerrigan.

"Priest," Father Kerrigan reminded her. He delivered the five dollars, saying: "Your daughter, Bernice, was very anxious that you spend this money on yourself. Get yourself some medicine, or a new pair of shoes."

Hester Proddy seemed more perturbed over how Bernice had got five dollars than what she herself intended doing with it.

"I do hope she's taking good care of herself," she said. "Pa's awful mad at her for leaving home just when she was big enough to really help around the farm."

Mrs. Proddy's maiden name had been Callahan, the priest discovered. "Weren't you raised in the Catholic faith?" he asked.

"I don't rightly know, Preacher Kerrigan. My real father was killed in the War between the States. Ma married again . . . some man from the North. I had four half brothers and sisters but none of us went to church much."

Jesse Proddy had crept up outside the house and was going from window to window, peering in. Hester saw him. "Jesse's outside afraid to come in," she said to the priest. "He's askeered of preacher folks. They always scold him for not taking better care of his family."

"I'm not what you call 'preacher folks,' but I'd like to scold him, too," Father Kerrigan said grimly. He took his hat and went outside, but Proddy had sensed his coming and had taken to his heels.

"I want a word with you, Jesse Proddy," he called, "and I want to see the children."

At an interval of fifty yards Jesse's fear of priests subsided. "They be hiding in the timber and they ain't coming out 'til you're gone, you fiend o' Rome," he shouted. "Now git off'n my land."

"Stay where you are . . . I want to talk to you," Father Kerrigan insisted grimly. He started toward Jesse but the farmer retreated again, keeping the same distance between them.

"I'll have the law on you," Jesse threatened.

The absurdity of exchanging threats at fifty yards was apparent to the priest. The children were leaping and grimacing at the edge of the woods, like gamins. "A poor excuse of a husband and father you are," Father Kerrigan shouted, determined to have the final word. "And I'll be back."

He returned to the house and found Hester Proddy standing in the doorway wringing her rough, toil-hardened hands. "You mustn't mind Jesse," she pleaded. "He's askeered. We ain't got a friend in the world, and he don't trust nobody . . . leastways preachers."

"Listen to me, Hester Proddy, and mark what I say," Father Kerrigan said sternly. "I'm not a preacher, I'm a priest . . . your priest . . . because you were born a Callahan and a Catholic; and once a Catholic always a Catholic."

Hester seemed gratified by his words, though their significance had plainly escaped her. "I'll be back to see you as often as I can so that you and those children will get proper religious instruction," the priest continued, "and mind you, keep that five dollars away from your husband."

He had learned later that Hester hadn't succeeded in keeping the money. Her husband, Jesse, was part fox where dollars were concerned. He had suspected that Father Kerrigan came upon more than just a friendly call. By shrewd and persistent questioning he had made Hester admit that the priest had brought something. Then, with the eagerness of a child on a treasure hunt, Jesse had set out to find it. He was vastly good-natured about the search, making no threats and never losing his temper.

"I wonder just where you coulda hid it, wife," he would say to Hester. Or rummaging about in the kitchen, he would plead for some clue. "Won'tcha tell me if I'm gettin' warm?"

There weren't many places to hide things in a three-room shack and Jesse soon found the five dollars. Hester had cried and pleaded and finally admitted the money had come from Bernice, which made Jesse so mad he had walked all the way into Atlanta and got himself drunk on his wayward daughter's earnings.

That had been Father Kerrigan's first experience with the Proddys. After that the girl, Bernice, brought him five dollars every month. "Tell Ma to hide it in the barn," she would suggest. "It'll be harder to find out there."

Once Bernice brought two five-dollar bills. "If Ma hides them in separate places she's sure to save one," she said.

For nearly a year Father Kerrigan had been Bernice's monthly emissary. During that time he and Jesse Proddy had never come closer than fifty yards to each other. The children learned to watch for and shrill the news of his approach, but never did they speak to him or answer his queries. Even Jesse grudgingly came to look forward to his visits. He no longer hurled insults and sometimes crept to a window and listened while the priest spoke consolingly to Hester. If Father Kerrigan stayed too long, however, Jesse would grow fretful. He was eager to get on with the search for whatever prize the priest had brought. Sometimes the children sneaked near the house for a look at what their father called the "fiend o' Rome," but Jesse promptly chased them.

"A man's gotta pertect his offspring," he would say, taking a stick and flinging it in their direction so that they scattered like quail.

As he turned Brian Boru into the lane, Father Kerrigan saw their pinched faces peering at him from around the house and barn. The children ranged in ages from five to fifteen but seemed stunted for their years. When the priest's horse came to a grateful halt in the yard, they scattered squealing like little gnomes.

Father Kerrigan waved good-naturally and climbed from the buggy. He was halfway toward the house when he heard a noise behind him and turned. The youngest Proddy, a boy of four or five, stood only a few feet away, cut off from his brothers and sisters and immobile with fright. He had been playing on the other side of the house and failed to hear the cry of warning until too late.

"What's your name, little man?" the priest asked, extending his hand. The child drew back, poised to flee like an animal.

"Sure now you're not afraid of me, are you?" Father Kerrigan continued cajolingly.

The little boy gave no sign that he heard. He was hatless and shoeless, and a great swatch of uncut, uncombed hair hung almost to his eyes like a tangle of wet straw. Beneath the curls was a face of extraordinary beauty, dominated by an enormous pair of blue and frightened eyes. The child stood staring at the priest until a shrill whistle cut the air, then he bounded away with the speed of a wild thing. Down the hill Father Kerrigan saw Jesse Proddy beckoning to the boy.

Like he would whistle for a dog, the priest thought grimly.

Inside the house Hester Proddy was in bed. She spent more and more time there now. It was chest pains again, she said. "I scarcely been outta my bed the whole week, Father. Nighttimes my chest feels like it was on fire."

"Wouldn't you like the doctor to come and see you?"

Hester appeared genuinely frightened. "Lawd-o'-me, no. Jesse don't hold with doctors. Besides, there's no money to pay."

The priest asked about the children. "I saw your youngest one up close today. He's a fine little boy, Hester."

"The baby? He ain't quite right, Father. He ain't never spoke a word, not since he was born."

"That's a pity," the priest said sympathetically. "What's his name?"

Hester was confused. "His name? I declare, I don't rightly think Jesse's given him a real name yet."

Father Kerrigan was shocked. "You have to call the child something!"

"The other children generally calls him 'little Number Seven,' but Jesse just whistles when he wants him," Hester said apologetically.

The priest had learned long since that he couldn't wage the battle for Hester's immortal soul on moral or theological grounds. Christ and the Virgin Mary, the Trinity and the saints, were characters from a book she had never read and were quite devoid of meaning for her. The question of sin was also remote. There had been as little time for sin in her life as there had been for salvation. They were abstractions existing in a far-off, nebulous world of other people and other places.

Father Kerrigan had discovered one route by which he could enter and capture the simple Hester's imagination. On each of his visits he talked about her father's family, the Callahans.

"What's happened to you, Hester Proddy, is that you've lost your most precious possession—next to your immortal soul. Your identity . . . your name, that's what you've lost. And it's a terrible thing to lose your name . . . especially a fine one like Callahan."

He began reciting the ancient Irish legends, tracing the history of Ireland through the centuries as if it were nothing but the personal record of the Callahan clan. Hester's faded eyes grew bright with childlike fascination and wonder at the tales.

"Great chieftains they were, and kings, too, Hester Proddy," the priest said. "They wore an O on the front of their name in those days, like a blazoned shield, proclaiming their superiority. But humble in the sight of God they were, too. Wherever St. Patrick knelt to pray, sure a Callahan was there kneeling beside him. And when Brigid was a young girl and laid her rain-wet cloak upon the dancing sunbeams to dry, and the blessed sunshine held it suspended in the air, sure it was a Callahan that witnessed the miracle and tried to do the same thing—without succeeding, of course. Then who do you suppose had the courage to stand all alone on the shores of Ireland's bottomless lake and answer the fearful question of the giant sea worms, when they rose from the depths on the fateful day and asked in Irish: 'Is it tomorrow'?"

"A Callahan, maybe?" Hester said hopefully.

"A Callahan, positively," answered Father Kerrigan. "Sure he faced the prehistoric monsters, and while the remainder of the population took to the hills, this mighty Callahan made the sign of the cross, and shouted—with a voice that shook, I'm thinking: 'No, it is not'; thereby sending the creatures back to the bottom of the lake for another seven years."

Hester closed her eyes in dreamy rapture. Father Kerrigan took her thin, worn hand. "Now do you understand the wonder of a fine name, Hester Proddy? It's like a suit of armor, helping you fight life's battles; and when your fighting days are finished, it honors you in your old age."

He glanced toward the door in time to catch the flash of a blue eye peering through the crack. The little nameless boy had crept back to listen outside the door. Before the priest could call him in, Jesse's shrill whistle sounded again, and boy and blue eye vanished once more.

"Who takes care of the children when you're sick like this?" Father Kerrigan asked.

Hester opened her eyes but they were still dreaming in a

far-off time. "Jesse can cook up a mess o' greens and fat back as good as anybody. I'll be all right tomorrow. The pain in my chest is almost gone."

"I'm going to leave you this little book. Will you study it and teach it to the children? It's your catechism."

The sick woman nodded. The excitement of listening had left her weary and spent. Father Kerrigan took two five-dollar bills from the money Shiel Harrigan had given him and put them in Hester's hand. "Better put them away before Jesse comes back," he advised.

Hester roused herself. "Put them in the book, Father," she said, indicating the catechism. "Jesse'd sooner pet a rattle-snake than touch a church book."

Obediently the priest folded the money between the pages. The sick woman thanked him, and as he slipped quietly from the house, she was holding the book clasped in her worn hands as if in prayer.

VII

NEXT day brought more and more groups of horse traders, until the woods beside the Chattanooga Turnpike were crowded with tents and laughing, chatting people. With each arrival, the newcomers swarmed from the wagons and buggies to be met with hearty but dignified greetings. Even the children showed well-mannered restraint, extending a polite welcome to playmates not seen for a year, as if their separation had been only for a day.

The women grouped themselves about the tables and stoves, their fingers busy with knitting and mending while they chatted of births, deaths, engagements, and marriages. The men wandered in small groups to examine each other's horses and mules, exchanging jokes, trade secrets, and the ever-present problem of animal sickness, its symptoms and remedies.

Among the first group arriving was Travis Bunn, Maeve's fiancé. Jamie recognized him instinctively. He was taller and older than Jamie, with dark hair and eyes, and arms and shoulders like a blacksmith's. The men in the camp greeted him pleasantly but without undue cordiality. His overbearing brusqueness and freedom with his fists had made him somewhat unpopular with the men, but the women considered him a great catch. In business he was one of the shrewdest of the horse traders.

He swept through the camp, laughing and calling greetings right and left. "And where is Maeve Harrigan and why was she not by the turnpike to meet me?" he shouted good-naturedly. "Have I worn the axles of my wagon thin to get to her—and for this kind of welcome?"

Bunn's appearance and arrogant assurance so filled Jamie with loathing that he left the camp to avoid meeting the man. He found the solitude soothing. Woods and fields were unbelievably beautiful to a man in love. The green, rolling hills were gashed here and there by plowing, exposing the moist red earth to glisten like new bricks in the April sun. Against the grayish green of new-leafing trees were splashed the early dogwood blooms, white as a bride's veil. Jamie walked for miles before turning back.

When he returned to camp, the merrymaking had begun. Dan Devlin was playing his pipes accompanied by an old man on the fiddle. The sight of Maeve dancing with Travis Bunn made Jamie sick with rage. He tried not to watch and took no part in the dancing, but he was unable to keep his eyes from the couple.

Seeking Owen Roe Tavish, he was told that the Speaker had caught a ride into Atlanta, intent upon finding his cousin, Power O'Malley.

"He sought you, Jamie," Jaunting Jim Donner said, "but you were nowhere about."

Jamie spoke his thanks and went back to the exquisite torture of watching Travis Bunn dance with the girl he loved. A devious and half-diabolical scheme began to form in his mind. Thrusting his hands in his pockets he began to stroll back and forth beside the throng of dancers. Not for an instant did he remove his eyes from Maeve. Aunt Bid saw him and muttered under her breath:

"Now what is that one scheming? Like a caged animal he is, full of malignity and mischief."

Tavish had ridden into the city with Me-Dennis O'Ryan, one of the shrewder traders of the camp who often acted for the group in collective business deals. Me-Dennis' mother had referred to her son so constantly as "Me-Dennis" when he was a child that the name had stuck. He was a wry, dry little man, whose wife had borne him seven children, and now patched his trousers at the seat and knees with leather. It gave him the odd appearance of never being completely separated from a saddle.

"If you be coming back tonight, Tavish, you can ride in style," he said. "Six more surreys for Sunday, I'm renting; to bring the women and children to church. Some years we hire every hack in Atlanta."

"Oh, no," Tavish said, with the loftiness of a man whose future is assured. "I couldn't be leaving my blood cousin with just a 'how-de-do' and 'good-by'; and after coming all these thousands of miles to visit him. Power O'Malley would never forgive such a slight."

"How long do you figure to stay?"

"A month or a month of Sundays. Who can say? Cousin Power may even want Jamie and me to make our home with him. He's quite rich, 'tis said." Tavish savored the prospective meeting with his long-absent cousin with satisfaction. "He has no family of his own."

Me-Dennis had lost interest. "Should you change your mind, I'll be at Rush's livery stable on Marietta Street. I won't be taking the horses out until after feeding time. That way I'll save oats. Oats for twelve horses is no small item."

"It's more than forty years since I've seen Cousin Power,"

Tavish said, ignoring Me-Dennis' muttering. "Och, what a lad he was at home. Generous to a fault. Sure his right arm grew longer than his left from the giving of gifts to others. Oh . . . he'll want Jamie and me to bide with him until I'm ready to go back home. Maybe he'll go with me . . . for a visit. . . ."

Me-Dennis didn't answer. He was busy pursuing his own line of thought. "Let Rush furnish their supper. After all, they're his horses. What kind of a man is it that expects someone else to feed his horses?"

"Sure it would be a piece of wonder to come home in style, with a new vest and shillings clanking like bells in my pockets," said Tavish dreamily.

Me-Dennis had worked himself into a full-scale row with the absent livery stable proprietor. "If Rush don't like it, then I'll take my business elsewhere. Who does he think he is, asking me to feed twelve horses?"

The vehemence of his companion called Tavish back from woolgathering. He asked the horse trader where he might find his cousin's shop.

"He's a stonecutter . . . a very dignified profession," he said.

"Now that I put my mind to it," Me-Dennis answered, "there's a stonecutter some of the camps do business with— named O'Malley. Could that be your cousin?"

"It could or it couldn't," said the Speaker. "I haven't seen Power in over forty years. He came to America when he was eighteen."

"Would you say he was a thin man, taller than most and balder than many, wearing thick glasses?"

"That I wouldn't . . . because I don't know," Tavish replied, peevishly. "He probably has changed some in all those years."

"That wouldn't be the O'Malley I'm thinking of any-way," Me-Dennis admitted. "The one I know is short and wide, with hair thick or a beaver's, only gray, and eyebrows that stand out to here."

To quiet the conversation Tavish agreed that this undoubtedly was the right O'Malley.

"He has a shop on West Peachtree Street," said McDennis, and for the remainder of the trip brooded in silence.

Tavish left the garrulous trader examining and faulting horses as if he intended buying the animals instead of renting them. Rush, the livery stable proprietor, directed him toward West Peachtree Street, and after a brief walk he came to his cousin's stonecutting establishment.

The shop was in the lower half of a ramshackle, two-story house, badly in need of paint. It sat some distance from the street and the yard was crowded with granite slabs and objects of the stonecutter's art. There was no proper fence, but two tall shafts of gray granite upheld a third slab of pink, forming a stern but celestial arch for an entrance, though no entrance was required. Chiseled perpendicularly upon the upright shafts was the name: O'MALLEY, while POWER was graved horizontally across the top.

The porch, like the yard, was littered with stone angels of all sizes and descriptions: cherubim and seraphim. Tavish made his way into the house through the open front doorway. The interior was dim and quiet as a cathedral, and charged with the pungent smell of rock dust. Almost obscured in a far corner was a high, old-style, slanting bookkeeper's desk. Perched behind it on a tall stool was a gnomelike little man absorbed in reading a letter. Had it not been that his lips were moving as they audibly spelled out the words, Tavish would have mistaken him for another piece of statuary. His short, crisp hair was so matted and whitened with stone dust that it appeared carved.

"Speak up or go away," the little man said in a voice as abrasive as the dust on the floor.

"Is it you now, Power O'Malley, my cousin that left Ireland forty years ago a little green-coated boy, and set out on the rocky roads of the world to push his fortune?" Tavish said, unconsciously keeping his voice low as if he were whispering in a graveyard or a church. " 'Tis I, your darling relation, Owen Roe Tavish, that you haven't laid eyes on these many years."

Power O'Malley blinked at Tavish but gave no other evidence of interest or surprise. "What took you so long, Cousin?" he said finally with disconcerting mildness.

His lack of surprise left Tavish taken aback. "Sure 'twas the roughness of the crossing," he hastened to explain. "The worst in the history of steam navigation. One minute the ocean was spitting at us, whiter than white, and the next minute hissing away, greener than green. Sure with our ups and downs we traveled enough to circumnavigate the globe."

"Did you now?" said Power, chuckling to himself as if he relished some small private joke. "I'm just after reading this letter from our cousin, Meg O'Leary, in Donegal. She's written a whole page about you and another cousin, Jamie . . . what's-his-name. . . ."

"McRuin . . . he's with me here. . . ."

Tavish's mouth was open, ready to explain that Jamie was stopping temporarily with the horse traders and would be along later, when Power O'Malley interrupted crossly: "I see him . . . I see him; and a fine looking lad he is, too. Good day to you, lad. Sure you must be weary after your long trip. Sit yourself on a slab. I'll read you both what Cousin Meg writes about your glorious funeral."

The old stonecutter was affably addressing the dust-laden air beside Tavish, and the Speaker felt the hair at the base of his neck rise. At the same moment he experienced a sinking sensation in the pit of his stomach.

"Cousin Power," he said gently, "Jamie I left behind with the Irish Travelers. He's not with me just now."

Power O'Malley seemed not to have heard. He was busy scanning Meg's letter, which was many pages in length.

"Travelers?" he said. "Fine people. Do a lot of work for them. Respectful of their dead, they are. Ah, here's the first page."

Without further ado he began reading snatches of the letter aloud in a fast mumble.

Your welcome letter received and me and your Uncle Esme thank you for the money you sent. We had masses said for your father and mother, God rest their souls . . . your cousin by marriage, Tade MacFigg, was hung in Belfast last week for killing a policeman. May God rest his soul—and may God's curse be on Prinny Butt, the informer, and may she burn in Hell, God forgive me. . . . We had a grand time at Pat Cullinan's wake . . . he was eighty! Some young roughs shouted at him last week, 'Give us the wake, Pat Cullinan'—and he obliged. Brigid O'Flaherty, that you once went to school with, has married again . . . an Englishman—and at her age! She'll have no luck. . . .

"Ah, here it is," said the stonecutter, shaking a rumpled page at Tavish.

Bless your heart, I almost forgot to tell you about your distant cousins, Owen Roe Tavish, him that was the matchmaker, and young Jamie McRuin. Both drowned, they were, in the gap of Dunriggan, and their bodies never recovered. The double wake was the talk of the countryside and went on for three days while they searched for the bodies. What a lively time! Some dirty, thieving upstart stole the priest's offering from off the coffins, but old Shanahan, him that was the tinker, replaced the missing money, believing, 'tis said by them that know, one of his own sons took it. Sure no one knew his sons better than Shanahan himself, and if he suspected them, then there's no one in the county to gainsay him. Things have turned out well, all in all. Dennis McRuin married the Shanahan girl, keeping the fortune in the family. His sister, Kate, was married to Waddie O'Dowd and now Old Dan is snugly kept, with plenty of tobacco for his pipe and a warm fire to toast his shins. . . . May God take care of you and keep you from sudden death. . . . P.S. Keep sending the money. . . . Your loving cousin . . .

Meg

Power raised his eyes from the letter and surveyed Tavish through the shaggy brows veiling his bright little eyes. "Think of that, Cousin Tavish, a three-day wake. Sure now that's something to warm the souls of drownded men."

The suspicion that had been growing within Owen Roe Tavish was now an awesome certainty. Power O'Malley believed him to be a ghost. The old stonecutter had lived so long among the symbols of the grave that he could no longer discern between the quick and the dead.

"Hear me now, Power O'Malley," Tavish said sternly, though his voice shook slightly: "I'm no more of a ghost than you are. Jamie McRuin dragged me from Dunriggan Gap and 'twas us snatched the money from off our own coffins to buy passage to America. We're here, man, flesh and blood. Feel my hand. . . ."

Power smiled patiently. "'Tis but the reaction to the reaction of being kilt, Cousin Tavish. Them that dies by drowning finds it hardest to believe at first. You'll get used to it. Hardly a day goes by but what a ghost or two drops in. Only last week Cyprian O'Leary, him that was kicked to death by a horse, was here to see me. He didn't believe he was dead either. And him with a hole in his head from the horse's hoof I could put my fist in."

A young man wearing a black arm band, and accompanied by two older women also in mourning, came to the door of the shop. "Don't go way, Tavish," Power said, going to meet them. "When I'm done here we'll pick out a nice stone for you."

"Sure wild horses couldn't drag me away until I've got it through your doddering head that I'm live as you are . . . liver," Tavish shouted after him.

He stuck by his determination until he overheard Power O'Malley explaining to the customers that the man inside was really the ghost of a drowned cousin who had crossed the wild Atlantic just to visit him. This was too much for Owen Roe Tavish. He swept past the startled women and the staring young man, smothering a Puckish impulse to give out a wild banshee wail.

"Sure that would send Power's customers shopping for a tombstone somewhere in the next county," he told himself grimly.

"Are you off so soon, Cousin?" Power queried solicitously. "Say a word to the blessed Brigid for me."

Tavish was still a small boy at heart. Before a towering stone angel with wings outspread, he paused dramatically and faced the women and men. Spreading his arms wide as if about to take flight, he said solemnly: *"Beir bog ar an saoghal agus beirfhidh an saoghal bog ort."*

One of the women seemed on the verge of fainting. When she opened her eyes Tavish had vanished. Power O'Malley, pleased with the excitement, translated Tavish's words from the Gaelic.

"Twas an old Irish proverb that says 'if you bear easy on life, sure then life will bear easy on you.' Just think of it," he added happily, "they're speaking Irish in Heaven."

VIII

TAVISH rode back to the horse traders' camp with Me-Dennis. The livery stable proprietor with his five strapping sons followed in the cavalcade of surreys. They brought saddle horses on which to ride back into town. It was a pleasant trip for everyone except Owen Roe Tavish. A bright half-moon tipped the tree-edges with spring silver and the air was filled with the thudding of hoofs, the smell of hay and horses' sweat and leather. The steel rims of the carriage wheels sang a thin, sweet obbligato as they sliced through the carpet of red dust on the road. But Tavish found small pleasure in the sights or sounds. He was depressed and homesick for familiar things. The steady drone of Me-Dennis' voice, reciting how he had bested Rush on the rental of the surreys, flowed over him unheeded.

"Why so silent, man? Have you lost your spark?" Me-Dennis demanded.

"That I have. I'm a ghost on two continents," replied Tavish sadly.

The cryptic answer silenced Me-Dennis, who was fond of worrying with words as dogs worried with bones. The glow of fires shone through the trees as they neared the camp in the pine grove, and the rollicking music of Irish dances was borne to them on the warm night air.

"Sounds like the Travelers are all come in," Me-Dennis cried. He whipped up the horse, anxious to end the trip and take part in the festivities. Beside him, Tavish pondered his and Jamie's doubtful future when they were set adrift by the migratory horse traders.

Two more musicians had joined with Dan Devlin and the old fiddler. The orchestra perched in a wagon bed to play "The Siege of Ennis" and "The Walls of Limerick," and others, while the dancers stepped, clapped, and swung in rhythm. Some of the men passed a jug among themselves but there was no rowdiness. Occasionally some oldster, fired by the liquor and the music, would hop into the arena and attempt to match his steps against the flying feet of the younger people.

Tavish found Jamie among the inner circle of watchers, his eyes following Maeve's every movement in the line of dancers. "You're wearing the Day of Judgment in your face. Do you be wanting everyone in the camp to know your feelings?" the old man queried crossly.

Jamie shrugged without removing his eyes from the girl and her partner. "They know them now, except the black one there, dancing with Maeve." He nodded toward Travis Bunn in the square of dancers.

"And how long do you think the secret will be kept from him, with you glowering up and down the length and breadth of the man, as if measuring him for a beating. And if that's what's in your mind—forget it. We'll not repay courtesy with rioting."

Tavish's warning was not without reason. Travis Bunn had already become conscious of Jamie's steady stare.

"Who's the one that's trying to stare me out of the county?" he asked Aunt Bid, between dances.

"A spalpeen with a heart as cold as charity and a tongue like a rasp. Picked up along the road out of the goodness of our souls, he was . . . him and the old one," she added, jerking her head in Tavish's direction.

Shiel Harrigan had little more to say about Jamie than had Aunt Bid. "He's a green lad from the old country who rode with us for a few days. He'll be going his own way tomorrow or the day after."

Bunn would have accepted these dismissals of Jamie's rudeness, but Maeve's evasiveness and the covert whispering of the women made him suspicious. The hopeless love of the stranger from Ireland for Shiel Harrigan's daughter was now common knowledge in the camp. Mothers ringed about the dancers kept one eye on their offspring and with the other watched the mounting tension between Bunn and Jamie.

Maeve, too, sensed the impending clash. She tried to draw Bunn away from the dancers. "I'm tired. Let's walk along the road a little way," she said.

Ordinarily he would have leapt at the chance to be alone with the girl he loved, but now Bunn suspected something was behind her request.

"Maybe it's dancing with me that has wearied you," he said sourly. "Another partner you might find less tiresome."

"The music and the dancing and the noise has tired me," Maeve replied coolly. "The music and the dancing and the noise would be the same no matter who was my partner."

She would have quit the reel but Bunn held her. "What's this coldness that's come over you, Maeve Harrigan? I have no liking for it in the girl I'm going to marry."

Maeve pushed his hands from her and walked away. Bunn stood while the dancers whirled about him and the wrath inside him mounted until it throbbed at his temples. Then he turned and pushed his way to where Jamie stood.

"Did no one teach you at home 'tis not polite to stare?" he said, with deliberate sarcasm.

Jamie smiled an aggravating smile, as if he were receiving a bit of pleasant news. "Sure now you're that nimble on your spags I couldn't keep my eyes off you, Mister Bunn. Did you have your lessons from a mountain goat? Or is it that you're part pooka, with hind legs like a rabbit?"

Bunn's mouth tightened and he crouched as if to spring. "I thought as much. 'Tis you that's set Maeve against me. Walk with me to the timber, for I'm of a mind to teach you a lesson."

Jamie's eyes were hard as crystal but his lips continued to smile. "If you're as lively with your fists as you are with your tongue, Mister Bunn, sure then you could outbox the wind."

"Do you come, or do I put your head on the other side of your face here and now?" Bunn's cup of rage was running over but Jamie's voice stayed soft and his lips continued to smile.

"I'll not go with you out of kindness, Mister Bunn," he said. "It's in my heart to kill you, but you're hers, and because of that I won't lay a finger on you."

Bunn swung at Jamie's taunting face before the words were fully out. His fist caught the Irish boy a glancing blow on the nose and cheek, staggering him. "Put up your hands," he snarled, circling catlike around Jamie.

A trickle of crimson crept along Jamie's upper lip from one nostril. He faced Bunn still smiling. Deliberately he slid his hands into his trouser's pockets. "Though his fists are weak, sure he slays armies with his tongue. 'Tis not in your power to hurt me, Travis Bunn," he jeered softly.

The dancers had lost interest in the dancing with the first blow, and the music collapsed immediately. By common instinct a ring formed solidly about the two men. Tavish, who was deep in conversation with Tade Hennessy and Me-Dennis, heard the crack of Bunn's fist and turned in time to see Jamie recovering his balance, the blood oozing from his nose.

The horse traders were bound together by blood ties and ties of self-interest, like a family. There could be quarrels and even blows among them, but against any and all outsiders they presented an unbroken front. The faces tightly ringed about Bunn and Jamie expressed only grim impartiality or open hostility toward the stranger. They watched without show of sympathy as Bunn struck again and again. Jamie made no move to defend himself, only weaving and pulling with the blows to avoid their full force.

"Jamie, for the love of Heaven, lad, defend yourself," Tavish shouted.

"What . . . from the pillows that this bowsie calls his fists?" Jamie retorted through bloody lips.

He was bleeding profusely now from mouth and nose, and purple splotches marked his white skin. Bunn had lost all control. With fists flailing he crowded in for the kill. Through battered lips, Jamie continued to whip the other man's nerves until they were raw.

"What a wonder of a man the girl must think you, Travis Bunn," he taunted, "seeing you waving your fists and beating at the wind."

"Sure if it's smashing you want, you'll get it," Bunn snarled. He feinted and caught Jamie solidly on the jaw—a blow that would have dropped a young bull.

Jamie saw the lacy tops of the trees shimmering in the moonlight. A sigh that could have come from the crowd, but probably came from the wind in the branches, hummed in his ears. His head thumped against the ground and he lay still while galaxies of stars exploded inside his skull.

"I must get up," he drove himself. "Half a beating won't do. Bunn must hammer at me 'til he himself is sick of the sight."

He staggered to his feet, hands still in pockets. "Sure you've got the ground on your side now," he rasped. "It's thumping me from one side while you're blasting at me from the other."

Bunn was sick of the slaughter but he had to go on. He had to stop that mocking, taunting, bloody mouth. From a corner of his eye he saw Maeve. She was standing back from the crowd, on a small rise of earth. Her face shone deathly pale in the light from the ring of fires. Her eyes were wide and staring, but she followed every motion of the two men. Tavish went from man to man, pleading with them to stop the one-sided struggle. They shook their heads. A fight was finished only when one of the participants could no longer rise, or was unable to continue and said so.

"But it's murder," Tavish pleaded. "The boy won't defend himself."

The men shrugged. That was Jamie's problem. Some of them turned away, sickened. The women had long since withdrawn, drawing the children as far from the unequal battle as possible. Finally Jamie went down and could not rise again. Tavish knelt beside him, almost in tears.

"Why did you do it, lad? Why did you do it? Have you lost your wits entirely? Or are you so torn inside that only the father and mother of a beating will cure you?" The old man lifted the body tenderly to his feet. "Come along. I'll walk you to the stream and wash your face."

The ring of watchers dissolved as swiftly as it had formed, but there was no further call for music and dancing. Bunn sought Maeve but she had disappeared. Nor did Shiel Harri-

gan or Aunt Bid know where she had gone. Still angry but
with a growing uncertainty, Bunn moved through the camp
seeking her. Some of the men drew aside when he approached.

There was little approval of his conduct among those who
had watched. Bunn found himself explaining over and over
again that Jamie had begged for it.

"There was nothing to do but give it him," he argued.

Jamie lay in a semistupor beside the stream. As through
a mist he heard the water bubbling in the brook and felt
someone bathing his hands and face and squeezing drops of
water between his swollen lips. There was an exquisite
pleasure in lying perfectly still, though every inch of him
ached like a broken tooth.

"You're very good to your wayward cousin, Owen Roe
Tavish," he whispered.

"Shush," a voice said soothingly. It was a softer, gentler
voice than Tavish's. Jamie strove to open first one eye then
the other, but they were both swollen fast.

"Maeve?" he whispered.

"You mustn't talk," she answered firmly.

He lay a long moment without speaking. Finally he said:
"Sure now I know I do be dreaming . . . dreaming."

Maeve had brought bandages and salves from her tent
and treated his wounds. Her fingers were deft and gentle but
every spot she touched brought a wince of pain from Jamie.

"Does it hurt so terribly?" she asked.

"Only where I'm flesh and blood," said Jamie. "Would
you not lift one small corner of an eyelid so I can see your
dear face? Sure there's more healing in the sight of you than
in the blessed hands of Brigid, herself."

Maeve rested her finger tips on his swollen eyes. "Why
did you let him beat you? Why didn't you fight back?'"

"Lay hands on the man you're going to marry?" Jamie protested. "Sure I'd sooner kill a robin . . . and a robin is that sacred, to kill one raises a lump in a man's hand and he can never work again."

"There's more behind all this than robins and lumps in the hand," Maeve scolded sagely. "Anyway, he's raised lumps on every other part of you."

Jamie's lips struggled with a smile. "Sure I'd like to keep them always since your two hands have blessed them."

"Never mind," Maeve consoled. " 'Tis your fate to be always getting newer and better ones."

"Aye," said Jamie, "but will you be there to soothe them always?"

"Aye," she said simply. "That is my fate . . . to be there . . . always."

It was thus that Travis Bunn found them. Jamie was asleep, his head in Maeve's lap. The anger and ferocity had gone from Bunn. In its place had come a great uncertainty. Loving Maeve desperately, and sensing the girl's superiority, he had waited out the long year of their engagement with mounting eagerness. Now he stood before her silent and humble.

"Go away," said Maeve, without looking at him.

"They were worried about you at the camp. You'll be coming back soon?"

"When I am ready."

"Is that what I'm to say to your father?"

"Say to him that you've no longer the right to speak for me," Maeve flashed, "and that Shiel Harrigan did not raise a daughter to marry the likes of one who beats another who will not defend himself."

Jamie awoke as Bunn went humbly away to lay his case before Shiel Harrigan and Maeve's relatives.

"Did you send him away?" he asked.

"Yes. Are you surprised?"

"No. It was fated."

Maeve laughed the light, delicious laugh that Jamie loved. "And getting yourself beaten into blood and oblivion had nothing to do with it?" she challenged derisively.

The memory of the beating made Jamie wince. "A man must give fate a 'leg-up' ever now and again," he conceded ruefully. "But that you were meant to be mine I knew from the beginning, though how I was to go about getting you, I didn't know. 'Travel and the love of the woman of my choice,' I was promised. . . ."

"Promised?" said Maeve, "and who promised you?"

"The Queen of the Fairies! Three times she appeared to me in a dream. Travel I've had already—halfway around the world! And the woman of my choice I met cooling my feet in a mountain stream. There I saw her golden hair outshining the sun."

Maeve bent and kissed his swollen, battered lips. "I think I knew it, too," she said, "though there was no Fairy Queen to tell me. Maybe a woman knows without being told."

"Shall I speak to your father?"

"Father will do the speaking . . . to us," she answered wryly. "But when all the words have been said . . . and a bucket of tears shed . . . and me banished—and brought back—and banished again . . . then I'll marry with Jamie McRuin."

"If you're that sure," Jamie said with a sigh, "then I'm that comforted."

"I'm that sure," Maeve teased him: "And I didn't need any nodding from the Fairy Queen to help in the making up of my mind."

IX

MAEVE'S quiet announcement that she would marry Jamie McRuin, an outsider; a stranger and a penniless wanderer; a boy with no fortune who fought for his love with his hands in his pockets, shocked and scandalized the entire camp. All the Harrigan relations, including children who were old enough to understand the issue at stake, were called into solemn conference. Hour after hour and spokesman after spokesman hammered at Maeve for the breaking of her troth. It could not be done, they said. Her father's word had been given. The bond had been sealed by a handshake. There could be no going back on such an agreement. Maeve must go through with her marriage.

"Travis Bunn is a devil," Maeve said simply, "and I'll not marry with a devil."

"Better marry with a devil you know than a devil you don't," Auntie Bid warned.

"I'll marry with Jamie McRuin or no one," Maeve insisted.

"Then you'll marry no one," Shiel Harrigan declared.

"Is this the respect a good girl shows her father's wishes?" a cousin from another camp demanded.

"You know that outsiders are not accepted into our families," said another.

"He would be accepted if Father said the word," Maeve answered.

"That I'll never do," said Harrigan.

Maeve showed no sign of wavering, and Me-Dennis was dispatched in haste for Father Kerrigan. "Tell him it's a matter of life and death," Bid roared, loud enough for the entire camp to hear.

Travis Bunn kept to his tent and Jamie and Tavish also stayed apart. The usual festivities were suspended and a pall of inactivity hung over the camp. Tavish had asked permission to speak for Jamie but his offer had been sharply declined.

"She can never hold out against them," he said to Jamie, as the rumble of male voices resounded from the Harrigan tent.

But every masculine roar was matched over and over again by the tempered steel of Maeve's reply. She gave as good as she got.

"Think of it, now," said Tavish, after hours had passed, "a slip of a girl in the full presence of her youth, standing against the entire clan. They named Maeve well . . . after the great warrior Queen of the West."

"She'll never give in," said Jamie confidently.

"They may wear her down."

"There's a great rock in a salmon leap near Kiltartan," said Jamie. "When the salmon are making their run they have to jump this rock. Some of them make it, but others slide back across the rock on their soft, white bellies. There is a legend that when the bellies of the salmon have worn that rock away to no bigger than a hazelnut, then the cry of the Old Kings will be heard and Ireland will be united. Maeve is that rock, and the words of her relatives are like the soft, white bellies of the salmon."

Jamie's words were brave enough, but when he saw Me-Dennis drive up with Father Kerrigan, a fearful ache rose inside his chest. The priest went directly to Shiel Harrigan's tent and for a while his voice could be heard speaking firmly to Maeve. At first she answered steadfastly enough, but after a time she fell silent, and the listeners outside could hear only the priest's voice raised in steady remonstration.

"They've beaten her," Tavish groaned.

Jamie said nothing, but the hope and exultation went out of him. After a while Shiel Harrigan and the relatives came out of the tent, leaving Maeve and Father Kerrigan alone. Jamie waited until he could bear no more, then impulsively he crossed to the tent and let himself in.

Maeve was sitting humbly before the priest, her face streaked with tears. Father Kerrigan turned toward the intruder with surprise. "Who are you?"

"It's Jamie McRuin, Father," Maeve said.

"Oh," said the priest sternly, "you may as well come in. I've some things to say to you, too."

He rose and paced back and forth. Finally he paused in front of Jamie and looked at him severely. "Well, young man, you've stirred up a pretty kettle of fish."

Jamie's throat knotted so that he could not speak. The pain inside his chest ached like a wound that would not heal. This, then, was the finish of his second wish; for no one—not even Maeve—could stand against the combined pressure of parent and priesthood.

Dropping to his knees, Jamie bowed his head to hide the great, hot tears that clung smarting to his eyelids. "I know it, Father," he said, striving to hold his voice steady. "Forgive me. The fault is mine—not Maeve's. I'll do what I can

to make it right . . . anything you say! I'll go away   . .
disappear . . . now . . . at once! Only promise me one
thing . . . make them leave Maeve alone. They've been at
her for hours . . . like dogs after a doe! Harrigans—thicker
than pine needles on the ground—hammering at her . . .
never letting her be. Make them stop it, Father. . . ." The
words stuck in his constricted throat and he could say no
more.

The priest drew Maeve toward the entrance of the tent.
"Go sit with your Aunt Bid," he said quietly. "You've been
forward, disobedient, and sharp-answering. Try being silent,
modest, and humble. Sympathy has melted more stony
hearts than tongues like hammers."

With Maeve gone, he turned back to Jamie. "So you'll go
away? And just where will you go, lad?"

"Anywhere . . . everywhere. Just so there be water
enough to drown a man . . . wood enough to hang him
. . . and earth enough to bury him," Jamie said.

"Here now, don't be giving me any of your flossy speeches.
What I want to know is, do you really love that girl . . .
and just how certain are you?"

Jamie extended his right arm. "This I'd have cut away at
the shoulder, Father, and lopsided go through life, would it
spare her a moment's pain," he said simply.

"Are you that sure? 'Tis common enough for a young man
on a spring day, with his feet in a cool stream and his head
in the clouds, to fall in love with a pretty girl," the priest
warned.

"Father," Jamie said earnestly, " 'tis common as the sun.
I only know that there was a locked door inside me, and the
sight of Maeve has opened it. If you say she's not to come
in, then I'll go away and live an empty man all the rest of
my days."

The priest studied the boy's face. "I'll see what can be
done," he said at last. "Go and wait in the woods."

Jamie rose from his knees. "I'm a nobody, Father, but they do wonderful things in this country . . . as wonderful as the fairies do at home. I'll be somebody. You wait and see. I'll . . ." Jamie's voice stumbled and broke under the weight of his feelings and he could not go on.

"It's a fine girl that's found it in her heart to love you," Father Kerrigan said. "Should you ever lose that love . . . there'll be small hope for your immortal soul in this world or the next, I'm thinking."

With Father Kerrigan on the side of Maeve and Jamie, events moved rapidly. The priest wielded great influence with the devout horse traders, but even he could not arbitrarily set aside a marriage contract. Shiel Harrigan was a stubborn man, jealous of his reputation for integrity, so Father Kerrigan shrewdly by-passed him, appealing to Aunt Bid. She had raised Maeve and loved her as if she were her own child.

When he told her that Maeve had sworn to become a nun if she could not marry Jamie, the old spinster's eyes filled with tears.

"Oh, this is a terrible calamity that's been inflicted upon us," she said. "Saving your pardon, Father, I'm not speaking of her becoming a nun, but of the disgrace. What are we to do?"

"I've talked with the boy . . . and I find much good in him. Since there're hearts to be broken no matter which way we turn, maybe Shiel Harrigan could be made to see that it's more economical to break one than two."

"You mean cast Travis Bunn aside and let Maeve have her way?" said Bid aghast. "Sure Harrigan would never do that. He's sworn an oath that she would marry Bunn or no one . . . and he's not one to be breaking an oath."

"Does he prefer breaking his daughter's heart to breaking an oath made in anger?" demanded the priest.

"Sure I never cared much for that Travis Bunn anyway," Bid said slyly, when she saw that the priest was on the side of the lovers. "He had a hand for every man and a heart for nobody."

Shiel Harrigan presented a tougher problem. As a parent he was interested in Jamie's ability to earn a living. "I want a son I can someday turn over my business to," he argued. "The lad has sweetness, but he's not a practical man, Father."

"Blather," said Father Kerrigan. "Practical men have never accomplished anything worthy of note in this world."

"They have the running of it," Harrigan insisted.

"Aye . . . and take a look at it," retorted the priest.

When Bid went against him, Harrigan weakened and finally gave in. "Who's to tell Travis Bunn?" he asked glumly.

Father Kerrigan stroked his chin thoughtfully. "It's the kind of news he'll take from no one but yourself, Shiel Harrigan, but I'll go with you."

Travis Bunn was standing before his tent chewing nervously on a straw. He seemed to read the answer in the faces of the two men before either of them spoke. "Is it your given bond and word that you've come to break, Shiel Harrigan?" he demanded.

"My daughter will not wed with you, Travis Bunn," Maeve's father replied flatly. "I'll make good in kind if it's settlement you want."

"Make good in kind?" Bunn said bitterly. "Have you another daughter as fair to give in her place?"

"No . . . but of what I have you may take your pick. Either mules or horses or my chestnut mare in foal."

"I hold you to your promise. I'll have Maeve or nothing."

"Then you'll have nothing. She'll not marry with you."

Travis Bunn turned to the priest. "Will you stand by and see him break his word, Father?"

"The breaking of hearts comes before the breaking of words, my son," Father Kerrigan said kindly.

"Is the breaking of my heart nothing then?"

"She'll not marry with you, Travis Bunn. Give her up and find another to love," the priest urged.

"You've all turned against me," Bunn said slowly, setting his face like stone. "Maeve, Bid, Shiel Harrigan . . . yes, and you, too, Father." His eyes grew wild and his mouth worked convulsively. "God's curse on the lot of you, then. You'll see no more of my face, in or out of church. No, nor in the camps of the Travelers, either. God's curse on Maeve Harrigan for making of my life one long despair . . . and on Jamie McRuin for taking her from me. . . ."

"Travis Bunn, for shame . . . hear me," Father Kerrigan cried, holding out his arms and advancing toward the maddened man. Bunn backed away, mouthing a confused mixture of ancient, half-remembered curses.

"Shortness of life and Hell to them that break their oath. May the hungry grass grow wherever they make their camp. No butter be on their milk. . . . No down on their ducks. . . . No children be born to them. . . . And greater and broader be the flames that consume their souls in Hell than the mountains of Connemara, and they all burning. . . ."

His voice had risen to a hoarse shout. He turned his face to where Maeve and Jamie had come from the tent and stood apart, numb with pity. The curses caught in Bunn's throat and became a strangled sob. With a moan, he threw his arm across his eyes as if to blot out the sight; then he turned and ran toward the woods.

"Sure now the man's that crazed," Harrigan said, troubled, "calling curses on a priest of the Church."

Father Kerrigan shook his head sadly. "He loved your daughter. Maybe the quiet of the woods will ease the pain and bring him to his senses."

Darkness fell, but there was no sign of Travis Bunn. In

the deep middle of the night, when the camp was fast asleep, he crept back and silently hitched up his wagon. Loading the tent and all his belongings, he drove quietly away.

In the morning, bolts of linens and fine laces and silks for dresses were found strewn about the site where his tent had been. These were the wedding gifts Travis Bunn had brought for his bride. Of all his possessions, and he was counted a wealthy man among the Irish Travelers, nothing else was left behind.

X

MRS. FLUKER, Father Kerrigan's housekeeper, viewed the swarms of Irish horse traders that descended upon the priest and the parish each spring with resentment. Since early morning their long caravans of surreys and wagons had rolled up to the doors of the church, discharging cargoes of well-combed men, women in hats and gowns treasured from year to year for the occasion, and the swarms of thoroughly clipped and scrubbed children. All day Father Kerrigan heard their confessions, christened their babies, and blessed the old ones who cried out emotionally whenever he came near them: "Raise your hand over me, Father."

By late afternoon he was exhausted. When the last of the horse traders had finally climbed into their wagons for the return to camp, he breathed a sigh of relief and settled comfortably into his favorite easy chair. There Mrs. Fluker brought him a glass of cold lemonade. The housekeeper was a tall, thin widow, dry and crisp as an autumn leaf.

"Wearing yourself out over them nomads," she scolded.

"Why don't they settle down and come to church on Sundays like regular Christians, instead of trying to crowd all their religion into just two or three days of the year?"

Father Kerrigan reminded her mildly that if the rest of the parish showed half as much devotion to the Church as the horse traders, his job would be comparatively simple. Mrs. Fluker sniffed her disagreement and rustled away to answer the front doorbell.

She was back a second later. "It's another one of them gypsies," she announced haughtily. "He asked me would I mind 'alarming' the priest. 'Alarm' the priest, indeed. Shall I send him away?"

The priest shook his head. "Show him in," he said wearily, adding pointedly, "they prefer to be called 'Travelers,' Mrs. Fluker."

She disappeared and returned again, followed this time by Jamie. During the exchange of greetings she waited disapprovingly by the study door.

"That will be all, Mrs. Fluker," Father Kerrigan said.

"Supper will be ready in a few minutes," she reminded him.

"Good. Jamie McRuin, here, can stay and have supper with me."

"Och, no, Father, I couldn't," the boy protested.

"And why not? Set another place, Mrs. Fluker."

The housekeeper whisked resentfully away. "Now, what's on your mind, Jamie? It must be something important to keep you away from confession this afternoon, yet bring you here tonight after the others have gone?"

"Sure, Father, I'm in trouble now up to my neck," Jamie said solemnly. "I think I've committed a mortal sin."

Father Kerrigan stared at him in amazement. The boy's handsome face was set and troubled. He was wearing a stiff, new blue serge suit, the creased confines of which made him appear awkward and uncomfortable. The suit was a gift from Maeve's father, the priest surmised.

"Do you want to talk about it now, or shall we have our bit and sup first?" he asked kindly.

"I couldn't eat with this on my soul, Father. Not a mouthful. It isn't 'dirt in a well' or any small mischief. 'Twill probably require a special dispensation from the Pope."

The priest repressed a smile. He had dealt with imaginative boys like Jamie before. When they were convinced their problem was unique and solvable only by the Holy See, it generally proved to be something any parish priest could settle with a wise word.

"All right . . . out with it . . . before it burns a hole in your conscience," he said.

Jamie blurted out the story of how he and Tavish had left Ireland. "It seemed a shame to spoil such a lovely wake, so Tavish and I set our sails for America without speaking a word to anybody."

The priest rose and walked to the window. There he took out his handkerchief, blew a blast on his nose and wiped his eyes.

"Are you laughing or crying, Father?" Jamie asked, sensing vaguely that he was appearing slightly ridiculous.

Father Kerrigan returned to his seat, keeping his eyes removed from Jamie's troubled face. "I think this matter can be settled without going to His Holiness," he said evasively. "We will write a letter to your family explaining that you are alive and in America. . . ."

"Could we wait until I have some money to send? Sure the news would be more acceptable with a little money. An empty letter was always a great disappointment at home," Jamie said eagerly. "We could say that Tavish and I were swept out to sea. There we were picked up by Queen Una in her magic boat—the one that's small enough to fit in the palm of your hand, yet will hold all the people in the world, and six hundred more besides. . . ."

"I wouldn't add any more tales to those you've already told," the priest hinted mildly.

Jamie was disappointed. "They do love a good story at home, Father," he said.

"And you're to repay the money you took at the wake," Father Kerrigan continued.

"That I will, Father. Already I'm on the way to being a rich man. Did you know that Maeve brings a fine fortune with her? I'm to be a partner in her father's business. 'Tis a tradition or something for the son-in-law to join the wife's caravan. And Shiel Harrigan just this day presented us with a splendid team of horses and a new tent and wagon. Aunt Bid furnished a bed and table and chairs from a place in town where everything can be bought, from a pair of boots to a coffin; and all so new and wonderful they haven't been unwrapped yet."

Mrs. Fluker came to announce that supper was on the table. All through the simple meal Jamie babbled of the wonderful thing that had happened to him. "Is it a sin, Father, to believe in dreams coming true?"

"Not sinful . . . foolish, maybe."

"What would you say if I told you I had dreamed all this in a dream . . . and everything promised me in that dream has come true?"

The priest studied the boy's vivid, handsome face. "There's an old country word my father used to use: Rameis. It meant 'talking through one's hat,' " he said, smiling.

"It's God's own truth, Father. How else could a poor, ignorant boy like myself marry the loveliest girl that was upon the ridge of the world. There's a finger of magic in it somewhere—and no mistake."

"There are some things I should tell you about the group

of people you are marrying into, Jamie," the priest said quietly. "In the first place, they're the descendants of a group of Irish tinkers that came to this country about the time of the great famine."

"Sure, Father, I knew they were tinkers from their green tents. At home we spit on them. For Maeve, I'll be one myself, and proud," said Jamie magnanimously.

"There will be no gay life for you on the road. The Travelers work hard. Many of those they do business with are prejudiced against them. You'll be called a gypsy and a thief. They'll say you steal babies and sell them—or worse. You can't go into the towns alone, but always in a group, because there are gangs of toughs lying in wait, eager to pick a fight with you."

"In the old country they'd have had small trouble. I was famous there for using my fists. But that's all behind me, Father. I'm a changed man. The girl I wanted most in the world I won by not fighting. With Maeve beside me they can't touch me. Sure I'll smile and put their hard words to music."

"Finally, Jamie McRuin," the priest continued, "you may see things in the camp which will shock your Catholic soul. There are ancient rites and customs among these people which can be traced back to pagan times. Some of the young people still go through the tinker ceremony of Jumping the Budget; that is, they leap through fire and wade through water to demonstrate the indissolubility of their marriage."

Jamie was aghast. "Sure they wouldn't be asking a Christian boy like myself to do that, would they, Father?"

Father Kerrigan laughed. "I haven't seen any signs of such pagan shenanigans among this group. But I'm warning you, it's a lonely life."

"I'm that full of happiness there'll be small room for any loneliness to crowd in," Jamie said simply. "And sure I'll not be forgetting that it's to you I owe everything. Give me your blessing, Father, and I'll say good night."

He knelt and the priest made the sign of the cross over him. "Are you walking back to the camp?"

"The long walk will be a comfort, Father. There'll be no sleep for me this night. I'm afraid I might wake and find it's all another dream. Good night. While you're sleeping, I'll be walking the fairy paths and listening to the music of things that happen."

The priest smiled. "Don't let anything change you, lad. You've something very precious that America—and the whole world—needs. You'll find a fever here for getting and spending. Don't be consumed by it. Now God be on the road with you."

He watched the boy's tall, buoyant figure swing down the walk and through the wrought-iron gate into the street. "The music of things that happen," he repeated softly to himself. For the first time in his twenty years' service as a priest of the Church, Father Kerrigan felt lonely.

XI

THE climax of the Irish Travelers' rituals always fell on April 28th in Atlanta. On the final day funerals were held and marriages performed. In the morning the bodies of those who had died during the year and their caskets sealed and held in vaults until the time for interment, were committed to the ground in one great group funeral.

Father Kerrigan, in the years in which he had served as priest for the nomadic horse traders, had never been able to discover why they fixed upon this particular day for their mass obsequies. He had come to the private conclusion that the date was linked with the tinkers' ancient and possibly pagan history, but whatever that relationship was, the present-day Travelers had apparently forgotten it entirely.

The weddings came last. Early in the afternoon the eight brides, including Maeve, arrived at the church escorted by their parents. Among the Travelers, anything as solemn as a wedding or a funeral was always left to the management of the women. Aunt Bid, her eyes red from weeping but hawk-ike for any details that might go wrong, hovered over Maeve,

121

readjusting the lace flounces of her satin gown, or disengaging the veil when it caught over the end of a pew. Shiel Harrigan stood ineffectually with the other fathers outside the church, waiting for the Mass to begin, shaken and a little bewildered by the endless details with which women garnished the events most important to them.

Between activities Aunt Bid whispered final bits of advice. "Don't stay for the wedding games. When the Mass is over and you've had your three tastes of oatmeal and salt, take your man and whisht away. 'Breaking the Bride's Cake' and 'The Race for the Bottle' are better left for the olders who can hold their liquor. A drunken husband on a wedding night is no better than a beast . . . so I've been told."

The grooms arrived next, accompanied by their families. In tight, nervous little groups they assembled at the rear of the chapel. Few words were exchanged, and those in whispers. Jamie entered the church by a side door. His eyes were slightly red rimmed from lack of sleep, but he was freshly shaved and his shoes greased and buffed. He ran his eyes eagerly over the cluster of girls in white assembled at the opposite side of the church. Tavish, hurrying to overtake him, tugged at his arm.

"What ails you, man? You don't go thundering into the House of God like a runaway horse. Don't forget there be others getting married besides yourself. And don't let your eyes be taken out of your head looking for Maeve. It's considered bad form for the bridegroom to look at the bride until after the wedding. Among the upper classes the groom always acts as if he wishes he was someplace else."

Across the church, Aunt Bid buzzed an alternating current of warnings and advice into Maeve's ear. "There's your Jamie now. Don't be looking at him with a light in your eyes he could light his pipe on. Where's your modesty? If you're a wise girl, you'll let him know right off how lucky he is. Tell him as how you had suitors standing one in the shadow of another, as indeed you had."

The older woman's eyes brimmed with sudden tears and she covered her face with her already moist handkerchief. Maeve embraced her, pressing her check against her aunt's. "Darling Bid," she whispered, "my own mother couldn't have done for me all the things you've done. I've been rude and thankless, but never for a moment have I not loved you as if you were she."

Aunt Bid was gratified and kissed her with trembling lips. "One last thing . . . when you're kneeling before the priest, be sure to be the first to rise after the final blessing. The bride who rises ahead of her husband will die before him. And take it from one who knows, child, living after the man you love is gone is worse than not living at all."

Maeve had been on the verge of tears all morning. Now her eyes flooded. She had heard camp talk since childhood of how Bid had loved a handsome young Traveler who had been kicked to death by a mule scarcely a week before their wedding. Bid had never looked at another man.

Lifting her aunt's rough hand she kissed it tenderly.

"It isn't fair for me to be so happy and not be able to share some of it with you," she said emotionally.

Bid withdrew her hand and fussed about, straightening and restraightening Maeve's veil. "Sure you can't keep happiness to yourself, no more than you can sunshine. It spills all over the world, warming the ones you love. There's the music. Now go to your kneeing . . . and God love and keep you, my treasure."

The organ music swelled and the line of brides formed and began to move down the aisle to meet the grooms before the altar.

XII

THE road out of Atlanta led southeastward toward Savannah. The surroundings were both new and strange to Jamie, but Maeve had driven the way many times. She sat beside him slim and erect, her eyes fixed upon the shiny brass knobs glinting on the collar of Big Red, the off horse.

Jamie's eyes, too, were on the road ahead. The excitement of the wedding festival and the games had deserted them. They were alone for the first time and painfully conscious of each other. The shyness which had grown between them seemed to increase instead of diminish as the miles rolled beneath the crisp, new wheels of the wagon.

Jamie drove, pretending absorption in the operation of the new wagon. Though he never turned his head to look at Maeve, she sat clear and perfect in every detail in his mind's eye. When he reached for the foot brake to ease the strain on the horses as the wagon lurched downgrade, he could glimpse the thin, red rim of dust around the edge of her wedding slippers. He had an impulse to halt the wagon and flick away the offending earth, so that nothing might mar the picture perfection of the girl beside him.

The sun was setting and the road ahead glowed the color of deep burnt orange. When the wagon lurched through a gutted place in the road, Maeve was thrown against Jamie's shoulder. She did not draw away and the muscles of his left side tensed and vibrated as if plucked by an unseen harpist.

"I'm sorry," she said shyly.

"I like it." The words sounded both false and futile, even as they left Jamie's mouth.

Maeve said nothing more and they were strangers again for a few hundred yards. "There's a small camp ahead . . . about a mile. We've stopped there before." She tried to make her words sound matter-of-fact.

"Stop now?" Jamie protested. "And us barely on the road? Sure the horses haven't even a sweat. 'Tis a lovely night for driving," he added lamely.

The thought of stopping and making camp, of going to bed with Maeve, of becoming her husband, overwhelmed Jamie with a mixture of terror and tenderness. In all the years of his adult life he had never been intimate with a girl. The blending of poverty, parental vigilance, plus the romantic aura which surrounded relationships between the sexes in Ireland, had made experimentation difficult . . . if not impossible.

His headlong courtship of Maeve had so absorbed Jamie there had been little or no time for him to get really acquainted with her. They had fallen in love, but did not know each other; were married, but had never exchanged the simplest kiss.

Through the jumble of his contradictory emotions, Jamie found himself wishing for Tavish. Tavish could help him. The old man would have a bachelor's objectivity. He would have precedents, too. They might date back to the ancient Irish, but just now a thousand-year-old precedent was better than none.

"Are you tired?" he asked awkwardly.

"I don't mind."

"It's been a big day."

"A day to remember," she agreed.

The road dipped downhill and sliced through a stand of tall pines and red oaks. The sun had disappeared and the twilight deepened into darkness. With the coming of night, Maeve's manner underwent a subtle change. Some instinct made her sense the emotional turmoil seething within Jamie. She slipped her hand beneath his arm and drew herself closer to him.

"You haven't once looked at me since breaking the Bride's Cake," she said reproachfully.

Jamie stole a glance at her and flashed a smile that shone white in the darkness. "Sure now it's true," he admitted, "But the reason's not far to seek. There's about you a light . . . like the one that shone from heroes in ancient times. It hurts my eyes."

"Could it be the love light?" Maeve teased. "And could you never have seen it before?"

"It could . . . and I could not . . . and there's my oath on it," Jamie said emphatically.

Maeve made a small sighing noise. "I think that's why I chose you over Travis Bunn."

Jamie didn't answer, so she persisted. "Don't you think it's the reason I chose you over Travis Bunn?"

"I'm that modest, sure I wouldn't dare speculate. Though I'll admit there's small comparison between us for manly beauty. My hair is curlier and my flesh pinker."

"It wasn't your curly hair, nor your pink flesh," Maeve said, suppressing a laugh.

"Faith, it must have been for my fine brain. At home no man in the county was more respected for his wisdom," said Jamie, joining in the spirit of banter.

Maeve shrieked with laughter. "Of that I'm sure."

"It's God own truth. 'Twas said of me, I had only to look at the smoke from a cottage chimney to tell the number of people around the hearth inside . . . and if any of them was ailing . . . and what the sickness was . . . and the sort of physic the patient should take. . . ."

Maeve had collapsed and was rocking back and forth holding her sides before Jamie finished. "Musha . . . don't . . . I have pains," she gasped.

The constraint born of their mutual shyness had vanished. Wagon tracks leading off to the right from the main road appeared and Maeve reached across Jamie and tugged at the reins, guiding the team along them and into the woods. Jamie, now thoroughly enjoying himself, gave no heed to where the horses were taking them.

"Sure now I know why it was me you took," he crowed. " 'Twas the fine tenor voice of me raised in song. At home they said I sang that sweetly, sure the cows gave more milk."

The camp site was well shielded in the timber, a hundred yards or so off the main road. A small brook furnished fresh, cool water. Jamie unhitched the horses, fed and watered them. While they were eating, he and Maeve unfolded the new tent and set it up by lantern light. There was no more laughing and talking. Each was busy with the multitude of chores: Unloading the wagon; unpacking tent furnishings; storing food and supplies—all gifts from Shiel Harrigan and the other horse traders.

As he handled the items, Jamie felt the first breath of pride that the possession of things gives a man. From nobody he had become somebody; from having nothing he suddenly had emerged as a man of means.

"Your father was against me because he thought I was

more for dreaming than for business," Jamie told Maeve. "Well . . . I'm going to show him, and all the others, too. At home they were ever flinging the word 'money' at me. Now I'll be showing them. Sure, if it's money they want, then I'll make it by the tentful . . . like King Midas. We'll be rich—so that when we're old and eaten by the tooth of time, we can love each other for the money."

Maeve laughed indulgently. "Be as rich as you like, my darling," she teased. "Only don't change. I fell in love with a boy who had nothing. . . ."

"Nothing, is it?" Jamie exclaimed, pretending to be incensed. "Would you be calling three wishes nothing . . . and the first two of them granted already, with the third . . ." he checked himself abruptly, and was glad of the darkness, for he felt himself blushing.

If Maeve noticed the reference to the third wish, she gave no indication. The tent was up and she went inside to change her wedding dress.

" 'Tis plain," Jamie told himself with boyish arrogance, "whatever I want out of this life I shall get. Everything the Fairy Queen said has come true! The woman of my choice is mine; there's travel enough ahead and behind me for two lifetimes."

Mentally, he thanked the Fairy Queen and discharged her from further duty. "For the wonderful son I'll be getting—sure I can do that for myself. There's but to flash my antlers in the air. . . ."

As Jamie worked, he could see Maeve's form moving about the tent and it added to his sense of well-being. When he had finished and a fire was roaring in the fire pit, he called to her, saying that they should have some supper. There was no answer from within the tent and her shadow had ceased to flit to and fro.

Jamie crossed to the opening, but before he drew the flap

aside, a sudden sharp tightening inside his chest made him hesitate. "Maeve?" he called softly.

There was still no answer. Pulling back the flap, Jamie entered. The bed was already in place, its lace spread gleaming the color of ivory in the yellow light of the lantern. Other furnishings had been distributed in their proper places. Small throw rugs were spread upon the pine-needle-strewn ground.

Maeve stood beside the center pole of the tent, where she had hung the tiny crucifix given her by Aunt Bid. Her hair was tied loosely with a strip of ribbon, and fell below her shoulders. It caught the warm rays from the lantern until it glowed in spots like heated copper. She had changed into her wedding nightgown.

The garment was of soft white silk and reached to the rug upon which she stood. The neck and shoulders were of finest lace, with tiny, exquisite ribbons of different colors escaloped about the throat. The picture created was one of such absolute perfection that Jamie stood speechless, afraid to breathe.

Maeve waited for him to say something, but a great lump had risen in his throat, rendering him incapable of uttering a sound. "Aunt Bid made it for me. Do you like it?" she asked simply.

Jamie nodded numbly. Maeve flashed him a little smile, turned to the lantern and blew it out, "Come to bed."

As she lay listening to Jamie undressing in the darkness, her thoughts turned to the torrent of events that had brought her as a bride to the bed of a man she had known but a few brief days. "I'm not afraid any more," she told herself. "The man drawing near me in this warm, pine-scented darkness is no longer a stranger. It's as if I had known him since he was a little boy and have always wanted to mother him."

A deep sense of security stole over her. When she had stood out against her father and all the relatives, including Father Kerrigan, a strange prescience had guided and given her strength. She knew with a certainty deeper than any born of logic that Jamie was her mate. He was the poet and warrior of ancient days. He would be, with her help, a child to children and a man to men. Whatever he made of his life would largely be her doing, for a wild and open nature such as his could be blown by every wind.

Jamie's hand reached out and fumbled with the bed covers. She turned them back for him and a trembling seized her that was not from the night air. Jamie's body burned against hers through the nightgown. His fingers touched her cheek, and with a cry that was almost a sob, he buried his face against her bosom.

The trembling left Maeve's body and she held him in her arms soothingly. An exultation swept through her that was almost savage. For the first time she knew the overwhelming sense of possession which complete and abject surrender can give a woman.

Outside the tent the fire fought its losing battle with surrounding darkness. The flames flickered and sank. The horses munched contentedly on the hay Jamie had spread for them, while the smaller night sounds were lost in the gentle moaning of the pines. And over all the full and ancient moon sailed in silent silver splendor.

XIII

JESSE PRODDY sat on his lean, hard haunches, his back braced against the gray, warped planks of the barn. It sheltered him from the sharp March wind whistling through the cracks and around the bleak edges of the building. His faded gray-blue eyes were fixed upon a circus of buzzards spiraling slowly earthward near the scrub pines at the edge of his property. Glumly he chewed on a piece of oat straw.

"My mule," he mourned, "my last and only dad-gummed mule . . . dead . . . buzzard bait . . . and right at plowing time. I reckon God's a-punishing me, but I don't rightly know why. I loved that mule."

He rose stiffly and ambled toward the house. The seventh and youngest child whipped around a corner, his uncombed blond hair flying in the gusty wind and his great blue eyes fastened upon some imaginary quarry he was pursuing. Jesse caught him with one hand as he sped past.

"Whoa, little Number Seven," he said. "Where's your ma?"

131

Images deep in the boy's eyes shifted from dream figures to the shabby, unshaven reality of his father. He pointed toward the hen house where Hester was emerging with a few eggs gathered in the folds of her apron.

"Wife," Jesse called to her plaintively, "Old Luke is dead."

Hester stopped in her tracks. "Oh, no," she said despairingly.

"Yep," Proddy continued bitterly, "lay down not ten minutes ago, with his four feet pointin' toward Heaven and leavin' me in a hell of a fix. If you don't believe me, just cast your eye over toward them pines. There ain't no better proof that somethin's dead than buzzards. And that somethin's Old Luke."

The little boy had been listening with mounting excitement. At seven, "death" was only a word, but its vibrant sound sent ripples of meaning into every corner of his being —like a heavy stone dropped into the placid waters of a well, wrinkling the surface with mysterious portent. Death, the wild, dark shadow that lay in wait for every living creature, had struck Old Luke. Old Luke, upon whose back he had ridden so many times. Death, that invisible chasm separating "to be" and "not to be"—its opening, narrower than a razor's edge yet deep enough to engulf every living thing, had swallowed their plodding, gentle old mule.

Drawn by a mixture of fear and fascination, the child started toward the spot where the first of the circling buzzards were settling about the dead animal. "Number Seven," his father shouted, "git back here."

He emphasized his shout with a shrill, ear-splitting whistle. Regretfully the boy turned back. "When the other kids git home from school we'll go down and bury him. You can come along and watch," Jesse comforted him.

"What are we gonna do?" Hester said, miserably. "It's

time the crops were in the ground. And now no mule for the plowing."

"The Lord's done turned his face against me," Jesse cried angrily. He shook his fist skyward. "From now we're quits. I'm a infidel. You hear that, Lord? Me and You is finished."

Hester listened to her husband in shocked amazement. The past year had wrought a remarkable change in the poor, slatternly creature who had listened so humbly to Father Kerrigan's tales. Physically she was wasting away, but a new fire burned within her. It showed in her eyes and in her speech. "Do you know what's happened to you, Hester Proddy?" the priest had said to her a few days before. "You've found your immortal soul. And it's made a new woman of you."

Now she flew at her husband with a violence that staggered him. "For shame, Jesse Proddy," she cried, "blasphemin' before your own child. You can burn in Hell if you like, but not my children. They're gonna have Christian raising."

The abruptness of his wife's attack left Jesse speechless. What's come over her? he thought, watching perplexed as she hustled the child into the house.

Muttering, he retreated to the shelter of the barn. "Sass . . . that's what I git around here . . . sass. I wasn't even talkin' to her. I was talkin' to the Lord . . . and she flew at me like a nestin' she-eagle. Ever since that fiend o' Rome's been snoopin' about, things has been goin' from bad to worse. First he sent the county policeman out to make sure the younguns went to school; and now he's turned my own wife agin me. That settles it. If he comes on the place agin I'll set the dog on him."

"Shucks," he amended after a moment's consideration, "I ain't got no dog. Old Blue's been dead a couple of years.

No mule . . . no dog. Things around here is sure goin' to Hell in a handbasket."

With his original determination blunted by the lack of means to execute it, Jesse surrendered with a grunt and fell to brooding upon the harsh uses to which fate had put him. When the other children came trudging from school, he took Trace, the oldest boy, and Tolbert and Todd, the next two, with him to bury the mule. The two girls, Beth and Bella, who were twelve and nine, he left behind despite their clamor to come along.

"Buryin' mules ain't fit work for girls," he told them.

The youngest boy was waiting outside with his brothers. When Jesse saw the look of eagerness on his face, an impulse to be cruel came over him. "Ain't no use you waitin' around, Number Seven. You can't come with us," he said, covering his feeling of guilt with a show of anger.

The child's blue eyes were swimming in great, unshed tears as he watched his brothers grab up a battered assortment of shovels and spades and follow Jesse toward the pine grove. This was a double injustice. Old Luke had been his friend and he had been promised he might watch. Besides, he had never seen a burying. It sounded mysterious and exciting.

From below he could hear his brothers' laughter and the dull "chuck" of their shovels biting into the soil. What was there to laugh about in Old Luke's being dead? he wondered. The mule had been a member of the family as long as he could remember.

Creeping along the back fence, the boy made his way toward the grove of jack pines. Overhead the disturbed buzzards floated in protesting spirals. When he was close enough to observe everything, he hid. Trace was standing waist-deep in the hole, shoveling out the soil. The boys took turns digging, while Jesse sat staring moodily at the dead mule.

"Dig that hole deep, boys," he ordered. "Old Luke was a tall mule."

From the protection of a tangle of weeds, Number Seven watched the grave sink lower and lower. Tolbert was digging now, and his tow head bobbed in and out of the hole like a cork. By the time enough dirt had been removed, long shadows from the pine grove were creeping across the land and darkening the pile of raw red earth beside the open grave.

The boy watched with combined horror and excitement as his father approached the dead mule. Jesse and Trace seized the two hind legs, while Tolbert and Todd took hold of the front. Straining and tugging, they dragged the inert body to the edge of the freshly dug hole and tumbled it in without ceremony.

From his place of concealment, the child felt the jolt at the pit of his stomach as the mule's torn carcass thudded into the grave. So this was what burying meant. With a mounting sense of suffocation, he watched the loose dirt being shoveled into the hole. When nothing was visible but the mound of red earth, the three boys leapt upon it with whoops of laughter and began to trample it flat.

Watching his brothers stomping upon Old Luke's grave, the boy's sensation of suffocating became so intense it seemed impossible to breathe. He wanted to cry out in protest; to ask his father how Old Luke was going to get out of the hole, with all that dirt packed on top of him? For the first time the full tragedy of his inability to speak came home to him. Like Old Luke, he, too, was entombed. For the mule, the walls were Georgia's soft red soil; for himself, the crystal and more intransigeant barriers of silence.

The job finished, Jesse and the three boys picked up their tools and trudged jokingly back to the house. Neither poverty, deprivation, nor death could check the natural buoyancy of their youth. They jabbed at each other, laughing and cavorting like colts in a pasture. When they were out of sight, Number Seven crept quietly to where the flattened grave lay like a dull red scar upon the green and silent earth. This was another aspect of death: The returning of the body to the ground. The March wind, no longer warmed by the sun, sighed downward through the pine branches and struck a chill through the boy's thin clothing. Faced with one of life's great imponderables, he drew his own child's conclusion. The earth was an Indian giver. She gave life to all creatures at birth . . . and took all creatures back to her bosom at death.

With a feeling of loneliness made doubly intolerable because he had no words with which to express it, and no person with whom to share it if he had, the boy turned away from the new-made grave and walked drearily homeward.

XIV

MRS. FLUKER showed Maeve into Father Kerrigan's small, plainly furnished reception room. The walls were dullish gray and needful of a coat of brightening paint. A few holy ornaments were spaced about, while in the stray beams of trespassing sunlight the dust of many yesterdays danced in bright irreverence.

Maeve seated herself quietly on a hard, straight-backed bench and folded her hands in her lap. It was restful and soothing to be sitting quietly, without the jolting movement of a wagon beneath her and the smell of sweating mules in her nostrils. To think a whole year has passed, she mused, so quickly. It seems like only a few days. Last year at this time Jamie had come to me in the night with his hands bashed and torn from smashing them against the trunks of trees—as if the breaking of his knuckles would mend the breaking of his heart. So much has happened since then . . . and yet so little.

She fingered the heavy gold bracelet weighing on her slender wrist. Jamie had given it to her a few days before, on

137

the anniversary of the day they had met. One small, perfect diamond was mounted in the bracelet.

"That's for our first year," Jamie had told her. "And there will be another like it, or maybe bigger, on this same day every year, until the acid of time has eaten us away, and only the love we had for each other is left."

"How long do you think that will endure?" she had teased.

Jamie had pretended to calculate seriously. " 'Tis not easy to figure," he had demurred, "for it runs into numbers not yet invented. Let me see: Of the days I loved you before either of us were born—count the stars of the heavens, the sands of the sea; then add to that total the flakes of the winter snow! For the days I will continue to love you—until time runs out and the King of Sunday calls us all home—add the dewdrops on the lawn, the hailstones after a summer storm, the grass under the feet of herds, and Manannan mac Lir's horses, with their white manes tossing as they ride the sea waves in a storm!"

He had kissed her then and said seriously: "The day a year ago when I saw you by the rivereen, I called and crossed you to myself before God and all the saints. As long as there's sight in the eyes of me, you'll be that young girl with the buckets heavy enough for a man, and the eyes that laughed deep down inside herself."

The memory of his words sent a glow through Maeve and a warm flush rose in her cheeks.

From outside the church came the squeal of high, childish voices. The children were coming from confession. A few minutes later she heard Father Kerrigan's footsteps entering the back door and coming toward the waiting room.

"Maeve!" he greeted her cordially. "Mrs. McRuin . . . you're back before the others. Where's Jamie? Sit down—tell me about yourself."

"Jamie stopped to see someone on business, Father. We came early because we're burying Aunt Bid this year."

"I know that," the priest said sympathetically. "Mr. Yates, the undertaker, told me. What happened?"

"We were wintering in Alabama. Auntie Bid took with a bad cold and it went into pneumonia. She was gone almost before we knew how sick she was," Maeve stated simply.

"She was a fine woman. God will give her rest," the priest said.

Maeve crossed herself and was silent. Something in her manner drew and held Father Kerrigan's attention. "Is everything else all right?"

"Yes, Father."

"Was it a good year with the horses?"

"Yes, Father, a very good year."

He tipped Maeve's chin upward with his forefinger. "You may be a married woman but you're still a little girl to me. Come . . . out with it. What's wrong? Is it Jamie?"

"Oh, no, Father," Maeve said earnestly. "We've been wonderfully happy. There's just one thing. . . ."

"Go on."

"We're not having a child this year." Maeve felt the warm flush creeping into her cheeks. The subject was difficult to discuss, even with someone as genial and understanding as Father Kerrigan.

"And is that a reason to wear such a long face?" he chided her. "God sends babies . . . and in His own good time."

"I know that, Father. It's sinful to ask for something more when already we have so much . . . but Jamie has been bragging among the men about the wonderful son he was going to have. Now, a year has passed and there's no child. He feels humiliated and ashamed."

"So, Jamie McRuin, like most pigheaded Irishmen, has been clamoring for a son, has he?" Father Kerrigan said sternly. "Well, you tell him he can just bide his time. Or better yet, I'll tell him."

"No, Father, please don't say anything," Maeve pleaded, genuinely disturbed. "He's hurt and bewildered—like a child that's been promised something and the promise not kept. He was so sure, Father. . . ."

"You've been married but a year! 'Tis a little soon to start fretting," the priest reminded Maeve. But inwardly he was disturbed. To a dreaming romanticist like Jamie, a child in the home was a necessity. It was an angel direct from Heaven; the deep and lasting proof of God's favor.

"I'll find a way to speak with him without mentioning our little talk," he assured the girl.

Maeve thanked him and rose to go, but she was not entirely comforted. "Father," she said hesitantly, "you don't think Travis Bunn . . . the curse he put on us . . .?"

"Nonsense," Father Kerrigan snapped. "I told you it was in God's hands—not Travis Bunn's—nor Satan's neither!"

"We heard from other of the caravans that he had paid a spoiled priest to do the Reversed Journey, invoking the power of evil . . ." Maeve said in awed tones.

"Maeve McRuin," the priest said sternly, "rid yourself of such thoughts. You're a child of God and no witchcraft or owree magic can stand in the way of your bearing a son . . . if it be God's will! Pray . . . and if it is His will, in time your prayers will be answered."

The doubts that had gnawed at Maeve's heart through the past months were dispelled. Father Kerrigan seemed so wise and sure. Around her he had thrown the protection of the saints, backed by the power and majesty of the Holy Church. Let Travis Bunn do his wicked worst. Mary and Her Son were on her side.

When the rumors had first reached Maeve of Bunn's practices, she was stunned by the enormity of the man's hate. Travis Bunn had loved her once—she knew that as women know such things. Was it possible that love's unstable chemistry could be changed to hate, as light was changed to darkness by the mere snuffing out of a candle?

Jamie had laughed at the reports of Bunn's traffic with the Devil. "Sure Old Nick will end up with a Monday haircutting if he does any business with Bunn," he asserted.

But the fear had grown in Maeve until it became obsessive: Bunn's curses were taking effect. Why else, then, was she not having a child? The idea haunted her, poisoning the perfection of her happiness. She couldn't wait to get back to Atlanta and the consolation of her priest. Now Bunn and his owree had been exorcised by Father Kerrigan's stern, sure judgment. Comforted, she went across the churchyard to light altar candles and pray for the peace of her own and Aunt Bid's soul.

The Travelers had made their camp on the same site used the year before. Membership of the individual groups assembling changed only slightly from one season to another. Marriages brought new husbands from their own camps to that of their brides. Or, since the horse traders were possessed of lively Irish tempers and temperaments, it was not unusual for loyalties to shift and families to become uncongenial. Disagreements occurred that could not be amicably adjusted, and the "road" settled the dispute. The disputants packed their belongings and departed in opposite directions.

As a rule those of like blood and temperament stayed together in the same group. Leadership was never formal or final. There were no kings or chosen chieftains. Ability, wisdom, character, and courage found their own level without question or challenge. When those qualities were outstanding in any member of a group, he automatically drew his own following.

Because of their leader's forthrightness, as well as shrewd-ness, the members of Shiel Harrigan's group had remained much the same year after year. Under his leadership the traders had grown prosperous. From his father-in-law, Jamie learned the rudiments of buying and selling horses and mules. There was a fascination in trading animals. It was like gambling. Men swapped horses and mules as small boys swapped pocketknives. There was an inner excitement in backing your judgment against that of other men. As in gambling, luck played a part, but in the end knowledge and skill were the invariable winners.

The nomadic Travelers had developed horse trading into a pleasant and profitable profession. This ability to judge quality, plus a shrewd understanding of human nature, had made them top men in their field. In the wide range of their dealings certain tabus became established. They never com-peted with each other for customers or trespassed upon each other's territory. No sale was pushed when a buyer appeared reluctant; nor was a trade urged when the trader seemed undecided. Salesmanship took a more dramatic form. When Shiel Harrigan led a string of horses and mules into a town's square on a Saturday, the animals were plumed and polished as if they were competing for a prize. On a vacant lot rented for the occasions, the animals were ringed about the traders' wagons in groups of ten or twelve, while Shiel Harrigan strolled among the interested farmers and townspeople, whip in hand, like a ringmaster.

"Which one shall it be, gentlemen?" he would call, punc-tuating his cries with sharp cracks of the long whip. "Take your pick or name your top price and I'll pick one for you."

No buyer who wanted to pay a hundred dollars for a mule was shown a hundred-and-fifty-dollar animal and urged that the higher-priced one was the better buy. What he asked for he got: the best animal available at his own price. As a result of this reputation for hard, fair dealing, whole communities came to rely upon the Travelers for supplying their working stock.

It was a healthy, happy life, and Jamie took to it with an eager and natural aptitude. Most Irishmen are born horsemen. To his native talent Jamie added his own guileless and engaging manner. He learned the technique of praising only those animals he had no intention of buying, pretending to ignore the horse or mule that made his teeth water. Before the year was out, he could judge the soundness of animals with the best of the traders, and won grudging praise from his father-in-law, plus a sizable share in the season's profits.

"Sure something has been directing me on the road of my luck," he told Maeve happily. "Look at the wonder of things that have happened: The love of my heart I've won. Travel I have, up and down the length and breadth of the land. And now money to buy with. Can you know what it means to have been without all your life, then suddenly to have plenty? Sure it's like having the Curse of Four and Twenty Men removed."

But Jamie's enthusiasm showed signs of wavering in the late winter months. When the caravan turned southward, following the warm weather, he suddenly became aware that Maeve was not having the child he had boasted would come with the springtide. He felt cheated and bewildered and shamed before the other men.

To make matters worse, Me-Dennis O'Ryan's daughter, Doreen, was expecting a baby. Doreen had married Tom Sherwood, from another camp, at the same time Jamie and Maeve were married. For the past three months her husband had been strutting about the camp crowing because his wife was having a baby while Maeve was not. Sherwood was a big, crude fellow who meant his joking good-naturedly enough, not suspecting how deeply the jibes galled Jamie.

Now added to Maeve's worries was the growing fear of a clash between her husband and Big Tom.

Maeve had stayed late in Atlanta, making the final arrangements for Aunt Bid's funeral. There were the usual details to be taken care of, and such functions always fell to the women. By the time she returned to camp Doreen Sherwood was in labor.

The men and older boys had retreated to the corral, humbled and a little frightened in the presence of this thing called "birth." Tom Sherwood had supplied a gallon of mountain whiskey for the occasion, and every time Doreen emitted a groan he took a hasty drink. As a result, Big Tom was well afloat.

Jamie sat with the circle of men but was not drinking. The talk was low voiced and desultory except for the expectant father, Big Tom. He was tearfully berating himself.

"Doreen will never forgive me . . . there's a thought for sorrow. Oh . . . the pain; sure it's killing her now. Oooooh . . . did you hear that? The moaning . . . hand me the jug, man. I'm a beast, that's what I am. All men are beasts, to do this to their wives. God stiffen the lot of us. Poor little Doreen. . . ."

"Wait till she's had as many as her mother," Me-Dennis grunted wryly. " 'Twill take no more effort than a loud sneeze."

Big Tom was drunkenly shocked at his father-in-law's callousness. He raised his right hand solemnly. "I swear . . . never again. Before God I swear it."

Me-Dennis laughed. "Doreen's gonna be just like her ma. May-Flo had nine kids in the first ten years we were married."

Tavish had been sitting quietly, occasionally turning a thoughtful eye in Jamie's direction. "There's a sudden silence from up at the tents," he said. "Maybe it's all over, Tom. Why don't you run up and see if the little one has arrived?"

"You think maybe. . . ." Tom stood up unsteadily, wiping his mouth with the back of his hand. "I'll go see." He lurched away, trying furtively to straighten his rumpled clothes.

"He'll be used to it in a few more years," Jaunting Jim Donner said slyly.

A ripple of laughter circled the ring of men. From the direction of the tents sounded a wild whoop of joy, and on the heels of it, Tom Sherwood came staggering back, his wide, plain face beaming.

"It's here . . . it's come . . . a boy; think of it . . . a boy!" he shouted excitedly. "Let's all have a drink to my son."

The men crowded good-naturedly around him, offering congratulations. Big Tom picked up the jug and sloshed the contents near his ear. "There's plenty left. Who'll be first?"

From the corner of his eye, Tavish saw Jamie turn and start away. "I will," he called out quickly, reaching for the jug.

"Wait a minute," Big Tom said belligerently. He, too, had seen Jamie leaving.

"I've got a better idea." With quick strides he planted himself in front of Jamie, blocking his way. "Here," he said with drunken menace, "I want Jamie McRuin to be the first to drink."

Big Tom held out the jug, but Jamie made no move to take it. Instead his eyes began to glow with the cold, impersonal hatred of a panther. "Why Thomas boyo, sure I'd love to share with you a seldom drink," he said softly, "but I'm thinking maybe the strain of being a father has worn you to a thread. Save the liquor for yourself."

Big Tom's face grew set and ugly. "No man refusing to drink with me will stay on his two feet longer than it takes me to knock him off them," he said warningly. "Say out, will you drink or no?"

Jamie's lips curled into a tantalizing smile, but his eyes were more menacing. "Sure the brave words of yourself have thrown me into a terrible flustration. Take the advice of a friendly man, Tom—don't let your newborn son witness the wreck I'd make of you."

Big Tom's rage was strangling him. "Make a wreck of me? You? With one hand I'll take you apart bone by bone . . . and I'll make a solemn oath on it."

The older men had hesitated to intervene, but now Tavish pushed his short body between the two younger, bigger men. "That's enough now," he said jovially. "Sure and the wind of your words has already blown the tails off the mules. Be a grown man, Jamie. Drink to the boy's first born. The bairn has never harmed a hair of anyone's head."

"He's that despairing because he hasn't done as well himself, for all his boasting," Big Tom said. "I say Jamie Mc-Ruin is not man enough to plow a proper furrow."

Jamie's face turned bluish gray in the shadow of the pines and his jaws locked in a rigid line. Tavish shoved Big Tom back. "What sort of drunk man's talk is that, Tom Sherwood?" he said sternly.

The smile had not wavered on Jamie's lips. "Never mind, Cousin Tavish," he said softly. "I'll drink with Tom. The fierceness of his talk has convinced me. Hand me the jug."

With a swagger, Big Tom passed the jug to Jamie. Still smiling, Jamie lifted it to his lips and filled his mouth with the clear, burning liquor. He passed the jug to Tavish, then deliberately spat the whiskey into Tom Sherwood's face.

"Sure I'll say when I'll drink . . . and to what I'll drink . . . and where and who with," he gritted savagely.

Big Tom, blinded by the liquor, struck wildly at the blurred, taunting face. Deliberately Jamie stepped in close, measured, and swung heavily. Sherwood went down, the back of his head striking a steel shackle on the wagon tongue. He lay still while Jamie stood over him, shaking with rage.

Tavish seized the boy's arm and dragged him away. "That's enough . . . he's down, Jamie. Come with me, lad. We'll walk it off," he said soothingly.

Jamie's tongue was thick and he could barely speak. "I could tear out his heart with my two hands and feed it to the dogs," he said hoarsely. "Not a proper man? Did you hear what he said, 'Cousin Tavish? Och, the villain . . . kill him slowly by inches, I could." A dry sobbing shook his body.

"Shh," Tavish said, gently. " 'Twas only drunken talk. Don't speak of it and don't think of it. Just walk."

They walked until the color had returned to Jamie's face and the violent trembling that had shaken him like the ague had gone. Then they turned back toward the camp, following the road.

At the turnoff leading to the camp site, Jamie said goodby to Owen Roe Tavish. "I'm not ready to go back there yet," he said. "I'll walk on into Atlanta."

He made no mention of Maeve and declined Tavish's offer to accompany him. With his heavy shoes splaying the soft red dust into a rosy cloud, he strode away alone. Tavish watched until the first bend in the road swallowed the boy from sight.

"Jamie boy . . . Jamie boy, will you always be laying life on the anvil, and trying to beat it into shape with your fists?" he murmured aloud.

With a sigh, the old man turned and walked slowly along the narrow trail leading to the camp in the pines.

XV

A BEDRAGGLED cab rocked unevenly along the dark, cobblestoned street, drawing to a halt before a square, two-story house. The colored driver tapped his sleeping passenger on the leg with the butt of his whip to rouse him.

"Heah we is," he said cheerfully.

"What . . . where?" Jamie asked, awakening and looking about stupidly.

The street was dark and empty, with few lights showing. Jamie gazed questioningly at the driver, striving to fit his blurred thoughts into some sort of logical pattern. Why had the driver brought him to this depressing spot? He had been drinking—all through the early part of the evening; but now he felt reasonably sober. He remembered getting into the cab, but falling asleep seemed to have blotted out whatever purpose was in his mind.

"That place I wuz to bring you to. There it is . . . right yonder," the driver reminded him, pointing with his whip.

Jamie found himself looking at a house with a remote aura of past, unpainted, and gingerbread elegance. The shades were drawn at the windows, but thin edges of light were dimly visible around the curtains. Then he remembered. "What do I do?" he asked.

"Nothin' . . . you don' have to do nothin'," the driver chuckled good-naturedly. "Jes' ring the doorbell an' from then on they does everything for you."

Jamie climbed stiffly from the cab. His mouth was sour and his tongue felt thick and not yet under control. "How much do I owe you?" he asked, fishing in his pockets.

"I mostly gits a dollah for a trip like dis," the colored man said hopefully.

Jamie handed him the money in silver. "I just ring the doorbell?" he repeated doubtfully.

"Dat's right. Ring de doorbell and watch de activity begin." The driver burst into a peal of deep, rich laughter. He saluted Jamie, and with the same motion urged his tired horse into a trot.

Standing on the curb, Jamie's eyes automatically examined the animal pulling the cab. "What a sorry garraun he be driving," he muttered irrelevantly. Vaguely Jamie wished he hadn't launched himself upon this wild expedition. It must be very late. Maeve was probably in bed and sweetly asleep. "Still I've got to go through with it," he told himself. "Not a man, am I? Sure now we'll be seeing about that."

He adjusted his wrinkled clothes and tried to smooth his rumpled hair; then he mounted the porch steps and twirled the doorbell. No sound of ringing came through the thick panels, but the door opened almost immediately and he was greeted by a trim colored girl wearing a maid's uniform.

"Please come in, suh," she said politely. Jamie was hatless and was led directly to the empty, dimly lit parlor.

"Madame Blanche will be right down," the girl announced, as if that pat particular phrase was one used often on the premises.

When she had gone, Jamie stared about the large, high-ceilinged room, impressed by the rich paneling and the worn elegance of the red plush furniture. Paintings of flossy ladies, their white and ample bosoms veiled only by a frosty breath of chiffon, hung in gilt frames around the walls. It was Jamie's first introduction to art and he found it awesome.

Madame Blanche swept into the room enveloped in an elaborate, off-the-shoulders gown of red silk. Its yards of heavy material presaged her approach with a gentle, rustling sound remindful of dry leaves in an autumn breeze. Her broad face was heavily rouged, and her dyed red hair was blown into great puffs that sat balanced on the top of her head like a coppery, wind-filled cloud. She flashed Jamie a broad smirk, the width of which could be measured by a scattered array of gold teeth spaced like milestones along the path of her smile.

"Gude evening, sir," she said in cultured tones, at the same time appraising Jamie with sharp, shrewd eyes in the same manner he would examine a horse. Satisfied, her air of false elegance dropped from her as if by default.

"Stranger in town?" she asked in a husky, good-natured voice.

"Yes . . . er no," Jamie said, flustered. "I've been in Atlanta before."

Madame Blanche gave a vulgar chortle and jogged him with a fat elbow. "I'll bet you have, big boy. Do you wanta drink first, or d'you wanta go straight upstairs?"

Jamie muttered that he'd prefer a drink. The thought of "going upstairs," with all that it implied, left his flesh clammy.

"Sure," said Blanche, flashing her gold-and-white smile. "I'll send one of the girls to drink with you."

She sailed from the room, wafting an aura of perfume in Jamie's direction that made his eyes water; the heavy folds of her red silk gown creaking and rustling like a schooner straining under full sail.

"Bernice," Jamie heard her call up the stairs, "gentleman in the parlor."

Glumly he wished he were somewhere else. The stubborn bravado that had brought him to Madame Blanche's, after a round of drinking places, was gone. He was hung over emotionally as well as physically. I should have gone back to camp with Tavish; given the Sherwood bairn my chestnut colt for a birthday present; and then let Tom Sherwood break my jaw in return for the beating I gave him, he ruminated.

A tall, slight girl, with fair hair and a pale sort of under-nourished prettiness about her, came into the room. "Hello," she said in a flat, southern voice, "I'm Bernice. Blanche said you wanted a drink."

Jamie nodded uneasily. The colored maid arrived almost on Bernice's heels, bearing a tray crowded with bottles and glasses. She set up a temporary bar on a small side table, then stood waiting.

"Y'gotta give the girl something," Bernice told him. Jamie fished in his pocket and handed the maid a dollar. He had no way of knowing if it was too much or too little. The girl took it and whisked away.

"How y'want your drink?" Bernice asked, acting as bartender.

Jamie shrugged distastefully. "Straight whiskey," he said.

Bernice handed him a small bar glass filled to the brim. He downed it with a grimace. She brought her glass untouched and sat beside him on the red plush sofa. "You a farmer?" she asked disinterestedly.

Jamie shook his head.

"I didn't think you talked like a farmer." She took a small sip of her drink.

"I buy and sell horses . . . mules," Jamie said.

Bernice looked at him, her pale eyes brightening. "You do? I was raised on a farm. We had an old mule . . . name was Luke. He just died a few weeks back."

Jamie was grateful for any sort of common ground. "Sure now I wish I'd seen your mule. Maybe I could have saved him."

"Think so?" the girl said dreamily. "I dunno . . . he was pretty old."

"I've got the way of a way with animals," Jamie assured her. "At home it was said I could take a horse cut in two and sew the pieces together, leaving the animal good as new, except for a slight stitching around the middle."

Bernice laughed. "Aw, you're spoofing me."

"As sure as there's truth in this world. Do I look like a man who would tell a lie like that?"

"It'd take more than stitching together to save Old Luke," the girl said. "He was worked to death. Just like my ma's being worked to death. Just like I'd a-been worked to death if I'd stayed there an' let him."

"Him? Is it your father you're speaking of?" Jamie asked, shocked and curious.

Bernice turned her pale eyes on him. "I like the way you talk. Kinda crazy. Are you a foreigner?"

"An Irishman is never a foreigner," Jamie told her. "He's at home anywhere . . . like a tinker's dog."

"Of course I'm talkin' about my pa," Bernice said, reverting to the original subject with disconcerting abruptness. "He used to drag me away from the mirror by my hair to chop cotton in the field. You think it's a sin for a girl to wanta look pretty?"

Jamie said that it wasn't, thinking of his sister, Kate, with her plain, good face and her toil-roughened hands.

Bernice swallowed her drink and her voice took on a bitter edge. "He used to be drunk, too; sometimes for days. Then he'd wallop us kids for makin' a sound. Got so we had to tiptoe round the house like mice. I won't never forget the look on ma's face when he was beatin' one of us and she was begging him to stop."

Jamie focused his eyes on the drop of amber fluid at the bottom of his glass. He was growing drowsy. Bernice droned on, reconstructing ugly fragments in the mirror of her early life.

"You know what? I'm glad I run away. I'm glad I'm a dollah fluzey. I'd rather be that than . . ." She paused while her mind fumbled for a comparison. "Anyway, I'm gonna make enough money to take my ma and the kids away from him."

Madame Blanche rustled in, her eyebrows arched like sickles. "Well, well; haven't you and big boy gone upstairs yet?" she asked Bernice.

"We been talkin' over old times," Bernice said shortly. She stood up, and Jamie also.

"Would you believe it," Jamie exclaimed in fake shocked tones, "I know her father."

The two women regarded him in dumfounded silence, and in the brief hiatus he marched to the door. "Sure it took the eyes right out of my head to find you here, Bernice, but your secret is safe with me." With a flourish, he drew his last twenty-dollar bill from his pocket, crossed back and pressed the money into the girl's limp hand.

"I knew her when the rose and the lily were fighting one another in her cheek," he said to Blanche sadly. "Finding her here has been one of the bruising moments of my life. Good-by, Bernice. God go between you and harm in all the empty places you must walk." He was out the door and down the block before either of the women found their tongues.

"You never told me you had a young man before you came here," Blanche said, hurt, "and such a good-looker, too."

The first merriment in years crept into Bernice's eyes and

face, and lifted the corners of her mouth. "A girl's gotta have some secrets," she said, and laughed.

Blanche heard her laughing all the way up the stairs. "Well it sure beats me," she muttered to herself, puzzled. "Handsome fella like that . . . he finds her, just like in a storybook; then away he goes again . . . and her laughin'. I don't rightly get it."

The spirit of the jest shortened Jamie's long walk to the camp. He hopped along the dark and empty road like a boy, occasionally laughing aloud at the memory of Madame Blanche and the perplexed look on her rouged face. "Oh, the poor pity of a woman. Another minute of my taletelling, and the tears would have been washing down the faces of the two of them."

Dawn was tracing the even line of hills to the eastward with a rosy crayon when he heard the sharp, rhythmic clop-clop of a horse trotting behind him. Jamie stepped to the side of the road and waited, hoping for a ride. In the graying half-light he saw a shiny, well-kept buggy, with a woman driving a familiar-looking horse. The horse was Big Red. The woman driving him was Maeve.

"Whoa," Jamie called as the vehicle came abreast. At the sound of the familiar voice, Big Red pulled up short and whinnied. "Madame," Jamie saluted his wife, "would you offer a poor, footworn traveler a bit of a lift in your fine new carriage, and accept his blessing in return?"

"I might," Maeve said unsmilingly. "Where has the poor, footworn traveler been?"

"To the Well at the End of the World, where I had a drink of the Water of Youth," Jamie said grandly, climbing into the buggy. "Sure this is the day of my luck: A ride in a fine, new carriage in the morning twilight along a road as red as a fairy path, and with a strange and beautiful princess."

Maeve leaned close to him and sniffed suspiciously at his clothes. "I feel the smell of a melodious, lying Irishman," she said coldly. "What have you been doing?"

"Now where did you pick up a fine expression like that?" Jamie asked, "melodious, lying Irishman."

"From Tavish, when he was telling stories to the children. But let's not change the subject," Maeve continued. "What have you been doing?"

"Slaying dragons, and that I'll make oath on."

"Male or female?" Maeve demanded.

"Female . . . but now how would you be knowing that?"

"By the smell of your clothes," Maeve said grimly. "There's dragon blood on them."

She whipped up Big Red and there was no more joking. Jamie sensed that he was in trouble and kept mouse quiet. When they arrived at the silent, sleeping camp, Maeve went directly to their tent, leaving Jamie to unhitch the horse. When he had finished and stepped inside the tent, he almost tripped over a washtub full of water.

"Now what might that be for?" he demanded.

"That, Mister Dragon Killer, is for you to wash off a certain smell before you sleep in this tent," Maeve snapped. "Hurry up . . . off with those clothes. Into the fire they go."

" 'Tis my best suit," Jamie wailed.

"Nothing less than fire will take out that stench," Maeve retorted. "Hurry up . . . give them me."

Reluctantly Jamie stripped to his underwear. "That, too," Maeve insisted firmly.

"No," Jamie cried. "Where's your modesty, woman? Were I laid out stiff and cold at my own wake, and they came to take my underwear, sure I'd raise myself up in protest."

"All right . . . you've protested; now take it off." While

Jamie moaned his objections, Maeve pealed the long union suit from him. "Now . . . into the tub."

"Ouch . . . it's cold, it is," Jamie complained, testing the water with his foot.

"Yes it's cold and it's not from the Well at the End of the World, but it will wash the stench of fluzeys from you." As Maeve talked her anger mounted, as much at herself as at her husband.

"Do you know how I happened along the road? Looking for you I'd been . . . all night, in Atlanta," she flailed at him, "expecting to find you sprawled in some gutter."

"Now that's a fine thing to say to your own sweet husband," Jamie protested.

"Well I'd rather have found you in a nice, clean gutter than where you were . . . doing what you were doing." Maeve's anger trembled on the verge of tears.

Jamie was conscience stricken. "Maeve, darling, hear me now . . ." he started to climb out of the tub but Maeve pushed him back.

"Don't you get out until every inch of you has been scrubbed raw," she ordered.

"I won't . . . I won't," Jamie assured her, "but please hear me out."

"I'll never listen to you again. I sat for hours at the police station, telling them you were sure to be fighting and would be brought in. I thought you would need me. When you fought Travis Bunn, I promised to always be there . . . to hold your head in my lap; to bind your hurts. Now you've made me ashamed. I hate myself for worrying about you." Maeve suddenly felt very tired. She went to the other side of the tent, undressed quickly and climbed into bed.

Quietly Jamie stepped from the tub and dried himself. He was aware now of how deeply he had hurt his wife. After blowing out the lamp, he crept silently between the covers and stretched himself at the farthest edge of the bed, while Maeve lay at the opposite, abject and miserable.

The gray of morning had invaded the tent, touching familiar objects with light and recognition. Outside, the chorus of birds chirped, whirred, and trilled. "Maeve," Jamie said softly after what seemed like a long time, "give me leave to speak—to tell you what truly happened?"

From her side of the bed, Maeve gave no sign she heard. "You've every right to be angry," Jamie continued. "I did go to one of those places. But nothing happened . . . I take oath upon that. Stand me over the Stone of Truth upon which St. Patrick knelt to pray and on which no man can utter a lie, and you'll get the same answer. I wanted to hurt someone—anyone; but mostly myself. Now I know it was the love of my heart I was wounding." He paused again but there was still no indication Maeve heard or was listening.

"You're there . . . beside me . . . within reach of my hand, and yet so far from me, were I the man with the third foot who had but to touch it to the ground and seven miles passed as one step, still I could not cross to you."

From Maeve's small, shadowy figure came a strangled sound. "Please don't," Jamie whispered, "please don't cry."

"I'm not crying . . . I'm laughing," Maeve said, her voice choking. She turned to Jamie and took him in her arms. "Och, what a child I have married. Jamie, my love, when will you learn to think first and act afterward?"

She was laughing and crying as Jamie smothered her lips with kisses. "My heart's darling," he said, "my treasure. I thought you had gone away, leaving the inside of me sacked and ruined; burned out like a captured castle of the olden time."

About them the camp stirred and buzzed with life, but Maeve and Jamie who had been lost and apart for a time, slept soundly, locked in each other's arms.

XVI

THE quarrel between Jamie and Big Tom had thrown a chill upon the camp. Me-Dennis O'Ryan and his clan were embittered and threatened to take their numerous members away and form a group of their own.

"Your Jamie has outgrown his boots. He's too much of a muchness," Me-Dennis told Maeve, when she sought to smooth the matter out. "Laying into Big Tom for small reason, and him with the drink taken."

Me-Dennis was speaking for Big Tom, who was not yet in a condition to talk for himself, with his scalp laid open by its contact with the sharp edge of the shackle. However, the gift of the chestnut colt soothed the leader of the O'Ryan clan somewhat, and he hurried off to examine the animal, muttering but mollified.

Maeve diplomatically kept Jamie out of sight until the matter was settled. When she brought the word that Me-Dennis was ready to forgive and forget, Jamie bussed her joyfully.

" 'Tis proof of what I already knew—I have a wife who

can walk in a river without wetting her shoes. What about
that great lump of a fellow, Tom? Will he kiss and make
up?"

"When the sense returns to his head that you knocked
out of it, he will," Maeve said, adding slyly, "but I'd speak
a little admiration of Doreen's baby if I were you. There's
an old saying: If you want a man's friendship, praise his
child or his horse."

"I'll do it now . . . and to his face," declared Jamie,
and departed to make amends with Big Tom.

By evening more Travelers' caravans had rolled into the
camp in the pines and pitched their spacious green tents.
Instead of music and dancing that night, Owen Roe Tavish
was called upon for a story. "A story it shall be, then," he
said, "and Heaven to everyone who shall remember this."

The men broke off their conversations, packed tight their
pipes, and shuffled closer, eager and attentive. Mothers
quieted their children and grouped with the women in a
body to listen. There was no intermingling of sexes. Men
and boys, married or not, sat or stood together, while the
women and children stayed apart.

Tavish was a self-trained, self-taught bard, but with a
power to put his own skin on the tales he told. As a master
storyteller, he warmed and breathed new life into the
ancient sagas of heroism and heartbreak, which had passed
from mouth to ear for untold generations.

In the time he had been with Shiel Harrigan's group, the
old man had won a warm and respected place. For the
grown people he had become the shanachie, or historian and
storyteller. With the children, he had taken Aunt Bid's
place, teaching them the legends and charms, the hundreds
of small prayers and blessings that wrapped their daily lives
in a mist of piety.

With the older men, he labored to bring their thick, strong fingers under control, so they might sign their names to deeds of sale, and not be shamed by making a clumsy cross at the bottom of a document.

"There's only one cross you should know about," he would scold them, "and that's the Cross of the Mountain, not one you scratch on a piece of paper."

Deliberately this night he chose the epic story of Ferdiad and Cuchulainn, the friends and foster brothers, who had battled each other to the death in the great Cattle Raid of of the Cooley, some two thousand years before. The formal telling of a story was a thing of magic to these semi-illiterate wanderers. Their literature had been lost in the loot and pillage of their country; its language shriveled by neglect and persecution from a rich and expressive seven or eight thousand words to a paltry seven or eight hundred. There remained for them only the spoken word, and Tavish was a master of that.

"It has been said," he began in a voice so soft his listeners had to strain to catch his words, "that a thousand years is as but a single day in God's time, and a single day as a thousand years. A small while since, then, by God's reckoning, there lived in the west of Ireland, a great and proud queen named Maeve, daughter of the High King of Tara. Such was the force of her beauty, 'twas also said, that men would close one eye when looking at her, as if peering at the sun, so bright-shining was her loveliness. Some historians make claim that this was how the 'wink' was invented. . . ." Tavish paused for the light laugh that swept his listeners like a sigh of eagerness.

"Sure I don't hold with that interpretation," he continued. "If the 'wink' needed inventing, then Maeve would have invented it herself. One day in the coolish part of the evening, she and her husband, a loud but lesser man than

herself, were engaged in light pillow-talk. It was the custom
in those uncivilized days among the melodious, lying Irish,
to boast a little. So said the king: 'Sure now 'tis plain my
cows and kine, my pigs and swine, my horses, sheep, cups of
gold and plate, my chariots, shields, spears, javelins, jewels,
rich-dyed feathers and furs, gold and silver, outnumber and
outweigh the likes of yours, dear wife.'

"Queen Maeve upon hearing this boast of the king, her
husband, laughed a queen-lady-like laugh that shook the
heavy timbers of her fortress in the West, and rattled the
shields hung upon the great walls there. With queenly
modesty she disputed the words of her king-husband, pointing out that so great was her dowry in gold and silver
brought from Tara that the wheels of the chariots bearing
the treasure sank to their hubs in solid stone, so heavy was
the burden of their riches; and her droves of cattle, horses,
and sheep threw up new mountain ranges with their
trampling hoofs, so multitudinous and violent was their
passing.

"Thus one argument led to another, until to settle the
mild dispute, king-husband and queen-wife ordered servants
to fetch and assemble all their possessions, that they might
be weighed and counted to determine which and whose out-
ranked the other's. Not one fishhook, feather, or jeweled
comb was to be overlooked.

"Now when all this had been done as ordered, Queen
Maeve found that the king was owner of one black bull
more than she. In all else their possessions were identical.
'How irritating,' said she, and over her queenly beauty a
shadow fell, as when some deep cloud obscures the sun,
casting shade and somber gloom across the surface of the
land.

"To the north and eastward where the great Connor—he
had been Maeve's first husband—was king in Ulster, there

was a famous dun bull, known throughout the length and breadth of Ireland. Straight at once Queen Maeve dispatched emissaries to the owner of the dun bull, asking the loan of the creature, and promising rewards and favors both rich and personal.

" 'Sure now 'twill be my deepest pleasure to gratify the queen,' said the owner of the dun bull like the gentleman he was. As one of Ulster's warrior chiefs, he received the queen's messengers with honor, filling them with food and drink and kind words. But while the emissaries were drinking and feasting they fell to quarreling. Said one, it were well their host had agreed to lend the dun bull, else would the great queen have been constrained to take it by force of arms.

"Sure now," Tavish commented philosophically, "this began the brannigan. When the Ulster chieftain heard of the drunken boast, he not only withdrew the loan of the dun bull, but told the queen of the west that she was lucky to get her messengers back with their skins. Och, but the queen was furious. East and west and north and south she sent, rallying the warrior chieftains of the land beneath her banner. Assembled, the heroes covered the plains outside Maeve's fortress as Manannan mac Lir's horses covered the sea with their foamy manes. Fierce and war-proud were these mighty champions; and none fiercer, none more proud, none fairer of face and form, than Ferdiad, son of Daman, son of Dare."

Tavish paused, as if lowering the curtain on the prologue of the mighty drama he was relating. The cooking fires had sunk to a soft glow of coals. From the ring of darkness edging the camp came the thin medley of small night sounds; the comforting little noises that underscored the deeper silences. Fireflies spotted the lower night with yellow, temporary stars that glowed silently for an instant, then vanished to flash their mellow radiance deeper in the shadows of the towering pines.

Step by step he led his listeners through the ancient tale—from humor to heroism and then to final heartbreak. Like an ancient tapestry maker, he drew the threads of drama in and out, until a vivid portrait of the times stood rich and true. He told how the wily Maeve launched one of Ireland's most famous and bloody wars. Then he described the magnificence of Connor's court and its hero.

"Strange and beautiful was the young champion, Cuchulainn. Seven toes to each foot, he had, and on either hand as many fingers. His eyes were bright with seven pupils apiece, and each one glittered with seven gemlike sparkles. On each cheek he had four moles—a blue, a crimson, a green, and a yellow one. From the top of his head, between one ear and the other, grew fifty tresses, long and yellow as the wax of bees, or like a brooch of white gold when it glittered in the afternoon sun. Of all the champions of Ulster, he alone was prepared to meet the onrush of Queen Maeve's men of Connacht. The others were taken with a sudden affliction, a strange weakness of the stones, which impaired their manliness. But that is another story."

Again Tavish paused and again his audience waited. Then in rich and measured tones, he related the last act of the drama: How Queen Maeve, through wine and lures and blandishments, had won from Ferdiad, Cuchulainn's friend and foster brother, a promise to meet the Ulsterman in mortal combat. There was the glint of tears in the eyes of his listeners, as the Speaker described how the two friends met and exchanged challenges with heavy hearts. He told of how they battled for three days, resting at night and returning to the fray in the mornings, until the water was driven from the ford of the river in which they fought, and the Bocanachs and Bananachs and wild people of the glens screamed from the rims of their shields and from the hilts of their swords and from the hafts of their spears; and of how, at the end of the third day, Cuchulainn struck the blow that slew his friend and foster brother.

" 'That is enough now, indeed,' said Ferdiad. 'I fall of that. Now, indeed, may I say that I am sickly after thee, and not by thy hand should I have fallen.'

"Cuchulainn ran toward him and clasped his two arms about him, and lifted him and his armor and his clothes across the ford northward, in order that the slain should be by the ford on the north and not by the west, with the men of Erin.

"He laid Ferdiad down there, and a trance and faintness fell upon him, from which he would not rouse. 'Good, O Cuchulainn,' said his charioteer, 'rise up now for the men of Erin are coming upon us, and it is not single combat they will give thee since Ferdiad, son of Daman, son of Dare, has fallen by thee.'

" 'Friend,' Cuchulainn replied, 'what availeth me to rise after him that has fallen by me is dead?'

"He wept, and there were those who said the tears were pure heart's blood. And that was the battle of the ford, between Ferdiad and Cuchulainn, friends and foster brothers, in the great Cattle Raid of the Cooley, two thousand years ago, which is but a day and a night in God's own time."

Tavish's voice was low and edged with emotion when he finished. The sadness was without relation to time or space, but universal. It had touched both speaker and listeners. Tears glistened in the eyes of the women as they turned silently toward their tents. The children, sensing a depth of feeling they could not understand, clung silently to their mothers.

The group of men dissolved with no exchange of words. The spell that had held them transported was too fine to be broken suddenly. Owen Roe Tavish had warmed into life a tragedy dead two thousand years, and for a little while, on the stage created by his words, men had loved, suffered, and died. The Hero's Light that shone from the foreheads of the ancient great had penetrated the dark in between, and its magic glow had fallen upon the listeners. Each went his own thoughtful, pensive way, possessor of some rich fragment of his jeweled and heroic past, to store the wonder of it in some inner temple sacred to himself alone.

PART THREE

A child to come with the springtime; it will have luck. . . .

XVII

DURING the summer months the caravans of the Travelers expanded northward, threading their way into remote rural communities with odd, provocative names familiar only to politicians and post office maps. Paprika, Doodlebug, Polkadot were as well known to them as Athens and Augusta. As nearly as possible their arrival was timed to coincide with the marketing of local crops, so farm wives would have money to spend on handmade lace and linoleum; or farmers ready to exchange old mules for new. When money was short, the Travelers took in exchange hams, bacon, eggs, butter, home-canned vegetables and fruit; or grain and fodder for the stock.

Older women from the caravans scouted the countryside near the camps, driving patiently from farmhouse to farmhouse, displaying their wares with cool, contained dignity. Meanwhile they kept a sharp lookout for animals in the barnyards, reporting back to their menfolk of mules and horses that might be likely prospects for purchase or trade.

In the spring of 1898, when the April rituals were over,

Jamie persuaded Shiel Harrigan's caravan to delay their departure from Atlanta.

"There's been a great booming in the market for mules and horses," he argued. "We should be camped close to an auction center, not moving about."

The older men listened and yielded somewhat resentfully. Since Jamie had been with the group, his influence had mounted steadily, especially with the younger men. They studied his methods and marveled at the swift ease with which he converted horseflesh into cash. As time passed, they tended to accept his leadership over that of Shiel Harrigan and the older horse traders.

One morning Jamie drove his new team of matched sorrel geldings into the camp just before the midday meal. Beside him in the buggy was a stranger.

"Meet Oran Talbot," he said to the men, introducing Talbot about. "He used to be a barber—now he's buying mules for the government."

Talbot was a lean, sly man, with pale, foxy eyes that were never still. He laughed easily and too often. "Yep . . . I been a barber fer ten years; but where can a man git on two-bit haircuts and fifteen-cent shaves! Now I'm a mule buyer fer Uncle Sam I don't know the south end of a northbound mule from the other, but I'm a mule buyer. Says so in my contract!" He laughed and slapped his lean thigh.

"Just why does the government want to buy mules?" Shiel Harrigan asked.

Talbot looked at the circle of faces around him craftily. "You mean you ain't heard about Spain and the war?"

"We're on the move so much there be little time to read the newspapers," Jamie explained.

"That so?" Talbot said, weighing the information. "Well . . . seems there's a little shooting war on with Spain . . . in a place called Cuba. Government needs mules and horses in a hurry . . . to haul guns and wagons. . . ."

"That's why the prices have been jumping higher and higher," said Shiel Harrigan, and the other horse traders nodded in agreement.

"They'll be jumping higher still, according to Mister Talbot, here," said Jamie.

"They'll go over the moon," said Talbot, "dependin' on how long the war lasts . . . which brings me to you fellers. I been told you can stuff a dead mule's skin with sawdust and pass it off as the first-class offspring of a Spanish jack!"

"Just what did you have in mind?" Shiel Harrigan inquired.

" 'Tis this," Jamie cut in. "Mister Talbot, here, has a cousin in Atlanta who is a livestock broker. He is buying up all the culls and rejected stock at the auctions; animals the buyers have turned down. He'd like to turn those animals over to us for feeding and sweetening. When they're ready, we offer them again . . . to Oran Talbot, here, who buys them for the government."

"Sounds profitable," was Shiel Harrigan's comment, "but is it honest?"

"Honest?" exclaimed Talbot. "Why, it's more'n honest! It's patriotic! There'll be money hanging on trees fer all of us."

Harrigan and the older men protested that to enter into a deal with Talbot would require their leaving the road. "We have regular customers . . . people we do business with year after year. Are we to give them up for this 'get rich quick' scheme?" they argued.

But the younger men under the leadership of Jamie were eager for the plan. The lure of quick and easy money beckoned them like green and distant pastures. Shiel Harrigan's caravan split on the issue. There was no bitterness or recrimination. The Donners, the Devlins, and the Hennesseys struck their tents and moved on.

"It's not that we're against the money," Tade Hennessey

told Jamie as they were leaving, "it's that we'd be lost without movement. Our people have had it in their blood for two thousand years. Maybe the young ones will change . . . but I hope not. When a man has more than he can put wheels under, 'tis too much for the good of his own soul, I'm thinking."

Shiel Harrigan stayed with Jamie's group. He did not approve of the plan, but Maeve was his nearest of kin and he could not bring himself to part with her. By common consent the new group's leadership passed to Jamie, and Shiel Harrigan's wise counsel was seldom heard in meetings, and then only when he was pressed for it by the others.

Occasionally he spoke of his fears to Maeve. " 'Tis not only this sudden hunger for riches," he said, "but the methods he is using will destroy the reputation for fair dealing we have been building these past fifty years."

The developments of the past months had disturbed Maeve, too, but she defended her husband. "The making of money is like a new game to Jamie," she protested, hopefully. "By and by he'll have had enough of it."

"The making of money is like the taste for drink," her father warned. "The more you have the more you want. You're a sensible girl, Maeve. Call halt to him before it is too late. For years we've had the freedom of the road. No one asked where we'd been or where we were going. But there'll be an end to that freedom if the outsiders turn against us."

"Why should they?" Maeve asked, troubled.

"Take my word for it, they will if we draw down too much attention on ourselves. Already they're talking about Jamie in Atlanta. There was even a piece about him in one of the newspapers—calling him the 'Mule Millionaire.' "

"I'll do what I can," Maeve promised, "but with Jamie, when the sun is shining, there's little to gain in talking of showers to come."

She spoke to Jamie that night when they were alone, broaching the subject of returning to the road. "We've been here almost a year. Don't you miss the rolling wheels and the wonder of what's ahead over the next hill?" she pleaded.

Jamie scoffed good-naturedly. "Sure the round dollars we're piling up will roll better than any wagon wheels made . . . and a lot more comfortably."

"But why?" Maeve persisted. "And who are we filling the banks with money for?"

The question was no sooner out than she wished she hadn't asked it. One subject she and Jamie had come to avoid by unspoken, mutual consent was the mention of children. In their nearly four years of married life, Maeve had come to know and understand her husband's every mood. She could read the thoughts in his eyes long before the words found expression on his lips.

For a fleeting instant Jamie's guard was down. He gazed at Maeve with such an expression of baffled misery that she felt her heart contract as if caught in the grasp of a giant fist. I've hurt him, she thought. He's never given up hoping for the child we never had. I've failed him in the chiefest way a woman can fail her husband. . . ."

"Sure now and there's always need for money," Jamie stammered. "We send it home in every letter . . . and they be always crying for more. Kate now has two mouths to feed besides her own and Waddie O'Dowd's. . . ."

He halted and his jaw knotted as it always did when he was trapped by a lack of logic. Maeve wanted to let the matter drop, but Jamie was disturbed and sought to hide his frustration behind the mask of anger.

"You've small liking for anything I do these days," he complained, edging his words with bitterness, "and sure 'tis for you I be doing it all!"

"Is it?" Maeve said. She tried to keep the acid from her

voice, but her words had a way of finding the chinks in Jamie's armor of self-satisfaction.

"Aye—it is that," he declared stubbornly, and began to point out all the new furnishings and luxuries that had been added to the tent. "Is there anything else you want? Anything your heart desires? If there be, sure you've but to name it and I'll get it for you."

Maeve could feel the quarrel gathering about them as electricity collects in a mounting storm, but she felt helpless to check it. "I've more than enough of everything," she said placatingly.

Jamie pounced upon her choice of words. "More than enough, is it?" he protested angrily. "And what kind of answer is that? How can a body have more than enough and yet still be wanting something else?"

"What I'm asking for isn't anything your money can buy," Maeve flashed at him, her anger rising, too. "Of course there's more money in the camp than ever before—but is there more happiness? Is there even as much? Where are the songs and the laughter we used to know on the road? You came with your Oran Talbot and your promises of bulging pockets and tents full of money, and you take from us a way of life we'd been leading for two thousand years! And what do you give us in return? Money! Too much of it! A golden mountain, with our people snarling and snapping like hyenas around the foot of it. Is that something to be proud of? I was more impressed with the boy I fell in love with—who had only the clothes on his back, but could put his ear to the ground and hear the grass growing, and who listened to the music rising from the fairy mounds. I'm not at all impressed with King Jamie, the 'Mule Millionaire.' "

The violence of her outburst left Maeve spent and a little sick. With trembling hands she began to undress. Jamie was hurt and angry, but a little frightened, too.

"Sure this tent will never be lacking a mule whip," he grumbled, "for 'tis yourself that has a tongue can snap the ears off any lead team. And there be no point in mentioning Oran Talbot. Sure I'm through with him, and have been for weeks."

He put out the light and undressed in the dark, muttering the while. It was the first of a series of short, sharp quarrels that raised and fed a barrier of glacial ice which threatened to spread and envelop Maeve and Jamie's entire marriage.

In the weeks that followed, Maeve sensed the ever-increasing chill that was nipping like deadly, destructive frost at her and Jamie's happiness. But she felt powerless to check it. Upon her heart she bore a feeling of deep guilt. It was her childlessness that had laid the foundation for this wall abuilding between herself and her husband. Each passing day—each flurry of cutting words—added fresh bricks and mortar to its insurmountability.

In his heart he no longer believes I'm the one Queen Una promised him: The girl of his choice who was to give him a wonderful son. With the repetition of this thought, Maeve came finally to believe it herself.

The heat of southern September lay oppressive on the camp in the pines. The younger children pleaded with Owen Roe Tavish to take them swimming. A wide, shallow lake was no more than an hour's walk, by following the edge of the stream that skirted the camp. Such a clamor was raised by the children when Tavish consented that the mothers hastened to agree. Most of the men were away on trading trips. They would be back by nightfall, but it would be a relief to have a few hours away from the noisy children.

"All right now," Tavish cried, assembling his charges, "let's count noses so there'll be no losing of any of you."

He lined them up, boys and girls together, and counted thirteen. Number thirteen turned out to be little Tommy Sherwood, eager to accompany the older children on all adventures. He was a bright child, large for his three plus years, with his father's flat, merry face and twinkling blue eyes.

"Tommy," Tavish told him, "you're too young to go on such a long trip. Stay and look after your mother and the baby sister." The little boy wailed in protest, and Doreen came from the Sherwood tent to call him. She was pregnant with her third child.

"Tommy, you're not to go with the big children," she ordered.

"I'll take you another time in the wagon," Tavish promised.

The child watched aggrieved as the others set off on their hike to the lake. When Tavish looked back, he was still standing where they had left him, head down, sullenly scraping the carpet of pine needles with his bare big toe.

"Little malrach," he said sympathetically, "they're that mad to grow up." He made a resolution to tell Tommy a special story that night—something to take the sting from being left behind.

Following the winding course of the stream to the lake, children and dogs ranged happily up and down the rocky banks. "Mind the snakes and lizards," the old man warned. "They've had no St. Patrick over here to banish the reptiles with a Christian word."

One of the more adventurous boys discovered an abandoned stone quarry near the top of a hill. It was almost full of water from the heavy summer rains, and glowed temptingly like a great, square-cut emerald in a jagged setting of rocks and trees. The children stood along the edges examining their vivid reflections in its shadowy, green-blue depths, and begged to swim in it. Tavish shook his head.

" 'Tis dangerous," he warned mysteriously. "There be some who say that a long time ago there was no pool here at all, but at the bottom a magic well. . . ."

The word magic caught every child's thoughts in the vise of attention. "No. . . . Really. . . . Tell us," they cried in unison. The square of emerald water assumed a new and wonderful significance to twelve pairs of eyes.

"A long time ago," Tavish began. . . .

"When cows were kine and pigs were swine . . . and eagles of the air built their nests in the beards of giants," the children interrupted gleefully.

"Now who is telling this tale?" the Speaker demanded with mock severity.

The children subsided with smothered laughter, and Tavish continued. "At the bottom of this pool was a magic well. One night, a rough, unlettered spalpeen came and uncovered the well to draw a bucket of water. But being an uncouth, careless sort of fellow, he went away without covering it again. Och, that were a foolish and dangerous thing to do, especially with a magic well. During the night the well began to overflow. It overflowed into the stream down there, and poured into the lake; sure it would have overflowed the whole red world if someone hadn't stopped it."

He paused, pointedly. "Who?" the children breathed in unison.

"The fairy people who live under the hills. Sure the water was pouring into their caves and washing them out of their beds."

"How did the fairies stop the water?" one of the girls asked timidly.

" 'Twere easy to answer that," Tavish said solemnly.

"They took away the bottom of the pool. Like ants, they swarmed in and carried off every sand and pebble of it. Now the water runs out at the other end as fast as it runs in from the magic well."

The children pondered this bit of dubious physics as Tavish led the way on toward the lake. He halted them once, thinking he heard a child calling, but when noses were counted, his charges were all present.

The afternoon at the lake was filled with boisterous play, and the children returned the way they had come, wet, tired, and happy. Most of the men were back from trading when they and Tavish trudged wearily into the camp. The women were bustling about, lighting the supper fires.

Big Tom Sherwood came hurrying to meet the cavalcade, his amiable face twisted between hope and anxiety. "Is little Tommy with you?" he asked eagerly. "Doreen said he's been gone most of the afternoon."

As he spoke his wife joined them. "He may have followed you, Tavish," she said desperately. "He wanted to go so badly."

"We came back the same way we went, now," Tavish assured her. "There was not a sign of him." As he spoke, the old man remembered the cry he had heard earlier, near the stone quarry.

"I did think once I heard a child calling as we were on our way, but I stopped to listen and there was nothing more." Tavish was deeply perturbed.

"He's lost," Doreen cried, covering her face with her hands and beginning to moan. Big Tom sought to reassure her.

"He can't have wandered far. We'll take the dogs and find him in no time."

The men were organizing the search as Jamie drove into camp. "What is it, Cousin Tavish?" he called as he stepped from the buggy.

Tavish explained that little Tommy Sherwood had wandered from the camp and Jamie immediately took a lantern to join the search. "Sure the boy is part squirrel; you couldn't lose the likes of him in these hills," he assured the weeping Doreen.

Tavish was tired from his earlier hike, but he guided the men toward the spot where he had heard a child calling. Spreading themselves into a wide, thin line, the men urged the prowling dogs to range even wider through the thick undergrowth. Darkness came swiftly beneath the trees, and they lit lanterns to continue the search, calling repeatedly "hallooooo, Tommy," which echoed back weirdly through the dusk-shrouded hills.

Shiel Harrigan and Jamie were the first to reach the deserted stone quarry. A child's straw hat was floating soggily, half submerged in the still, dark water. Maeve's father fished it out as the others converged upon the pool.

"Is this the lad's hat?" he asked, handing it to Big Tom Sherwood.

The boy's father took the wet, misshapen object and examined it with trembling hands. "It might be," he said hesitantly. "Where'd you find it?"

He knew the answer without following Shiel Harrigan's gesture toward the pool. Silence like a dull ache settled over the men. They stood along the edge of the quarry as the children had stood earlier in the afternoon. The glare from their lanterns lit deep, reflected fires in the depths of the water, changing now from blue-green to blue-black.

Jamie broke the silence. "Does anyone know how deep it is?"

"I saw it last year when the water was not so high," Me-Dennis spoke up. "There are two levels. The outer one is down about fifteen feet. The other is fifty or more."

The men looked at Big Tom. "I'm no swimmer," he said apologetically.

"Let me have a try." Quickly Jamie pulled off his suit, stripping down to his long, summer-weight underwear. Then he lowered himself into the pool. "I'll work this side nearest the camp first."

He took a deep breath and dove, swimming downward frog-fashion, with quick, vigorous strokes. The water near the surface was warm, but turned chillingly cold a few feet down. His lungs were aching by the time he touched the even stone shelf of the outer level. There was no time to make any search. He shot himself surfaceward with a powerful thrust of his legs; then rested against the smooth side of the pool, gasping for breath.

"Me-Dennis is right," he called to the men. "There's a shelf about fifteen feet down. I'll have a look around next time."

Sucking his lungs full of air, Jamie dived again. He swam with his eyes open but could see nothing. It was like swimming imprisoned in the depths of a great, dark emerald, as a beetle is imprisoned in amber. Tavish had once told him stories of the sunken continent of Moo, lost in the deep Atlantic off the coast of Ireland. There in the emerald underwater-land, all children who died prematurely came to live out their lives before going on to Heaven.

Jamie swam slowly along the side of the quarry, extending his arms in a wide breast stroke. He was out of breath and was turning toward the surface again when his fingers touched something. It was a child's hand that slid away before Jamie could grasp it.

Back at the surface, he rested, filling his lungs with deep gulps of air before he spoke. "Me-Dennis," he beckoned the child's grandfather. "I've found the little one," he whispered. "Better the news be broken to Tom before I bring him up."

As Jamie was diving, he heard Big Tom's broken voice saying: "O Mother of God . . . Mary . . . my little son . . . my little son. . . ."

The small crucifix glowed dully on the center pole of the tent. The flame of the altar candle beneath it wavered slightly, forming slender, upright shadows that danced without music on the dark walls of the tent. Jamie lay with half-closed eyes, watching them. He had returned from the ordeal at the quarry, saddened and exhausted. Maeve had put him to bed, then left immediately to be with Doreen. It was past midnight and she hadn't returned.

The slight golden flame of the altar candle nodded toward the entrance as the tent flap was drawn aside and Maeve entered. In the dim half-light her small face seemed haggard and drawn with fatigue. "How is she?" Jamie asked, sitting up.

"It's poor Tom I feel sorriest for," Maeve answered indirectly. "Every time Doreen sobs, it's like hitting him with with a whip."

"Who's with her now?"

"Father Kerrigan came out from town. She quieted down until the undertaker arrived to take the boy; then she got hysterical again. When she started blaming Cousin Tavish for what happened, I left."

"Och—crazed with grief, she is," Jamie exclaimed. "How could she be blaming Owen Roe Tavish? Sure he carried the wee drowned one in his arms all the way back to the camp. Big Tom was that weak he had to be helped himself."

"Doreen said he heard the baby crying and gave no heed. Had he turned back, little Tommy would still be alive."

"And where was she while her child was wandering in the woods?" Jamie demanded, indignant that Doreen should involve Tavish in any way.

"Sure, that's the poor thing's trouble. She feels guilty and is trying to shift some of the blame to someone else."

"Let her not shift it to Tavish, whose heart broke as much

as Tom's when I brought the boy up out of the water . . ."
Jamie declared.

Maeve undressed listlessly, blew out the crucifix candle,
and crept wearily into bed. She was exhausted but felt no
desire to sleep. To her childless self, the drowning of little
Tommy was a sort of double death. She relived Doreen's
grief with an anguish of her own. Had she been the mother
of a little boy, the same adventurous spirit might have been
his undoing. Some square-cut emerald pool might have
mirrored his child's face and smilingly beckoned him in.
The thought of a child never to be born, gasping out breath
it would never breathe, convulsed her slender body with
sobs. Tears she had stored unshed for years now rained from
her eyes in unchecked relief. Her weeping roused Jamie,
who had fallen asleep, and he strove awkwardly to comfort
her.

"My arms are around you this now, Maeve darling," he
whispered. "Tell me what's wearing your heart away. Is it
the death of the boy? Tavish told us coming back from the
pool, 'When a little child dies, sure a part of every other
child in the world dies with him.' Is it for the babe you never
had, or for the one that's lost you're grieving?"

Maeve made no attempt to answer, but her sobbing subsided. It had been some time since they had lain side by
side, drawing common strength from their closeness to each
other. Pillow-talk had ended when the quarrels began and
they stopped being lovers. With it had ended the tender
word probings that explored and examined the sealed com-
partments of their minds and hearts. For more than a year
they had remained physical strangers, sharing a tent but not
themselves or their thoughts occupying the same bed but
living in different worlds.

Now the tragic death of another's child seemed to heal
the breach. In the warm, medicinal darkness capsuled within

the green walls of the tent, words that had lately been impossible to speak—subjects neither dared broach—found easy expression and easier understanding. Time could have retraced itself to the first year of their marriage.

"I've failed you," Maeve whispered, pressing her tear-moist cheek against Jamie's shoulder. "You wanted a son so very much—every day has been like a reproach. I promised God to give the first born to the Church, if He would but hear my prayer. Then, you'll never know how I prayed to have one. When prayers and candles didn't help I asked Tavish to arrange a May Baby dance once when you were away."

Jamie caressed her cheek tenderly. "My Maeve . . . my heart's own love . . . my small, wee pagan wife. If Father Kerrigan ever learned you'd been trafficking with the Druids, sure he'd jump straight up through the hoop of his collar without stopping to unfasten it."

"I don't care. It doesn't seem right. Doreen's having a new baby nearly every year."

"Aye, but look what happened to her eldest," Jamie reminded gently. "Maybe 'tis God's way of punishing us for having so much and still asking for more."

Maeve was silent. Then she whispered with a catch in her voice: "To have a child and lose it would be more than heart could bear. I wouldn't want to live."

"There's the great hulk of your husband that's still part baby. Sure you'll always have him to take care of," Jamie teased tenderly.

Maeve laughed fondly, her face against his arm. "Aye, there's woman's problem in a nutshell: How to help them grow up and still keep them children."

"When we were first married and the sight of your sweet portrait of a face set my heart dancing with a kind of music only the fairies know, sure I was the richest man in all the round red world. I owned the mists of the mountains. Proud I was, and went about flashing my antlers in the air, so certain that a wonderful son like the one promised me would be mine. A daughter I'd have none of; it was a son or nothing. I never dreamed that the last of my three wishes, the one that seemed simplest and easiest of fulfillment. . . ." Jamie paused and Maeve caressed his arm sympathetically.

"Do you still mind so terribly?"

"About the wonderful gossoon who was to speak in the poetry of the ancient tongue? No. For a while, though, when that pink little tongue of yours grew more and more like a mustard plaster. . . ."

"It never," Maeve protested.

Jamie continued teasingly, ignoring the interruption: "Then I was that certain you were not the girl promised me. Now since I know you, and have lived and traveled and seen the world . . . I know better."

"You mean you know I am the girl promised you by the Fairy Queen?"

"I mean I know there's no Fairy Queen," Jamie announced calmly. Maeve was shocked.

"But what of the first two wishes? They came true!" she said dismayed.

"They'd have come about without any help from Una," Jamie assured her.

"I wonder," Maeve said seriously.

The more she considered Jamie's calm dismissal of the fairy folk, the more perturbed she became. Such sentiments from Jamie seemed vaguely sacrilegious. His half-serious belief that a power above nature was personally shaping his destiny had been such an integral part of him. Without it he would not be Jamie McRuin. Maeve had never taken his fantasies deeply to heart, but there was an intangible comfort in knowing that Jamie believed in them.

"Tell me one thing," she challenged him. "Had you not believed the girl of your choice was yours by Queen Una's promise—would you have stood up to Travis Bunn and let his fists pound hatred of him and love for you into my heart, with every blow he struck?"

Jamie considered the question for a long moment; then he laughed. "Sure I never thought of it that way. You're right as always, my heart's darling. Had I not believed you were meant to be mine by compacts made beyond the rim of the world, sure then there'd have been but one thought in my mind: Like a Kerry dog, to fight until I'd killed the man, or he had killed me."

"Come here," he cried exultantly, "we'll give Una and the fairies another chance."

Eagerly and happily he drew Maeve closer; and eagerly and happily she came to him.

XVIII

OWEN ROE TAVISH regarded Maeve and Jamie's reconciliation with deep inner satisfaction. The bitterness between them had infected the entire camp, already torn by petty quarrels and bickering.

"You're a wonder, now," he praised Maeve. "However did you work such a change in the stubborn malrach? Already he's on the way to being the darling he was when I brought him to America!" Tavish had quite forgotten it had been the other way round.

Maeve smiled happily. "He's promised we'll go back to the road—in two or three months—as soon as business matters can be arranged." She spoke with unconcealed delight.

"There's no need to tell the why of the coolness between you," the old man assured her confidentially. "I saw it begin and I watched the secret sorrow of it wear you, one against the other, like the grinding stones of a mill. If ever two people needed a little one to soften the friction that marriage brings, 'tis yourself and Jamie McRuin."

186

A wistful, far-off look clouded Maeve's eyes. "Aye . . . Cousin Tavish," she said simply.

"At home they tell the tale of a childless couple in the olden time who took in a little foundling left on their doorstep one dark Halloween. They cared for it and loved it as if it were their very own. The wee one, of course, turned out to be the little Jesus, come to test them; and after He had revealed Himself and gone His way, sure the man and his wife had seven wonderful sons . . . one right after the other. . . ."

Tavish spoke with such assured exuberance that Maeve laughed. "I doubt if anyone will be leaving a foundling on our doorstep—Halloween or any other evening. Few people even know we exist," she reminded him.

Tavish tipped her face up toward his own. "I'm thinking Father Kerrigan could find one, should you but whisper a word in his ear," he said pointedly.

Maeve was startled. "Adopt a child . . . and from the outside?" she exclaimed.

"Is the idea so frightening?" Tavish persisted. "Sure you're not forgetting that all little ones are arrows shot straight from Heaven?"

Maeve's deep-hazel eyes grew thoughtful. She shook her head slowly. "No . . . only I'd never considered anything like that."

"Then do," said Tavish flatly, "and now . . . while the mood of your husband is soft."

Jamie's team of matched sorrels trotted briskly along the Savannah Road toward Atlanta. He had been away from the camp one week, winding up odds and ends of business in towns to the south and east of the capital. His big body lounged comfortably on the seat, lulled by the song of the bright, new wheels singing their light, shrill Chinese tune to the rhythmic accompaniment of hoofbeats on the dust-muffled surface of the road. Soothed by the sound and swaying movement of the buggy, Jamie's thoughts had turned toward Maeve and an affectionate reprise of his reconciliation with her. With penitential zeal he berated himself.

The love of one in ten million she gave me, yet I let her wear her gentle heart to a thread because there was no child —as if the blame were in any way hers. She who took me in—and me without rus or raub—against the clamor of her kinsmen; and by the love in the heart of her, made a man of me—with horses and houses and money in the bank.

Money in the bank reminded Jamie that he was carrying nearly four thousand dollars in cash. I'll stop at the bank first thing, he assured himself, then to the stonecutter's and order some lovely monument for Little Tom. For 'twas the death of the little Sherwood that brought me to my senses.

Still held by the mood of happy penitence, Jamie resolved to buy Maeve a reconciliation present. Something for her lovely self so beautiful it will take the eyes right out of her head, he resolved.

Contrary to Traveler custom, Jamie managed the family money. Among the horse traders, the women always exercised that prerogative, just as they supervised arrangements for all basic functions such as births, deaths, marriages, and christenings. They issued whatever cash was needed for purchasing and trading to the men, but held the balance in matriarchal reserve.

Knowing her husband's love for fine clothes and grand gestures, Maeve had breached the tradition. Jamie went about carrying large sums in cash until the sudden war prosperity made it imperative that he open a bank account. With difficulty he and Tavish had persuaded Harrigan and the others to deposit their savings also. The men of the camp followed suit with reluctance and suspicion. Exchanging good money for small bankbooks and a sheaf of checks seemed rather foolish, and it fell upon Tavish to teach them the intricacies of signing the slips of paper which could be translated into cash.

"You're writing too big, man," he would say to those like Tom Sherwood, whose great fist needed a twelve-inch space to sprawl his name. "Squeeze it down. They don't make checks wide enough to fit the likes of your grand scribbling. Think of a fat woman squeezing into a tight corset. 'Tis confining but stops the spread and improves the appearance. Now confine yourself to that little space right there."

Some managed to master the finger-cramping labor, but others gave up in disgust, pretending to have suffered elaborate injuries to their hands when called upon to affix their signature to a check. Bank officials were aware of these childish fictions, but respected the deep pride which prompted them. Many of the traders carried accounts the size of which insured them courteous treatment anywhere.

Jamie's thoughts had gone daydreaming back to the time when he first spied Maeve moving gracefully among the green willows. *Without her I'm but half a man. Together we're something complete. In my heart's heart I want no more than that. Had we had children, sure they would have spoiled the sweetness. 'Tis selfish but true,* he rationalized.

With that rationalization, his inner discontent at being childless was somehow purged. From this instant his preference was postulated and fixed. The perfection of his newfound relationship with Maeve was not to be marred by any outside person or thing. It was God's will and his; and he was content.

At the edge of town Jamie chose a street which would take him past Power O'Malley's stone-cutting shop. When he arrived at the weird assortment of monuments which turned the front yard into a miniature cemetery, he drew the sorrels to a halt. Jamie had never bothered to visit his eccentric cousin, though Tavish had recounted in hilarious detail how Power O'Malley had believed him dead and mistook the Speaker for his own ghost.

As Jamie tied his team before the shop, a strange sight caught and held his gaze in complete fascination. O'Malley was standing on a low scaffolding in the yard, working on a group of stone figures which depicted the collapse of a hanging bridge similar to the one over Dunriggan Gap in Ireland. Two stone bodies were shown tumbling precipitately toward the serriform waves below, while from the banks above, stone soldiers stood with rifles leveled.

In awe and unbelief, Jamie entered the yard and drew closer. Power O'Malley was absorbed in his work, but finally became aware of Jamie's presence. He spoke without turning his head: "Just look around until you find something you like; then come tell me. I'm too busy to go showing you about."

"What in the name of the seven whiskies of Ireland is that?" Jamie demanded, ignoring the old man's lack of courtesy.

O'Malley turned and surveyed Jamie with hostility through his great shaggy brows. "What is it?" he echoed in a voice weighted with sarcasm. "'Tis only a small project that has occupied my talents for the past four years—my masterpiece . . . no less."

"That it is a masterpiece is plain," Jamie agreed unruffled, "but what it is is not so plain."

The old man climbed down from the scaffolding and viewed his work lovingly. Evidently his kin in the old country had neglected to tell him that Tavish and Jamie were alive and well.

"In the west of Ireland is a place called the gap of Dunriggan. There two of my kinsmen met heroic death resisting

the British constabulary. You speak like a man of the Gael
—have you not heard the story?"

"Not the way you be telling it," Jamie admitted wryly.

" 'Tis fast becoming one of the great legends of the west
of Ireland," O'Malley boasted. Like a man delivering an
illustrated lecture, he expounded a version of how Tavish
and Jamie had met their deaths that compared romantically
with a novel of the eighteenth century. According to O'Malley, Jamie was sort of an Irish Robin Hood and Tavish
another Friar Tuck. Tirsa was Maid Marian, and Jamie,
accompanied by Tavish, was on his way to marry her when
trapped on the bridge by the murderous constabulary.

"Rather than surrender, the two darlings of the Western
world sought escape from the British by leaping from the
bridge—may God and the Virgin give them rest," the old
man concluded.

Torn between incredulity and laughter, Jamie was on the
verge of protesting that there was not one bubble of truth
in the entire ocean of distortion, when the entrance of a
young woman into the yard distracted him. It required a
second look before he recognized Bernice Proddy.

A sensation of acute embarrassment shot through Jamie.
It was relieved an instant later when it became plain the
girl did not recognize him. She seemed paler than when last
he saw her, and her eyes reflected some deep inner suffering.

Power O'Malley greeted her with his usual gruffness, but
when the girl whispered that her mother had passed away,
his manner softened perceptible. "For your mother, you
say?" he repeated kindly. "How much do you want to pay
for the stone?"

"Does it have to be cash—all at once? I was hoping to pay
a little at a time," Bernice said wistfully.

"Terms are cash . . . but maybe we can work out something," the old man assured her. "Look around until you see a stone you like."

The girl turned away and began dejectedly to inspect the smaller monuments displayed about the yard. Jamie drew the stonecutter to one side. "Power O'Malley," he said, "I know you're a man to be trusted. I want you to give that girl the finest gravestone that money can buy."

"Aye," said O'Malley, "but whose money?"

"Mine." Jamie counted out a thousand dollars. " 'Tis all right," he said in answer to the old man's suspicious gaze. "All her life the girsha there wanted to do something fine for her mother. This will help her do it."

"You know her?" O'Malley queried.

"Yes and no," Jamie said. "Once she did me a great favor. She talked to me until I came to my senses. Is there any more you would like to be knowing, you nosy old shee-hogue?"

"Aye," said Power O'Malley, displaying a rare, wry grin, "what's to be done with the money that's left over?"

"Give it to the girl," Jamie said airily. "Tell her 'tis little enough, but less than that bought one of the Three Marys the brightest star in the Heavens. And tell her, if she really wants to do something for her mother . . . find herself another job. I'll come again another time to purchase a stone for the boyeen we lost a while back."

With a feeling of having given the strings of fate an irreverent pluck, Jamie sauntered to his buggy and drove away. After a time, when the feeling of playing God had worn away, he tried to analyze why he had paid out a thousand dollars for a girl he scarcely knew. "If anyone learned of this, sure they'd say I'd turned half-fool, and no mistake," he muttered.

But as he drove on toward the Five Points a feeling grew in him that the money had been well spent. The gift seemed to erase the one small stain that had marred his otherwise perfect relationship with Maeve. Now he felt that a phase in his life had passed—that he had survived some subtle test, the meaning of which was veiled in deep mystery and might never be revealed until the Day of the Mountain, when all things would be made clear to all men.

It was suppertime when Jamie reached the camp. The men were eating early, ahead of the women and children as was the custom. Tonight there was little of the genial raillery usual at mealtime. The drowning of Little Tom had left a pall that was not easily shaken off. In the hearts of these simple people, few of whom could read or write, children ruled as sovereigns by the divine right of birth. The death of one was a loss felt by all.

As Jamie seated himself at the table beside Shiel Harrigan, he caught a glimpse of Maeve busy among the women and children. She looked younger and more beautiful to him than she had since that first supper four years before. Then neither food nor drink had had taste or flavor for him.

"Sure someone should invent a potion to make men fall in love with their wives over again . . . every four years," he announced without preface.

"Huh . . . what was that?" Harrigan asked, startled.

" 'Twill take the place of all the excitement we had at mule auctions when we be back on the road," Jamie continued blandly.

Maeve's father studied his son-in-law out of the corner of his eye. "You've more wisdom than I gave you credit for, Jamie," he said quietly.

Owen Roe Tavish joined them at the plain pine table, his face still damp from the hasty wetting he had given it. "Too bad you weren't here for the christening," he said, looking at Jamie slyly.

"And who was named this day?" said Jamie, helping himself to the food Maeve set before him, "colt or Christian?"

"A fine broth of a boy," said Tavish, "though they're usually more colt than Christian. One can never be quite sure until he has counted the legs. And how were things to the south?"

The Speaker was unusually gay and talkative, it seemed to Jamie. Since Doreen's hysterical blaming of him for Little Tom's drowning, the old man had been sick at heart, given to long, brooding silences. Now he chattered on as merrily as before.

"Since when are boys named at this time of year . . . and in the camp instead of the church?" Jamie inquired.

" 'Twas all right and proper," Tavish hastened to say. "Father Kerrigan was here with three drops of the water of Sunday and made church beneath the trees."

"I still don't recall any bairn of the camp that was in need of christening," Jamie insisted.

Shiel Harrigan interrupted the cat-and-mouse conversation. "No bairn—a new boy the Father brought."

Jamie half sensed something behind the Speaker's evasiveness, but dismissed the matter without further questioning. When he finished eating he rose from the table. "I'll drop down for a quick look at the animals," he said.

"Sure now maybe I'll just go along with you," Tavish offered.

"Finish your supper, man; I'll be but a minute," Jamie assured him.

Tavish sat down again nervously. "On second thought I will finish my bit and sup," he said uneasily.

Jamie sauntered away toward the corrals but Tavish ate nothing more. Instead he kept his sharp eyes on Jamie's broad back. When it had disappeared into the pines, he rose from the table and beckoned to Maeve.

"Where have you hidden the lad?" he whispered.

"Will you stop acting as if we'd committed a crime, Cousin Tavish," Maeve said. "Kevin is waiting in the tent."

"Your husband has gone to the corral to count his mules," Tavish said meaningly.

"I know," Maeve said, distressed. "I was hoping he would meet the boy first—then I could have explained about the mule. Maybe he won't be missing the animal," she added hopefully.

Tavish snorted. "Your husband can count mules blind-folded, and he would be missing Big Ed if it was the middle of the night and he was counting with his eyes shut."

"Well, if there's no way to break it to him gently, then he must learn the hard way," said Maeve firmly.

Tavish pointed in warning toward the corrals. "Sure now let's brace ourselves, for here he comes with enough speed to overtake the wind that's before him, and a look of the Day of Judgment on his face."

Inside Maeve and Jamie's tent, the youngest of Jesse Proddy's seven children sat in a big upholstered chair, afraid to move. The last rays of the afternoon sun filtered through the green canvas, tinting the rich objects about him with a greenish gold luster. At one side stood a tall grandfather's clock announcing the seconds in solemn baritone. Near the foot of the great master bed was an elaborate dresser with high, oval mirror in which the boy could see himself by craning his neck to one side. He was almost afraid to look. The reflection that stared back from the glass was almost unrecognizable. A bath, haircut, and new shoes and stock-ings, plus a new suit so blue and stiffly creased that his back and shoulders ached from its rigid confinement, had worked a complete transformation.

As if to reassure himself, the boy tested his identity on the image in the glass with quick, furtive gestures. It was he all right, and not a dream. The mirror mimicked every move. The small lady with the bright, shining hair, and the eyes that seemed to laugh and cry at the same time, had really embraced him. He remembered her words and her light, clear way of talking.

"You're going to live here with me for a while," she had said, when Father Kerrigan brought him to the small tent city. "There'll be wonderful things for a boy to do: Horses to ride . . . children to play with . . . plenty of good things to eat. . . ."

"And most important of all," the priest had told him, "you'll have someone to love and care for you. If you're a good boy . . . and everyone likes you . . . maybe this will be your new home."

After that a little man with fierce eyebrows and twinkling blue eyes had ruffled his thatch of blond hair and said: "First off this boy needs a bath and a haircut." But the beautiful lady embraced him again and said: "First off he's going to have a name. Can't he be christened right here, Father?"

They had given him a name. Number Seven hadn't been able to figure why it seemed so important to everyone, but the priest had set up a tiny altar inside the tent and touched his head three times with water, all the while pronouncing strange and wonderful words. Then they had told him his new name—Kevin Roe Callahan McRuin—and the lovely lady with hair like sunshine had kissed him and wept. The men of the camp had come forward and shook his hand, calling him "Kevin," and the little old man with the eyebrows had boasted that as godfather, he had personally selected the name.

"Take any little mongrel dog, without home and spirit, and give him a fine Irish name, and immediately he becomes different from other dogs . . . a sort of supercanine," he had said.

After a bath, Tavish and Maeve had driven him into the city for new clothes and a haircut—the first he had ever had in a real barbershop. On the road, they passed the Proddy farm. Father Kerrigan was just turning into the lane leading to the house, and tied to his buggy was a huge black-and-tan-colored mule. The priest had waved to them but didn't stop.

The sight of the gray, unpainted shack where he was born had sent a throb of homesickness through the boy. He longed to cry out to be taken back. Better the familiar misery he had known there than the dark uncertainty of strange people and stranger places. The memory-anchors of his life were sunk in those bleak acres. There Old Luke had died and his mother—crying wildly of Callahans and kings, until the priest had come and smoothed her passage into eternity.

Something of the torment of loneliness seething within him had communicated itself to Maeve. She had folded her arms about him, racked and tortured herself by the spasms of soundless sobbing which shook him. "There . . . there . . . there," she crooned. "You're thinking of your mother. Sure her dying wish was that you come to us. Father Kerrigan promised her you would have a real name and a new life—and you shall, Kevin, you shall."

In the premature twilight of the tent, Kevin, once a number instead of a name, relived the happy, crowded hours he had spent that day with Maeve and Tavish. Confidence seeped back into his slight form as moisture returns to a footprint in wet sand. He wondered why Maeve had told him not to stray from the tent until she returned. He heard her voice outside, explaining something as she came nearer. The deeper voice of a man with her was raised in exasperation.

"Did it have to be the king of mules you gave the priest?

Wouldn't a lesser animal than Big Ed do? Sure you've given away my right eye."

"There was so much happiness in me," Maeve said soothingly. "I wanted to make a fine offering; and Father Kerrigan had special need of a good mule. 'Tis for the salvation of our souls."

"Big Ed is a bit of a price to pay for an altar candle," Jamie grumbled. "Sure there hasn't been that much sinning in the entire camp in a whole year."

The boy didn't hear Maeve's whispered answer. The flap of the tent was thrust aside and Jamie entered, his arm about Maeve's waist. He looked at the strange child in amazement, his arm dropping to his side. "God a' mercy, and what lad is this?"

"His name is Kevin. Father Kerrigan gave us the lend of him for a while," Maeve explained hastily.

Jamie was puzzled but not displeased. "Since when do they lend boys like they were cups of salt? Where's your home, little maneen?"

"I'm trying to tell you," Maeve said, lowering her voice. "Kevin is a sort of orphan. His mother just died and I promised Father Kerrigan we'd look after him for a bit of a while."

"Might this have something to do with my prize mule disappearing down the road in a cloud of red dust?" Jamie demanded suspiciously. He glared fiercely, first at Maeve, then at the trembling child. "I can see by your two faces it has."

Kevin shrank back into the big chair, while great tears rose in his eyes and clung there unshed. Maeve charged at her husband like a small mother bear. "Stop your eagle screaming this instant. Can't you see you're frightening the child? He's been through enough today without your roaring at him like a bull."

"Like a bull, is it?" Jamie protested. "Am I to stand idly by while my wife and a priest of the Church make off with my prize mule, leaving in his place this mouse of a boy?"

"You're away from the camp so much—it would be company to have a child about," Maeve said pleadingly.

"Aye, now we've come to the dirt at the bottom of the bucket. Father Kerrigan has gone about the soft side of you to find a home for some parish orphan. Well, I'll have no part of such a devil's package. Back he goes this night, and that's my final word."

Maeve's face was pale but she held her tongue. "Run find your Uncle Tavish, child," she said to Kevin. When he had slipped from the tent like a frightened shadow, she turned to face Jamie, her eyes hard with anger.

"You've had your final word, now let me have mine," she said, with forced quietness. "Father Kerrigan did not come to me—I went to him. There was no time to consult you. You were away and we didn't know when you'd be back. When the opportunity came to get Kevin I said we'd take him. Father Kerrigan has my promise!—I'll not go back on my word."

In the face of Maeve's determination, Jamie retreated. "But Maeve darling—why?" he pleaded. "Don't you see . . . a foreign child in a tent where there are no children makes me a shamed man. The camp will say: 'Take a look at the McRuin. Not able to get a child of his own, he had to borrow one from the outside.' "

"Is this my husband who used to cry: 'May the Devil fly away with the roof of a house where there's no welcome?' " Maeve answered scornfully, "afraid of what a few will say?"

With that the fight went out of Jamie, but Maeve's victory was a Pyrrhic one at best. She had hoped desperately that Jamie would accept the child, if not enthusiastically, at least with forbearance. With a wrench of conscience, she realized that her husband would never entirely give up hope of having a son of his own. The acceptance of an adopted child would only be an admission within his inner heart that the one promised him was part of a web of hillside fancy; a fairy gift as insubstantial as the morning dew.

Jamie had slumped down in the chair vacated by Kevin. "All through these past days the cold inside of me was kept warm by the thought you and I were together again. Now I come home to bitter words and the old wounds that were so long in healing are open again."

Maeve was at his side without knowing she moved, and her arms were about his head. "O my heart," she whispered, "please forgive me. 'Twas of myself alone I was thinking when I told the priest we wanted the little boy. Tomorrow I'll drive with him back to Father Kerrigan."

Halfheartedly Jamie protested that she had given her word, but Maeve had reversed her plan of attack. She seemed now as determined that the child should go as she had been that he was to stay. "What's the thread of a promise against my own husband's happiness?" she insisted, and Jamie was comforted.

That night, alone in the velvet darkness of the tent, they lay whispering. "It's not that I want to be hard about the boy," said Jamie, conscience-troubled, "but 'twould never work. We know nothing about the lad. . . ."

"His mother was a Callahan," Maeve supplied innocently.

"Was she now?" Jamie was impressed. "Truth is," he whispered, "I'd be jealous of the malrach, running to you with his tales and his bruises—taking your time and attention."

Maeve laughed her pleasant laugh. "There'd be small cause," she said. "Somewhere along the way the child has lost the power of talking."

Jamie digested Maeve's calm announcement in mounting horror. "A dummy," he said, shocked, "one of God's Fair Innocents, we say at home. Wirra . . . wirra . . . the pity of it."

"Yes," said Maeve, "that's what I thought . . . the pity of it. To be alone and with no way of sharing the loneliness; to feel pain and fear, without the release of crying out; to know love, without the power of putting it into words; we may well say 'wirra . . . wirra!' "

"Sure there be but one thing to do," Jamie announced firmly, "the lad must stay. There can be no shame at taking in a Fair Innocent."

Maeve kissed him lightly. "Whatever you say, my husband."

"And no one would make the mistake of thinking him truly my child," Jamie continued. "Jamie McRuin, known in two lands for his lip-liveliness, the father of one without the power of speaking . . . it wouldn't make sense at all."

"No, my husband."

"What is the lad's name?" Jamie asked, oblivious of the note of merriment lurking behind Maeve's placid agreement.

"Father Kerrigan said he'd never been christened. His father wanted all his sons to have names beginning with T, but he had run out of such names by the time this last one had come along. He called him 'Number Seven,' and that was his name until this afternoon."

Jamie remembered Owen Roe Tavish's odd conduct at the supper table. "Och, then he is the lad who was christened here in the camp. What was he named?"

Maeve smothered a little laugh against Jamie's shoulder. "Tavish was godfather and insisted upon naming him 'Kevin.' . . ."

" 'Tis a good saint's name," said Jamie.

"Next we called him 'Roe,' for Owen Roe Tavish. . . ."

"Fine . . . fine," said Jamie. "What else?"

"Then 'Callahan,' for his mother. . . ."

"None better in the whole of Ireland," said Jamie. "Now what's the boyo's last name?"

"McRuin."

"What?" Jamie shouted, ready to be angry all over again.

"Please, darling," Maeve cried, clinging to him; "if you knew how the heart of me has longed for a child named McRuin. Life is so empty for a woman without a bairn. Every baby wailing in the camp—every laugh from a playing boy—cries failure to me because there's no child of my own. Grant me this and I'll never ask anything of you again."

It was the humblest speech Jamie had ever heard his spirited wife make. She was almost in tears when she finished. "Och, my treasure, you shame me to myself," he whispered. "If it means that much to you, sure the boy is yours. I don't even mind the lend of my name; though," he added reprovingly, "the way you built a nest in my ear to get round me was a sly bit of sleuthering."

"I'll never do it again," Maeve whispered, "and I make that promise before Mary and all the saints."

Jamie sighed. "There be those who say three kinds of men never understand their wives: The young . . . the middle-aged . . . and the old."

Maeve laughed. "Isn't it better that way? When the time comes that men understand us, sure there'll be an end to the wonder of life."

Jamie remembered the present he had brought from town. "Och, I've forgotten the surprise I brought you. It's in the buggy."

He would have dressed and fetched it but Maeve checked him. "It will keep," she said. "Tell me what it is and I'll have the double pleasure in the morning."

"Only a lovely something for hanging in the tent."

"Another picture?"

He shook his head. "A wind harp."

Maeve was pleased but puzzled. "I've never seen one."

" 'Tis a rare musical instrument. It hangs in the tent and the wind plucks wonderful music from the strings. I bought it of a purpose," said Jamie. "Long ago in Ireland there lived a man and wife who had no children. And the wife had fallen out of love with her husband, so much so that she had lost the power of sleeping entirely. Finally she became maddened by the sleepless nights and the days filled with hate for the man she had married; and she fled away from her husband, wandering alone until she came to the sea. There on the shore was the skeleton of a huge whale, every white and gleaming bone in place. The poor, exhausted woman creature rested against the great carcass, and the wind rose, and the sound of wonderful music was heard. So soothing was the melody that she was lulled to sleep; and there her husband found her, beside the great ribs of the whale. 'Twas the wind blowing through the great, bleached bones that had created the wonderful music which had brought sleep at last to the unhappy woman."

"What happened then?" Maeve asked like a sleepy child.

"Sure the husband carried her back and built the first wind harp, so she might find happiness and true sleep at home. And so grateful was the woman that she fell in love with her husband all over again. And that's how the wind harp came to be invented . . . and it's a story that's all truth."

Jamie turned his head to look at the face beside him. Maeve was asleep. Silently, he crept from the bed and made his way barefooted to the buggy parked near the tent. In the warm stillness of the camp, he unpacked the wind harp and carried it inside. When Maeve awoke in the morning, the instrument hung near the entrance, singing softly. Beside her, Jamie slept, the shadow of a smile tipping the corners of his mouth as if traced there by some pleasant dream. The smile-shadows deepened when Maeve brushed his lips with a butterfly kiss.

XIX

MRS. FLUKER brought the morning mail to Father Kerrigan's study. He could count the housekeeper's slow, measured steps: Front door to the stairs; up the stairs to the landing; from the landing to the door of the study. "Some Christian soldiers march with a heavy tread," he mused.

The housekeeper knocked and entered. "The morning mail just came, Father," she said.

"Anything exciting?" The priest eyed the usual clatter of religious pamphlets, magazines, bills, and begging letters.

"I didn't look, Father," Mrs. Fluker said stiffly.

"Of course not. You're the only woman in the parish completely without curiosity."

The housekeeper accepted the priest's comment as a compliment. "Thank you, Father," she sniffed. "I try to do my Christian duty."

She retreated toward the door as if paced by fife and drum. "Sure it would be nice if Mrs. Fluker got a little fun out of doing her Christian duty," the priest sighed.

He sorted through the letters until a florid, unfamiliar

handwriting caught his eye. The envelope was postmarked from a town in Mississippi, and began:

Dear Father Kerrigan:

I take my pen in hand to acquaint you that once more the caravan is heading toward Atlanta. As we move eastward the trees along the road are tinted with the pale and urgent young green of spring. Here and there an early blooming dogwood raises its white branches like a flag of surrender to the vernal equinox.

It having been almost seven months since the little lad, Kevin, came to us, you'll be wanting to know how he is, and of the progress he is making. Father, the dear child is one of the rare, and flahooly ones; wedded to the hills and to the sea, they are, and in dreams so rich they are the envy of the earth. There is a budding project in my mind concerning the boy. Upon it I would ask your Reverence's blessing. Would his handicap of silence make it impossible for him to enter the priesthood? If ever a youth has felt the call, Father, 'tis he. I told him the story of when the young and beautiful St. Kevin was praying alone in the woods (the lad and I occupy the same tent and the nights are spent as the ancients used to say: A third in storytelling; a third with Fenian tales; and a third in the mild enjoyment of slumber and true sleep). He was standing, as was his custom, in the shape of the Irish cross, with his arms outstretched and his feet together, when a mother blackbird built her nest in the palm of his hand and laid her eggs there before the good saint was aware of it. "Sure then, the man of God," I told the boy, "rather than disturb the nesting mother bird, held his arm outstretched until the eggs were hatched and the birdlings flown away."

Father—and this is the truth; my right hand is raised toward Heaven as I write it—the very next day I found little Kevin standing alone in the woods, his wee arms spread wide with the palms up, trying to persuade another mother bird to build her nest in the palm of his hand. Now wouldn't you say that that was proof the lad had been called, Father?

I know your intent in bringing the boy to us was twofold: A home for the child and a child to mend the breach between Maeve and Jamie. But Cousin Jamie has never accepted little Kevin. Maeve loves him dearly and the lad loves her, but from the first she has been torn between the boy she married and the one she adopted. Upon my oath, Father, I love Jamie as if he were my own son, but in some ways he is more of a child than Kevin. As a result, the lad has turned to me as to a father. Now there is a secret plan brewing between us. I want to take the boy to Ireland, provide him with the finest education possible; then, if it is his desire and he is qualified, let him enter the priesthood. There is a deep personal reason for this, Father. I will explain it to you in Atlanta at ritual time. I am a reasonably wealthy man, thanks to Jamie, who has set aside a fourth of his earnings as mine, so there will be ample money, do you but give the project your blessing.

Be not too harsh in your judgment of Jamie, Father. He has a wonderful heart, though he can find no room in it for a child that is not his own. 'Tis the soul of him that's still undersized. It will grow, Father, in God's good time. I think he tried to love the boy for Maeve's sake, but Kevin is frightened of him. Jamie is not a happy man, Father, and if Maeve thought Kevin's leaving would ease the brooding in the dark heart of him, she would give her consent for the good of all.

Another month will find us near your parish, which is the only home we know. The blessings of the Virgin and of the man in the East and the man in the West be upon you, Father.

The letter was inscribed: "Your most obedient servant," and bore Owen Roe Tavish's looping signature. The priest folded the pages neatly and returned them to the envelope. His thoughts had gone many times to the tents of the wandering traders. Rumors were spreading that some of the counties and the state legislature were contemplating excessive license fees to drive the horse traders out. The presence of this unique group of devout Catholics in a dominantly Protestant community—their insular attitude and refusal to become assimilated—created an ever-active point of friction.

Father Kerrigan's thoughts shifted to Kevin. He had sensed something unusual in the child the first time he had visited Hester Proddy. I wonder what the boy is like after almost a year with Tavish and the Travelers? At least there will be something in his stomach, and he'll have had his basic religious training, he concluded. As for the priesthood —there was Maeve to consider. He had not forgotten the look on her face when she first opened her arms to the nameless boy.

Unless I be greatly mistaken, she'll not be giving him up for Tavish, or Jamie, or even holy orders. Anyway, time will be the storyteller, he concluded to himself.

XX

A FEW days after he had written to Father Kerrigan, Tavish had a premonition of returning to Ireland. He dreamed that Kevin came to him and said a strange man was waiting for him beyond a bend in the road ahead. It seemed entirely natural in the dream that the boy was able to speak. Furthermore, he spoke in purest Gaelic.

"Describe the man, Kevin lad," Tavish had said in his dream.

"That were easy to do," the boy replied. Fluently and in great detail, he drew a word picture of the strange man waiting in the road for Owen Roe Tavish.

"Not a small man, nor yet overtall," he said, "with a face round and ruddy red, brimful of humor."

"I know no such man," said Tavish. "How spoke he?"

"In a voice most fair, with music and laughter behind each word. His eyes were deepest blue, as when lightning flashes catch the rain clouds unaware."

"I know no such man," Tavish said again. "How was he dressed?"

"In a green coachman's coat that would take the sight from your eyes. It hung to his ankles, and had golden buttons in the shape of tiny bells that tinkled when he moved. A high hat to match his coat, he wore, and boots that shone black as a blackbird's wing during mating time. In his hand was a long coachwhip and two huge coach dogs crouched at his heels."

"Och," said Tavish, "I think I recognize the man."

In the dream he had put his thumb behind his Tooth of Knowledge, as he had shown Kevin many times to do, and straightway the truth was made known to him. The coachman waiting round the bend in the road was an omen.

" 'Tis sure now we be going to take our trip," the old man said, confiding his dream to Kevin. " 'Tis a great secret between us. No one else must know of it."

The boy nodded eagerly. Between Tavish and the child had developed an understanding possible only between two such spirits, so unlike and yet so complementary to each other. Tavish had few thoughts that escaped utterance at one time or another. To think a thing was to say it. Thoughts without words went nowhere. They had no existence until molded into language and the warm breath of life breathed over them. The result of this rationalization was that the two were perfectly matched; Tavish loved to talk, Kevin to listen.

In the old man's profuse outpourings, the child found a release from the ache of silence which walled him in. His wrapt attention to the Speaker's words was balm to the old man's pride. The boy's great, expressive eyes laughed, danced, sighed, and wept, according to whatever mood Tavish created. The two were inseparable.

Maeve regarded the first attachment between Kevin and the old man with tolerant eyes. The child's attempts to play with other children were complicated by his inability to express himself in the usual ear-shattering shouts and screams. He was active and as fleet of foot as any boy in the camp, but the terrible block of unnatural silence marked and set him apart from the others.

With the impulsive cruelty of the young, they sometimes teased Kevin because he couldn't speak, and the wounds inflicted were worse than any sticks and stones might make. The gentle companionship of Owen Roe Tavish was a relief for child and woman alike.

"I do be teaching the lad the fancies of life," the old man declared. "Sure any fool can learn the facts."

It was a rich, wonderful, and altogether fanciful education the boy received. The history of Ireland according to Tavish, began with the Little People who had inhabited the land in the beginning. "They were that small, Kevin, were you to walk among them you'd be called a giant. They ruled Ireland in those days, with kings and queens and warriors and noble folk just like now. Horses and cows and sheep and pigs they had, of a size like to their own. Then came Amergin Glunmar, king-poet and king-judge. He divided Ireland into two parts: the part above the ground and the part below. The part below Amergin gave to the Tuatha De Danaan— that's what the Little People were called—and the part above he reserved for mortals. 'Twas as good an arrangement as any, but from that day to this, those above the ground are constantly interfering in the affairs of those below, while the Little People themselves can't leave off meddling in matters that should concern only mortals."

After Amergin, Tavish explained, the land was divided by his two sons, Eremon and Eber. They cast lots to see with whom Cir, the poet, and Cennfinn, the harper, would go. By decision of the lot, Cir, the poet, went northward with Eremon and Cennfinn, the harper, to the south with Eber.

"And since that time," Tavish assured Kevin, "music and

harmony have dwelt in the south of Ireland, and poetry and learning in the north."

Together Kevin and Tavish explored the wooded hills and back roads around every camp. As they walked the old man talked and dreamed aloud. The boy listened enthralled, more at home in a world of wishing wells and straying stones, of fairy mounds and the legends of the great Finn, than any he had known. Even the now-familiar nomadic existence of the horse traders seemed foreign by comparison.

Tavish was very secretive about the dream he had had. He shared it with no one but Kevin. "There's no yer-a-no about it, the coachman waiting means I'm going home to Ireland, and you're coming with me," he told the boy. "Not to heed the warning of such a dream could bring seven years' bad luck."

The Travelers were encamped near Augusta, while Jamie and the men scouted the countryside on daily selling and trading expeditions. There had been light showers of rain, leaving a slight chill in the spring air. Here and there above the young green of the hills, hawks winged in sharp, predatory circles.

Immediately after breakfast, Tavish drew Kevin aside. "We're off to the deep woods . . . to cut two shillelahs; sticks to make a man walk with grandeur. We'll be needing them when we get to Ireland," he whispered mysteriously. "Not a word to anyone."

Kevin looked eagerly toward Maeve, who was clearing away the breakfast dishes. Five years of marriage had erased the young girl look from her face, but rewarded her in turn with a quiet gentleness. Whatever anguish she had suffered because of Jamie, had left no mark except the faint suggestion of lines at the corners of her eyes.

"And what are you two planning now?" she said affectionately, when Tavish and the boy approached her.

"Sure yesterday I spied an eagle nesting. I thought it might interest the boy," Tavish said slyly.

"Since when have eagles begun nesting in the low branches along the road?" Maeve retorted.

"That's the very thing I'll be asking the creature when we come face to face with it this day," Tavish replied blandly. "There's the mite of a chance it's that rare bird called the 'bush eagle.' 'Tis an outcast, and does everything opposite, like nesting in the shrubs instead of the upper branches, and hatching ducks instead of eagles of the air."

Maeve raised her hands in the gesture of defeat that mothers use. "Take him with you, but mind you bring him safely back. There may be more rain and I'll have nought to do with pneumonia in either of you."

"Your blessing is all we need to keep out the drop," Tavish said airily. "But a bit of bread and meat might come in handy toward the middle of the day."

Maeve wrapped great slices of bread and meat and shooed them on their way. She watched them trudging into the woods and an indulgent smile softened the shadows in her eyes. "Sure the naoidhean and the older are the same age in many ways," she said aloud, turning back to her work.

As Tavish and Kevin strode through the thickening timber, kicking aside the leaves of yesteryear, the Speaker explained the necessity of finding a proper stick with which to return to Ireland. "The stick a man carries is as important as the clothes he wears. A stick makes the man, you might say. I'd sooner go home in a wooden box than show my face in Ireland without a proper stick."

He continued his dissertation upon the importance of shillelahs throughout the morning. "They were called shillelahs after a place in Ireland famous for its oak trees, but when the English came the trees were cut down. Now the sticks are made from blackthorn and ash. I'm thinking the ones we'll take back with us will be of hickory. There's a good, tough wood, and not too heavy."

"It's more than something to help a man over the rough places," Tavish rambled on. "A stick is a comfort when you're by yourself. It's company . . . like having a dog with you. I've known men who never exchanged a civil word with their neighbors, but carried on the politest sort of talk with their six-foot shillelahs."

Toward the noon hour they stopped by a small spring and ate their meat and bread. Tavish had examined and rejected quite a few hickory trees. "A man should be as careful in choosing a stick as in choosing a wife," he commented expansively. "They be the two things that will walk with him in life and lie beside him in death."

The old man found a patch of leaves where a shaft of sunlight had warmed and left them dry after the rain. "If you'll stand watch, Kevin lad, I'll stretch out here for a minute's nap. Mind, you're not to go wandering away."

Kevin watched, attentive as a puppy, as the old man made himself comfortable, grunting and shifting from side to side on the pile of leaves. "Sure I need something to rest my head on now. Fetch me a smooth, flat stone, lad."

The boy darted away like a dog bent on retrieving a stick. He scouted along the low bluff that overhung the spring beside which they had eaten, snapping his fingers to attract Tavish's attention when he found a rock that seemed suitable to serve as a pillow.

"Bring that one along," Tavish called, "I'll see if it's soft enough."

Kevin lugged the stone to where the old man lay and watched curiously as Tavish turned it about, examining it with mock thoroughness. "A man must be careful about the kind of stone he lays his head on," he warned. "I don't know about over here, but in Ireland we have 'straying stones.'

To fall asleep on one of them is as good as your life. They'll whisk you away for a hundred years, and without so much as a 'God save you' when they bring you back. It happened to Mochae, when the good saint fell asleep listening to the singing of a bird, and three times fifty years passed between the closing of his eyes and the opening of them."

Tavish scrutinized the child's face for the effect of his words and found there a worshipful wonder that tugged at his heart. "Kevin lad," he said gently, "remember the things I tell you. They're the great truths and there's a mystery surrounds them, as there is mystery surrounding life and beauty. Any omadhaun can figure out a fact—and facts change from time to time; but the deeper truths, like the deepest water, never change . . . no matter what storms rage above on the surface."

With that observation, not a word of which the boy understood, Tavish closed his eyes, murmuring a little prayer from his childhood.

> Jesus, Father, Lamb, I pray
> Drive each evil thought away;
> Be with me till break of day;
> In my sleep or on my way;
> When the hour of hours shall sound,
> Jesus be within me found. Amen.

Kevin watched wraptly as the old man closed his eyes and appeared to fall asleep immediately. His lips relaxed and slight, easy snores vibrated within his throat. To the child's overstimulated imagination, sleep settled about his companion with a presence that was almost physical. It seemed on the verge of spiriting the old man away bodily. A terrible thought flashed in Kevin's mind: Maybe the stone under Tavish's head was in truth a "straying stone"! He edged closer, seeking to retain some contact with the sleeping man;

but the bond between them was broken. He felt alone, cut off, imprisoned in a tomb, the walls of which were silence and the door to which was speech—and he was dumb. A heavy stillness settled over the woods and the sinister shadows crept closer. The small, friendly agitation of insects and the light rustling of leaves became sounds fraught with menace.

Kevin sat without moving, feeling the pinpricks of fear that began at the pit of his stomach and grew and spread like so many faceless monsters, until every fibre of his being was contaminated. Seconds spawned and became minutes. He wanted to cry out and deep, silent shrieks formed in his throat, only to die there unborn. His chest became a great, convulsive ache.

Without being aware of it, he had crept closer until he was crouched trembling above the sleeping Tavish. A lone, hot tear fell from his cheek and splashed on the back of the old man's hand. The Speaker opened his bright blue eyes and found two pools of misery staring down at him.

"Wirra, wirra," he said gently. "Sure now I dreamt a tear big enough to drown a man fell on the back of my hand. And it woke me just in time, too. The coachman with the green coat that was in my dream before was back, and this time driving a black coach and four black horses. Their manes and tails fanned out in the wind until they filled the sky like clouds. I was about to step into the coach when that tear woke me."

With that the old man scrambled to his feet. "Now we'll be off to find the proper stick for Owen Roe Tavish and his young friend, Kevin McRuin, to walk the lanes of the world with."

He said not a word of the look of stark and lonely terror that had greeted him in the boy's eyes. Kevin, ashamed of the panic that had overwhelmed him, now dashed belligerently among the trees and shrubs, seeking to demonstrate his doughtiness.

It was late afternoon before Tavish found the hickory limb that suited him: a thick, low-hanging branch, gnarled but straight, stretched out above a seam of limestone rock that formed a shallow bluff. He boosted Kevin into the tree, and passed up his heavy-bladed pocket knife to the boy.

"Press the end of the limb down to me, Kevin lad," he instructed. "I'll be pulling on it while you whittle away. Mind you don't cut yourself . . . and chop as close to the trunk as possible. The knobbier the handle the better."

Kevin sawed valiantly at the tough wood, while below, Tavish strained the long limb downward. Suddenly, with a sharp splintering sound, the branch ripped away, trailing a long strip of hickory bark stripped downward from the trunk of the tree. Kevin had been concentrating furiously upon cutting the limb, so he did not see what happened. The first realization that something was wrong came when Tavish groaned. The abrupt giving way of the limb had caused the old man to stagger heavily and fall backward over the outcropping of limestone—a drop of some six or eight feet.

With fear drumming a charge inside his breast, Kevin slid to the ground and scrambled to where Tavish lay. The Speaker's face was gray with pain and his lips had turned the color of old blood. He held his eyes shut, but with his right hand he fumbled to touch the frightened boy.

"Listen closely, child, and hear me with both ears. I'm hurt that badly I can't move. You'll have to go for help. You know the way!"

The words seemed to cost Tavish great effort. He lay silent for a few moments, then opened his eyes and looked at Kevin. The boy saw that his eyes, once so blue-bright, were now blurred with pain. "You must hurry, lad; and remember this spot, so as not to lose it when you come again. I . . . I may be asleep and not hear the calling."

He rested, breathing painfully. Kevin made no move to leave, but stood transfixed by the horror of what had happened. About him gloom spread like a mantle through the woods. Here and there a patch of sunlight disappeared, swallowed by the lengthening shadows. "In the forests where night is born," Tavish had said once, when telling Kevin a story. Now the child felt he was witness to the birth. Darkness, newborn but menacing, was slowly wedging him in, driving him closer to the only comfort and protection he knew. It was physically impossible for him to stir from Tavish's side.

Something of what was going on inside the boy seemed to communicate itself to the injured man. "I wouldn't be sending you into the darkness alone without a special prayer," he whispered. "Come closer and stand in the sign of the cross."

Kevin obeyed and Tavish continued without opening his eyes. " 'Tis the mighty 'Cry of the Deer,' invoked by St. Patrick when he was on his way to Tara, bringing Christianity to the pagans. During his journey the pagan king planned to kill him from an ambush. But, with this prayer, St. Patrick changed himself and all his followers into deer, going safely through the forests to Tara. Repeat it after me, and should danger threaten you, sure you'll change in a twinkling into a great stag, with antlers flashing, and hoofs as sharp as sabers."

Laboring over each sentence, and with Kevin mentally repeating the words after him, Tavish spoke St. Patrick's mighty invocation:

> I place all Heaven with its power,
> And the sun with its brightness

And the snow with its whiteness
And fire with all the strength it hath
And the winds with their swiftness along their path
And the sea with its deepness
And the rocks with their steepness
And the earth with its starkness—
All these I place, by God's almighty help and grace,
Between Kevin McRuin and the Powers of Darkness....
Amen!

The effort left Tavish exhausted. "Go now, lad," he whispered. Drifting into unconsciousness, he heard as from a great distance the sharp crackle of twigs and leaves that diminished as Kevin sped away.

XXI

JAMIE drove campward in the moonlight. It was late and he was sleepy. He had been on the road since early morning, and for his day's work had sold a span of young mules and two mares in foal at ridiculously low prices. There had been small choice in the deals. The market was bad and either you sold your animals for what they would bring, or continued to feed them until they had devoured any profits they might eventually fetch. With a sigh of weariness, Jamie leaned back against the seat cushions. The tired sorrels slowed to an ambling walk and the muffled thrumming of their hoofs upon the dust-padded surface of the road lulled him into a fitful doze.

He must have fallen asleep, for abruptly he started wide awake, his muscles tensed and ready. On the surface all seemed serene. The road ahead glowed placid and empty in the moonlight; a strip of dull rust upon the bright blue steel of night. Nor did a closer scrutiny of the shadows lurking beneath the trees along the way give an answer to Jamie's sudden alarm.

A premonition that something was wrong seized him. It began to grow with every revolution of the buggy wheels. He urged the sorrels to a brisk trot, but the increased speed served only to increase his apprehension. By the time he reached the camp, Jamie was certain something terrible had happened. One look was enough to confirm his fears.

The entire camp was awake and dressed—even the children. Great fires were lit, illuminating the grove in which the camp was set. Men, women, and children stood silent in a deep semicircle outside Maeve and Jamie's tent.

A fear as dry as cotton lined Jamie's mouth. He leapt from the buggy, leaving the team to wander to the corral untended. "What's happened, man? Is it Maeve?" he demanded of Me-Dennis, standing on the outskirts of the group.

The horse trader shook his head. " 'Tis the old one," he said simply.

Jamie felt a momentary surge of relief. If it was Owen Roe Tavish it couldn't be very serious. The old man was indestructible. "Speak up, man; what ails him?" he said, relief showing in his voice.

Me-Dennis shook his head pityingly. "Ails him! Sure and the old man is only just there. It's a miracle he's lasted this long, and him with his back broken," he said.

Jaunting Jim beckoned Me-Dennis aside. The men were working in shifts to finish Tavish's stick, carving it from the same hickory limb he and Kevin had ripped from the tree at the time of the accident. They had peeled the wood and sanded the knobs, and now it hung in the smoke of one of the fires. Occasionally they took it down and rubbed fresh butter into the grain, then hung it back again in the smoke.

"It will be ready for the old one to take with him," the men assured each other. "He'd not like being separated from his stick."

Jamie pushed through the group to the entrance of his tent. There he hesitated, uncertain whether to go in or not. As he waited Maeve came out. She walked apart from the others and he followed her.

"How is he?" he asked.

"Done to death," Maeve answered wearily.

"Is there no help for him?"

"The doctor came from town and gave something to deaden his pain. Nought can be done for a broken back. There's only to wait."

"And the priest?"

"He's on his way."

"Where's the boy?"

"Tavish asked that Kevin stay with him as long as possible."

Mutely Jamie listened while Maeve briefly recounted what she knew of the tragedy.

"The boy returned without the old one at dusk. From the wild look of him, we knew something terrible had happened. He wouldn't rest or eat, but led us straight to where Tavish lay."

Jamie shook his head. The thought of Owen Roe Tavish dying was somehow incomprehensible. The old man was a fixed star in a shifting firmament; had always been—would always be. "I'll go in to him now," he said. "Get some rest."

Maeve shook her head wearily. "When he wakes there'll be things to say . . . good-bys to speak. I'll wait."

The small yellow flame of the crucifix candle curtsied toward the opening when Jamie drew aside the tent flap. Inside, Owen Roe Tavish lay on Jamie and Maeve's big bed. On a low stool near the foot sat Kevin, fast asleep. His blond head, leaning against the lace counterpane, was the shade of deep amber in the soft, mellow light. One arm lay stretched along the edge of the bed, palm upward toward the dying man, as if in supplication.

Jamie hesitated, uncertain whether to go or stay. Upon the old man's ashen face death's shadow had already fallen. He breathed slowly and heavily through parted lips. As if in response to Jamie's troubled scrutiny, he stirred and opened his eyes.

"Is it you now, Cousin Jamie?" he asked softly.

"Yes, Tavish."

"Come closer . . . and speak softly. I would not wake the boy."

A gush of pity turned Jamie's blood to milk. The Speaker, on his deathbed, was worrying about awakening a sleeping child. "Sure I'll speak no louder than breath, Cousin Tavish," he promised.

Kneeling beside the bed, his face was but a few inches from Tavish's on the pillow. "Are you in pain? Can I do anything? Get you anything?" he whispered.

"The doing and the getting has been done, lad," Tavish whispered. "I'm not afraid of dying. Sure the soul of me is hungry for the wonderful experience," the voice was barely audible. "I've a confession to make."

"The priest will be here soon. Maeve sent to Augusta."

" 'Tis to you and Maeve, as well as to the priest, I must confess," Tavish answered. "At home you heard the tale that I was a spoiled priest? Well, 'tis true. I studied for holy orders and was rejected. I was a fine scholar; too fine. I fell in love with the wild and bloody history of my own land. Conchobor and the great Finn, and the pagan hosts of Tara meant more to me than did the King of Sunday."

"Should you be talking so, Cousin Tavish?"

"Aye, Jamie, for in my heart I plotted to do you and Maeve a great wrong. Because I failed in my youth, I wanted to take Kevin away to Ireland, and make of him the priest I could not be. 'Twas wicked of me, Jamie, and God has punished me for it. It would have broken Maeve's heart."

Jamie felt great unshed tears sting his eyes. " 'Tis I who should be begging your forgiveness—not you mine. The promise I gave you has not been kept. When your time came, I swore you'd not lie in foreign ground."

" 'Twas a foolish request of my greener days. The mound of earth that's inviting me is the same here as at home. Besides, I've a pinch of Irish sod in a small sack which I wear around my neck. Sprinkle it on my coffin and what's left of me will feel at home."

A trace of the old man's former roguishness crept into his voice. "We've had some rare times together, Jamie. Remember that eating place along the road while we were walking our way to Georgia? When the girl waiting on the table set a large bowl of potatoes before us? In Ireland 'twould have been no more than a large individual portion, but here 'twas meant for all six others at the table as well. I'll never forget the look on that girsha's face when she came back and discovered you and I had eaten every pratie in the dish."

Jamie tried to laugh. "Aye . . . we were the babes in the wood in this rich new land where one man's food would feed ten at home."

" 'Twas cruel of your father and me to scheme to marry you to the daughter of the Shanahans. By a miracle you escaped. Forgive us for that."

"Aye," Jamie said softly, "a miracle that brought the two of us to America."

"Och, yes, and speaking of miracles, have you noticed how many small ones—ones we seldom notice—blossom along our way like forget-me-nots scattered by angels?"

Jamie's throat constricted and he laid his face against the bed, weeping unashamed. "Wirra, now—you mustn't cry," the old man soothed, touching Jamie's bowed head tenderly.

"I cannot help it. The middle of my heart is made of burning coal. Forgive me, Tavish, for the wrongs I've done you."

"You were always a darling of a boy—now you've only to be a darling of a man," the Speaker consoled him. " 'Tis part of the adventure of life . . . to grow and keep on growing. When a man has made his peace with God and is ready to climb the Mountain of Tears, many things become plain. Remember at home how you were ready to sacrifice yourself that Kate might have her own house and husband?"

Jamie nodded mutely.

"And straight off the miracle happened? Your first wish . . . for travel . . . came true. . . ." Tavish's voice rang with the excitement of a great discovery. "Then, to spare your Maeve from the hammering of her kinsmen when she said she'd marry you or no one, you offered to give her up and go away . . . sure then the second miracle came to pass? You had your second wish and the woman of your choice was yours?"

"Aye," said Jamie, unable to follow the thread of the old man's thought, "but somewhere along the way . . . between that and the last wish, something happened! Something went wrong!"

"Don't you see, Jamie," Tavish cried, " 'twas you! You went astray, spreading your wings like the eagle to go it on your own! For the first two wishes you were ready to give up the things closest to your heart! But what were you ready to give for the third wish? For the wonderful son you never had?"

The Speaker's voice slowed and drifted toward a whisper. Deep in the inner recesses of Jamie's heart, a gate unlocked, loosing a flood of understanding that swept through him.

" 'Tis true, my cousin," he cried, clasping Tavish's dry,

limp hand. "In the wonder of things that happened to me I forgot to bend the second knee! Can I make you one more promise? I swear by the things our people swear by—that Kevin will be my son, and he shall have his chance to become a priest! This oath I make before God and all His saints!"

Tavish looked at him through blurred eyes, trying to smile. "He's the bonnie child of my spirit, Jamie," he whispered. "He will make a great priest."

The old man's mind began to wander and his thoughts grew fanciful again. With his eyes fixed upon the crucifix, he told his last story on earth. "Once there was a man, and he was working in his field, and it came on to thunder and storm something fearful. The man ran for shelter to a stone wall, and he put his head in a hole in the wall, which was all the shelter there was, and he prayed: 'God save what's out o' me!' But he ought to have prayed for the whole of him, for no sooner had he said that than the wall collapsed and took his head clean off. Sure now it was a judgment on the creature, because it's not right to pray small, just for yourself. You should pray large, to save us all, Jamie. Pray big and openhearted."

The Speaker's voice had risen as he talked, and his mind became clear once more. The child sleeping against the bed was roused. His sleep-filled eyes searched Jamie's face. "Are you awake, Kevin lad?" Tavish said. "I want you to hear this. Whatever is my share of Jamie's savings is to be yours. Raise your right hand and swear by all that's holy that what's mine will be the boy's, Jamie."

"I swear it," Jamie said solemnly.

"Now take the lad to his bed. What I have to do is best done alone."

Jamie lifted the child in his arms. "He'll not be afraid of you any more," the old man whispered. "Good-by, Kevin; may the road rise with you, lad."

At the entrance to the tent, Tavish called again. "Send Maeve and the others in. I'll be saying my last farewells now. And Jamie, remember at home a window was always left open for the soul to pass through? Sure then raise the corner flap of the tent a small piece, will you?"

"Aye, Tavish." Jamie could not trust himself to say more.

"Good-by, Jamie."

"Good-by, Cousin Tavish."

"A little music would not be amiss . . . but no wailing, mind."

"No, Cousin Tavish."

"Any song will do. Anything from the heart of home," the old man said wistfully.

Maeve was waiting outside the tent. When she tried to take Kevin from his arms, Jamie drew back. "I'll be putting the lad to bed," he said. "Tavish is waiting to say good-by. Will you sing 'Eileen Aroon' for the old one? He's almost dark now."

Owen Roe Tavish was alone, as he wished. The farewells had been spoken and there was nothing to do but wait. Whatever life remained in the old man wavered as unsteadily as the small flame dancing irreverently on the remains of the crucifix candle. In the distance a rooster crowed. *"Moc na ho-ya slaun,"* it said in Gaelic: "The Son of the Virgin is safe." Another dawn. Somewhere beyond the greening hills, where the heart but not the eye could see, the light of another morning was gilding the edge of the world with sunrise.

The Speaker's lips moved, rummaging in the attic of his memory for familiar word pictures that crumbled as they became sound: "The long sweet spring, and the smell of honey from the heather—remember—a pair of scissors near the boy, and a horseshoe nail hung round his neck. They will keep the Good People from stealing him—Strike Angel's

Welcome on the bell—Bury me like the great Conn, up-right, spear in hand and hound at foot . . . Woe to Eman, roof and wall; woe to Red Branch, hearth and hall; tenfold woe and black dishonor to the foul and false Clan Connor."

His wavering consciousness moved among the memory shadows like a beacon light, touching and illuminating long-forgotten objects and incidents with a phrase, then passing on: "The little cows of Kerry, and the little Connemara horses; they turned their heads to me when I walked down the street. . . . If we remain here there'll be plenty of money but few souls will go to Heaven. . . . Every acorn must drop. . . . Come the Three Graces that were yonder; come the Three Marys from Rome; come the three demons from the East. . . . From dawn to sunset no man's shadow fell on mine. I was lonely as poverty. . . . Friday hair, Sun-day horn, better hadst thou never been born. . . . Look not with pride at the polished shoe; be not too proud of the cloak so nice; in humility walk the road afoot; and always salute the poor man twice. . . ."

A small center of clarity was forming in Tavish's brain, pushing back the shifting patterns of memory. If this is death—'tis not too unpleasant, he thought. In the distance he thought he could hear the soothing music of Fer Fi, the red-haired dwarf, played upon his three-stringed harp. There was a woman singing, too; in a sweet clear voice. The song sounded like "Eilleen Aroon." That would be Aine, the Ban-shee, whose whispering song of sleep, "Suantraighe," com-forted the dying. Och, the old man thought, I be one whose feet were set in one century but whose heart dwelt in another.

In the mirror near the foot of the bed, Tavish could see the raised corner of the tent left by Jamie for his soul to pass. As he gazed at the aperture, a mist seemed to form in it and begin to spiral like a miniature whirlwind, moving slowly toward him at the same time. As it neared the bed the whirlwind began to expand. Soon it filled the tent. Pieces of furniture were drawn into the spiral; then the bed, and finally the tent itself. Through the gathering dusk, the crucifix on the center pole of the tent glowed ever brighter, like a great beckoning star. With the sacred light for a pivot, the cavalcade began to swing round and round like a weird carrousel. Through the small opening, more and more objects came to join the fantastic spinning dance. Flying through the murky air, Tavish could identify famous objects in Irish folklore; The long lost Stone of Fal, which cried out each time the true king of Ireland stepped upon it at Tara. Next, through the ever-deepening mist came straying stones and slumber pins; pookas, merrows, leprechauns and shee-hogues; water horses, sea serpents and sea worms, half serpent and half fish. The phantom chariot of Cuchulainn flashed past, as did the ghostly figure of Garret Fitzgerald, on his great white horse with the silver shoes, on which he must ride once in every seven years around Lough Gur, until the silver shoes were worn away. The great swords—that when unsheathed spoke—sailed by, boasting of their feats in battle. Jasconye, the great fish that swam round and round the world trying to catch its tail in its mouth, floated lazily through the mist. Finally, a miniature, old-fashioned coach the size of a man's hat, and drawn by four black chargers no bigger than mice, galloped through the opening to join the galaxy circling in the mist. It was driven by a tiny red maneen the size of a workingman's thumb, and wearing a green coachman's hat and coat. Two infinitesimal coach dogs with amber, pin-point eyes trotted between the rear wheels.

"'Tis a miniature of the coach I saw in my dreams," Tavish remembered. Then he understood: The coach he had dreamed of was the Death Coach! "Och," he chided himself wryly, "and I thought it meant a journey!" He chuckled.

"Well . . . to dream of the Death Coach and dying . . . sure now that means a journey indeed . . . !"

The song of Aine grew louder; the objects in the whirling carrousel spun faster; the music of Fer Fi's harp swelled to its highest pitch—and Owen Roe Tavish fell asleep.

A heavy rumble of wheels, accompanied by a sharp swaying from side to side and the thunder of hoofs, roused him. He was no longer on the bed—or even in the tent. The ghostly carrousel had disappeared. He was the lone passenger in a strange, old-fashioned coach the like of which he had never seen, yet nevertheless was vaguely reminiscent. The paneling of the coach's interior was inlaid with a substance like mother-of-pearl, trimmed with faded gold leaf. The elaborate upholstering was of worn red-and-gold plush.

"Sure now what can this be?" Tavish asked himself. "Are they rushing me to a hospital in this weird relic? Hurt as I am, I should be lying on a board—the way I was carried from the woods."

But to his amazement the ravaging pain in his back had disappeared. Gone, too, was the heavy paralysis of his legs. Cautiously he drew the curtain covering the small window in the door aside and peered out. Outside was the gray half-light of morning. Great trees and fields were hurtling past at what seemed tremendous speed. Gaining courage, Tavish lowered the window and poked his head out. What he saw almost took the sight from his eyes. On the box was the little red maneen with the round red face, and wearing the green coachman's hat and coat. As he swung his whip toward the four black mouse-sized horses, Tavish could hear the musical tinkling of the buttons on his long green coat.

With a sigh he leaned his head back on the red plush cushions. An instant later he was sitting bolt upright. "Sure there must be some mistake."

Thrusting his head from the coach window again, he called to the little driver: "Now where on earth are you taking me?"

The tiny red coachman flashed him the merriest smile possible. "Nowhere on earth, Owen Roe Tavish! To the Land of Moo, where you're to be shanachie to all the children of the other world."

"Now what do you make of that?" Tavish exclaimed. "Storyteller to the little lost children of Moo."

"Surely you've guessed it, Tavish?" the little driver shouted. "You're one of us now, man—one of the Little People."

XXII

THE new sign over the barbershop at the western edge of Atlanta read: HAIRCUTTING EMPORIUM . . . ORAN TALBOT, PROP. It was a drab, one-room affair, with a weather-beaten exterior and a single, secondhand chair, but Talbot regarded it with the satisfaction of ownership.

"If'n the rest of the joint looked half as good as the new sign, it'd be all right," he assured himself. "Time enough fer that when I take in a little money, though."

The raising of the sign marked Talbot's return to his earlier profession of barbering. His venture into the horse and mule trade had not fared very well. The war with Spain had been short-lived, and his commission as a government purchasing agent even shorter. Talbot had emerged with little more than he had gone in with. He had, however, acquired a deep and lasting hatred for Jamie McRuin.

According to Talbot, Jamie had stolen his idea and had made a mountain of money, while he, the inventor, had been left out in the cold. "Serves me right fer ever trustin' an Irishman," he would aver bitterly. "There's two kinda crooks

—ordinary ones and Irish. The ordinary ones you can generally trust; but God help you if you git mixed up with the
Irish."

At midmorning, near the end of April, a large wagon
crowded with young boys drew up in front of the Haircutting Emporium. Talbot was alone inside in the act of
shaving. "Hell's afire," he swore, "I hope they ain't comin'
here."

Talbot was no lover of children, either professionally or
socially. For a moment he considered drawing the window
shade and announcing the shop was closed. It was too late.
The driver of the wagon had spied the new sign.

"Here be a place. Shall we give it a try?" he called.

The children shouted assent. They ranged in ages from
six to twelve, and while badly in need of haircuts, their
faces were lively and scrubbed clean. When the wagon
halted, they scrambled to the ground with the wild exuberance of hounds on the trail of a fox. "Quiet now," the driver
ordered. "Once inside the shop you're not to speak unless
you're spoken to. Is that clear?"

Peering through the grimy, fly-specked window, Talbot
studied the face of the man in charge of the children. "Now
where'n hell have I seen that feller?" he muttered. Then his
eyes widened with recognition. "O m'gawd," he exclaimed.

Jamie led his flock into the small shop and the children
expanded noisily into every corner. "Could you be cutting
the little ones' hair while I'm in town?" he inquired pleasantly, his attention taken with the boys' antics.

Talbot viewed the throng sourly. "All of 'em?"

"All of them . . . and a neat job done on every one,"
Jamie replied. "Oh, 'tis you, Oran Talbot! Well now—and
back at the barbering trade?"

"I am," Talbot replied sourly, "thanks to you."

"Sure you're that welcome," Jamie assured him, blandly

enjoying the encounter. "You'll be more happy in a shop. The mule trade is not for a man as soft as yourself."

He laughed and Talbot's rage rose in his throat until it threatened to choke him. When he could speak he shifted the subject back to the children.

"Lotsa wool on them sheep and I ain't got but one chair. Take me at least two hours."

"Take it, man. All the time you want. But I want a fine job done all around. This is a very special occasion," Jamie warned him jovially.

"One of the kids gettin' married?" Talbot sniggered.

Jamie gave him a look that erased the grin from Talbot's face. "One of the lads is being confirmed this Sunday. Hop up in the chair, Kevin."

Jamie launched into detail as to how he wanted Kevin's hair trimmed. "Take quite a bit off the back and sides and around his ears . . . but not too much off the top. Part it in the middle . . . let me see, about here . . . and make it stay down with oil or grease or something."

"You act like the boy's mother," Talbot said sourly. "Is he your kid?"

"That he is," Jamie responded proudly, "so see that you do a fine job."

When Jamie had left the shop, Talbot began methodically to snip away at Kevin's mass of blond curls with the clippers.

"So you're Jamie McRuin's kid?" he asked Kevin.

Talbot could feel the child tense beneath the folds of the apron. "Whatsa matter? Cat got your tongue?"

Kevin shook his head. "Well then, what's your name?" the barber persisted.

"Kevin Roe Callahan McRuin," one of the older boys volunteered.

"That's a lot of name for a little squirt like you," Talbot said, and again felt the child's tensed reaction. "So you're gonna be confirmed this Sunday, eh?" he queried. "That must be pretty important to a kid."

"It's more important to our parents," the older boys confided. "That's why we gotta look our best."

"You do, eh?" Talbot's mind spun a web to ensnare possibilities but trapped nothing. "Must be some way to git even," he pondered.

So absorbed was he in futile scheming that he forgot what he was about. "Look what you're doing," one of the children shouted.

The clippers had rambled high up on the side of Kevin's head. When they came away, a deep swatch of yellow hair came with them. The gap left the appearance of a mower run amuck in a field of ripened wheat. Over Talbot's smirking face stole a look of gleeful cunning.

"Now ain't that too bad . . . but I got an idea how to fix it . . . fix it just fine. Son, you're gonna git Oran Talbot's summer special." He chuckled as he plowed the clippers through the mass of Kevin's yellow curls.

When Jamie pulled up before the barbershop, he could hear the children inside screaming with laughter. "Och, the boys do be making a fine time of it," he grinned to himself.

As he entered the shop, the last boy was just climbing from the chair. He was grinning from ear to ear. Jamie stared about him, aghast at the sight that greeted him. The heads of every boy in the shop had been shorn absolutely clean.

Without their hair they looked disconcertingly alike. In one corner stood Kevin, his head as bare as the rest.

"In the name of the saints, what's been going on here?" Jamie demanded.

The children's laughter ceased. "That's the way the kids wanted it," Talbot said, with bland innocence. "Great for hot weather."

"Sure and whose idea was it?" Jamie's eyes moved angrily from face to face, seeking an explanation.

"Kevin had his this way . . . so we all wanted it," the oldest boy confessed.

"Wait outside in the wagon," Jamie motioned the youngsters from the shop. They filed out, chastened.

"Tell me now again—whose idea was this?" he turned to Talbot.

The barber shifted uncomfortably. "Why, your kid's . . . Kevin's. He was first."

"Kevin asked you to shave the head of him?"

"Sure he did. You don't think I'd do a thing like that on my own?" Talbot protested.

Jamie's eyes turned an ominous slate-blue, and he moved closer to Talbot.

"Look, Jamie, if you don't like the job I done . . . well . . . you don't have to pay me. That's fair, ain't it?" The barber moved away as he spoke.

"Sure I wouldn't think of going away without paying you, Mister Talbot," Jamie said grimly.

Quietly he turned and locked the door, then drew the battered green shade over the window. Talbot was thoroughly frightened now. "I tell you them kids wanted their hair cut like that," he whined.

"And I'll tell you a something," Jamie said, lowering his voice to a whisper. "You've just witnessed a miracle, Mister Talbot. The lad who asked you to shave his head . . . has never spoken a word in his life. He's dumb."

Talbot's mouth began to tremble and his face turned gray-yellow in the gloom of the shop. "It was all in fun, Jamie," he pleaded. "Can't you take a joke?"

"I be laughing," Jamie said, moving toward the cowering barber. "I want you to join me as soon as I fix your face so you can laugh on the other side of it."

A small crowd had gathered outside the shop when Jamie came out. They drew aside nervously to let him pass. "What's goin' on in there?" one man inquired.

"Go in and see," Jamie replied affably, climbing into the wagon.

Inside the shop the crowd half expected to find the place swimming in blood. Instead everything was in surprising good order—except for the floor, which was ankle-deep in a wide assortment of hair. Sitting in the barber's chair was Oran Talbot, his eyes fixed dully upon his reflection in the mirror. Gone was his shock of wavy hair of which he had been quite vain. Thoroughly stripped, his head shone naked and white in the half-gloom of the shop.

"Are you all right, Oran?" a man asked.

Slowly Talbot slid his hand across the sandpaper surface of his close-clipped scalp. "That two-legged devil! He's ruint me. I'll never be the same again," he whimpered.

The "Monday haircutting" he had given Oran Talbot left Jamie in high good humor. As the wagon rolled toward the camp, he laughed and sang with the children. "I'll be telling your parents 'twas all the barber's fault," he promised. "Don't go saying you saw Kevin's head looking like the side of a white rock and begged for some of the same. If you do, there'll be holly growing out of your hips from the lickings you'll get this night."

He ran his head affectionately over Kevin's prickly scalp, sensing the child's embarrassment at his freakish appearance. "Maybe we'll postpone the confirming—till some of the hair grows a bit," he suggested.

Beside him on the seat, the boy smiled gratefully. Sure, he has the smile of an angel, Jamie thought.

A warm and wonderful relationship had developed between them in the months since Tavish had died. The homeless boy had occupied the empty room in Jamie's heart. He wouldn't close a deal without Kevin's approval.

"Give me the nod, lad, and it's a deal," he would say. "Sure the boy has an eye for animals," he bragged to the other traders. "The Church is in the way of getting a fine livestock man."

He and Maeve spoke confidently of Kevin's coming priesthood, but in their hearts they were not so sure. No Traveler had ever taken holy orders; besides, there was Kevin's handicap to overcome. They had spoken earnestly with Father Kerrigan about schools and special teachers, but the priest had urged them to go slowly.

"You've only just won the boy's heart. Don't shake his confidence by shoving him off with this teacher and that. If he has been called, sure God will find a way—with or without speech."

As for Kevin, good food and camp life had made him strong and rosy. The memory of Tavish, which had been the furniture of his young life, had at last retired into a small, secret closet. The first few weeks after the old man had died, he had wanted to die, too. The loneliness was too much to bear. The Speaker had been the great oak around which his timorous spirit had wrapped itself, and when the tree fell there seemed nowhere to climb. Then one night Tavish had appeared in a wonderfully vivid dream.

"You've no cause to grieve, Kevin lad," the old man had chided. "There's Jamie and Maeve to cling to. They need you as much as you need them. Besides, you've but to call me and I'll be beside you like lightning through a gooseberry bush."

"But how can I call you when I can't talk?" Kevin had asked in his dream.

"Now what sort of nonsense is that?" Tavish had scoffed. "You're talking now, aren't you? Sure there's no more to it than that. Open your mouth and let your heart speak the words."

In the dream it had all seemed quite plausible. Tavish often appeared after that. He was like an unseen playmate to Kevin. They held long conversations together, the old man responding to the boy's eager questions with wonderful descriptions of the underwater-land of Moo, where children who had died went to live out their lives. " 'Tis their story-teller, I am," he assured Kevin, "a very important post."

"How many children dwell in the Land of Moo?" Kevin had asked.

"Let me see," said Tavish. "Add the number of stars in the heavens to the sands of the sea; the raindrops in a winter rain to all the heartbeats since time began; all these and twelve hundred more besides and you'll have the number of children in the Land of Moo."

"And you tell stories to all of them?" said Kevin, awed.

"Aye . . . I tell stories to every one."

In his dream, Kevin had asked Owen Roe Tavish the one question that was nearest his heart. "Will I ever be able to speak when I'm awake as I do in my dreams?"

"That's something beyond a poor shanachie's power of knowing or telling," Tavish had answered. "But I'll tell you a very important secret. I learned this as a boy at home. There's a time of petition—one instant in all the twenty-four of the day. Any prayer presented on that instant will be answered, phfft . . . just like that. I'll snoop around and find out just when 'twill be . . . and then when the time comes that you need it most—at the most important moment of your life—sure I'll have it for you."

When Jamie turned off the main road toward the camp, he noticed a strange buggy and surrey tied up at the edge of the woods. "Keep out of sight, you little bald-headed eagles," he called to the children in the wagon. "Sure it looks like we be having visitors."

As he drove toward the camp, Jamie could see that something was wrong. Father Kerrigan was standing with Maeve, facing four men. At first glance the men had all appeared to be strangers, but as Jamie halted the team at the edge of the clearing he recognized Travis Bunn. A second and longer look confirmed it.

The man was completely changed. A haunting fire glowed in his dark eyes. Hatred had consumed him, stripping the weight from his strong frame, and leaving him little more than a skeleton. "The man is truly hate-crazed," Jamie muttered. "Stay out of sight in the wagon," he instructed Kevin, who had remained beside him on the seat. "I'll see what this is all about."

Maeve was the first to glimpse him striding across the clearing and she hurried to meet him. "Kevin's father is here with the sheriff and a deputy. He wants the boy back," she whispered.

Jamie slipped his arm about Maeve's waist. The Travelers seldom showed public affection for their women, but Jamie sensed the terrible strain his wife was undergoing. She loved Kevin as if he were her own son. To lose him now would destroy her.

"He'll not have him. He's ours. And tell me—what's Travis Bunn to do with all this?"

Maeve shook her head. "I'm not sure. He was with them when they went to Father Kerrigan."

"Then he's behind the whole thing; 'tis plain enough," Jamie said angrily.

"God salute you, Father," he said to the priest.

The sheriff strolled toward Jamie. He was a solidly built man, with a square, granite face, but a quiet, easy way of speaking. "You Mister McRuin?" he said.

Jamie nodded warily. "I'm Jack Haynes . . . sheriff of Fulton County. Jess Proddy here says you got his boy."

Father Kerrigan stepped forward. "I told you, Sheriff, Proddy was only too glad to give the child away when his wife died. He took a two-hundred-dollar mule in payment." The priest's face was grim with anger.

"Things is different now," Jesse whined. "All my kids done run off. I need somebody to help me work the farm. I been to a lawyer . . . the boy's lawfully mine and I mean to have him."

"You'll not have him," Jamie said hoarsely. "You gave him to us and we're going to keep him."

"Don't try to obstruct justice," the sheriff warned. "If you got Proddy's son, the law says he's entitled to have him back."

Maeve had stood silent because it wasn't a woman's place to speak in such matters. Now she spoke carefully, striving to conceal her feelings. "We've clothed and fed and cared for the boy. He loves us. Does that mean nothing?" she asked.

Sheriff Haynes shrugged. "That's up to Proddy. If he wants to pay you something for feeding the kid. . . ."

"Sure . . . I'll pay 'em somethin' . . . anything," Jesse agreed.

"We're not asking for pay," Maeve retorted. "We're asking for the child."

Father Kerrigan turned to Proddy. "Where do you propose to get the money to pay for two years' keep?" he demanded.

The farmer was taken aback. "Why . . . I reckon I'll . . . well . . . as soon as I git the young'un . . ." he stammered to a halt.

"Is it just possible you've heard that the child has a trust fund established by Jamie, here, from money left him by Owen Roe Tavish?" the priest continued.

"Well . . . if there's money . . . he's my kid," Jesse said lamely.

"You've hit the nail with a nine-pound hammer, Father," said Jamie, "and I think I be knowing the man who told him." He glared at Travis Bunn, who stared ferret-eyed but said nothing.

"Don't see what difference it makes," the sheriff interposed. "If the boy is Proddy's, he's his, rich or poor."

"That's right," Jesse snapped. "Now you just trot little Number Seven out here."

" 'Tis over my dead body you'll be taking him," Jamie said through clenched teeth.

"We're with you, Jamie," shouted Big Tom.

The other horse traders echoed his cry. They had stood grimly apart as silent observers, but now they changed positions, surrounding the two police officers and Proddy and Bunn.

The deputy shifted his holster, squaring away for trouble. "You'll get nowhere resisting the law," Haynes warned.

"You've got no warrant for the boy," Me-Dennis challenged. "By the time you get back with one, we'll be out of the county."

"Then you'll be charged with kidnaping," retorted Haynes. "Bring out the child."

"Never," said Jamie.

The horse traders tightened their loop about the four men. Nervously, the deputy drew his revolver, a heavy Colt with a long, sinister barrel. For a moment violence lurked dangerously above their heads. A word or a move could set it off.

Father Kerrigan crossed to the side of the sheriff and faced the traders. "There's nought to be gained by fighting. The child and you will be the losers. We will fight in the courts."

"What chance have we there?" Jamie cried. "None! The place to fight is here and now."

The men of the camp shouted their approval of Jamie's stand. Father Kerrigan shook his head. "We've no choice but the courts . . . and I promise you a fight to the bitter end. We're not beaten yet."

"Och, Father, you lie finer than truth. If the boy leaves this camp, we've lost . . . it's written on your face and the face of everyone here," Jamie pleaded. "It's not Maeve or myself I'm thinking of—not entirely. It's the little one. He was only just beginning to find a bit of kindness in the world . . ." his voice broke.

There was a long silence. The sheriff shifted his weight from one foot to the other. "I'm sorry, ma'am," he said to Maeve. "Everybody knows Jesse Proddy ain't much good—but it's the law."

Maeve crossed to Jamie's side without answering. "Where are the children?" she asked. Jamie indicated the wagon. Maeve crossed to it and called:

"Come out, boys."

There were gasps when the group climbed from the wagon and moved timidly to the center of the clearing. Their shaven heads made them look like so many under-sized convicts. The sheriff surveyed each one grimly.

"All right, Proddy, pick out your youngster and let's get out of here," he said shortly.

Jesse Proddy moved with alacrity. "Sure . . . sure, Sheriff. Line up here, boys—let me have a look at you." He began peering into the faces of the children. "I cain't rightly tell which one he is . . . offhand."

"You mean you can't recognize your own child?" Father Kerrigan snapped.

"I ain't seen him for two years," Jesse whined. "He's growed some . . . and they all look alike without no hair."

Maeve and Jamie looked at each other with a flickering of hope. "If you can't tell which is yours it's a dead certain cinch nobody around here is gonna help you," Haynes snapped. He was rapidly growing tired of the whole affair.

"Help me, Father," Jesse pleaded. "You know which 'un he is."

"Help you take that child back to the kind of nameless existence you gave him before? It would be a mortal sin. You'll get no help from me, Jesse Proddy," the priest answered sternly.

"Where are you, son? Speak up, little Number Seven . . . it's yore pappy, remember?" Proddy was going plaintively from boy to boy. He passed Kevin by time and again.

Travis Bunn stepped forward, his dark eyes lit with a wild cunning.

"Didn't you say the boy couldn't talk?" he said to Proddy. The hope that had been glimmering in Maeve and Jamie's breasts flickered and died.

"Yeah . . . that's right," said Proddy.

"Then he ought to be easy to find," continued Bunn. He looked toward Maeve and Jamie, savoring his victory. "Just line them up and ask each one his name. The one that can't answer—he will be yours."

"Sure! Now why didn't I think of that? Line up there, you kids, and tell me your names." Proddy shuffled them into line.

Some instinct helped Kevin to place himself last. He had listened with sickening terror as the full realization of what was happening came to him in the wagon. Maeve's eyes sought him out. Her hands were clasped and her lips moved as if in prayer. Beside her Jamie stood clenching and unclenching his great fists. Father Kerrigan's eyes followed Proddy as he moved from child to child.

"Tell me your name, little feller?" Jesse would say cajolingly. "Dennis? That's fine. Who's next?"

Kevin's eyes went back to Maeve. He wanted to cry out comforting words to her. "We'll always be together—in your heart and mine," he would have said if he could. "The man who is taking me away won't be able to keep me. When I'm grown up I will come to you. I know the roads you travel, and the groves where you pitch your tents. I will find you and Jamie. For you are the mother and father of my choice. . . ."

Jesse was only two boys away. "Can you tell me yore name, little feller?" he was wheezing.

Kevin wondered if he shouldn't step forward and end the suspense. Maeve's eyes were closed and she was praying openly now. He thought of Owen Roe Tavish and the memory of the old man's promise about the time of petition came back to him. "When the time comes that you need it most—at the most important moment of your life—sure I'll have it for you."

I'll never need it more than I do right now, Kevin thought.

As if in answer, he heard a rumble of wheels and the muffled thunder of galloping hoofs. Against the dark background of the trees, he saw the strange coach Tavish had described to him. The same little man in the green coachman's coat and hat was on the box; the same four black horses drew the coach; and the same two dogs coursed between the rear wheels. There was only one difference. Now the coach was occupied! Leaning from the window and waving merrily was Owen Roe Tavish.

"Kevin lad, the time is now. Say your prayer . . . the hour of petition be's in it. Hurry . . . speak what's in your heart."

The boy felt himself borne upward in a great surge of relief. Owen Roe Tavish had not failed him. He opened his mouth to cry out his thanks, only to discover that Jesse Proddy was already standing before him. "Didn't you hear me, Number Seven? I said I done recognized you. It's yore pappy . . . come to take you home," his father was saying.

For an instant Kevin thought all was lost. Then he heard a strange voice that seemed to come from somewhere deep inside him, speaking words he did not understand. *"Cuevin moc Ruin is ainm dom, agus se seo mo baile,"* it said.

Jesse Proddy's face puckered with surprise and disappointment. He looked as if he were about to cry. Maeve's eyes had opened, wide and incredulous, as if she had heard sounds beyond the range of human ears. The circle of men and women stood stunned—too awed even to cry: "Miracle."

The long silence was broken by the sheriff. "The boy talked, but what he said I don't know."

Travis Bunn's mouth hung slackly open, while his eyes darted wildly about. "I be cursed," he muttered brokenly. "The boy spoke in the ancient tongue. 'Kevin McRuin is my name, and this is my home.' he said." He began to laugh wildly . . . hysterically. Jamie started toward him but Maeve held him back. "No, Jamie, no. He's that crazed —poor thing," she cried.

Travis Bunn's wild eyes sought and found hers. "Aye, Maeve," he said slowly, "you may well call me geilt . . . I, who would have lain on your grave sod to shield you from the rain. Mad I am, for who could be sane and hate as I have hated. I'm going away now—into the ground. I'll work no more spells. All the curses—Reversed Journeys . . . Turning the Anvil—they haven't hurt you or him. . . . They've hurt only me." His voice twisted and crumbled into a fit of sobbing. Covering his face with his hands, he turned and fled through the trees as he had fled five years before.

The sheriff beckoned to his deputy. "Let's get out of here."

They walked quickly toward their rig, tied near the road. "Hey . . . wait fer me," Proddy called, trailing mournfully after them.

"I cain't rightly figger it out," he complained to the two men. "One of them kids should've been Number Seven. And what sort of talk was that last one giving me?"

The sheriff's deputy spoke for the first time. "You heard what your runaway pal said. The kid was speakin' Gaelic. Looks to me like you and him had sorta been drinkin' out of the wrong jug."

At the camp, in the wave of rejoicing, Kevin was aware only of Maeve and Jamie's arms around him and their warm tears on his cheeks. Father Kerrigan was stroking his head.

"Break your camp and be out of this county before morning," he ordered Jamie. "Skip the rituals and don't come back until I send the word. Proddy is beaten now, but he may be back with his lawyer tomorrow."

They were packed and on the road within an hour. Kevin slept soundly behind the seat in the softly creaking wagon. Beside her husband, Maeve sat proudly erect. "Sure now, Travis Bunn and I are even," Jamie mused philosophically. "Had he taken the boy he'd have killed us both by inches."

"Och, the poor, demented man," Maeve sighed.

" 'Twas a judgment on the creature," Jamie assured her.

He was still trying to comprehend what had happened. "Do you know, if that shrieking gombeen in the barbershop hadn't cut off Kevin's hair, sure Proddy would have recognized the boy and been halfway home with him now?"

"Nonsense," said Maeve. " 'Twas a miracle—straight from Heaven. And miracles are not to be put off. If the boys had not all looked alike, then Jesse Proddy would have been struck blind—temporarily, of course. 'Twas the will of Heaven that Kevin stay with us."

"Aye," said Jamie, "there's no other explanation."

"Dear Tavish," said Maeve thoughtfully, "I wonder if he knows?"

"Sure he'll be standing the Seven Heavens upside down if he doesn't," Jamie replied proudly.

Abruptly he drew the horses to a stop. "Maeve darling . . . queen of my heart, a terrible and wonderful thought has just come to me. 'Twas no miracle that made Kevin speak. 'Tis but the last of my three wishes being granted! I now have a son that speaks in the ancient tongue!"

Maeve's silvery laugh pealed out into the warm spring night. Hers and Jamie's life together suddenly seemed to have completed a cycle. He was once more the boy she had loved and married; but more than that, he was now a man, too. Sure now the test of manhood is to be a child with children a man with men, she thought.

Just ahead—or was it behind—and around another bend in the road, another vehicle coursed their path. It was a strange, old-fashioned coach whose wheels left no tracks, and from the tiny buttons on the small, red-faced driver's coat, came the musical tinkling of little golden bells.

The road ahead unfurled like a ribbon of deep orange, glowing dully in the mystic moonlight like a fairy path across the ridge of the world.